CW01431424

never
let go

ALSO BY JILL SANDERS

never let go

JILL SANDERS

Montlake
Romance

This is a work of fiction. Names, characters, organizations, places, events, and incidents are either products of the author's imagination or are used fictitiously.

Text copyright © 2018 by Jill Sanders
All rights reserved.

No part of this book may be reproduced, or stored in a retrieval system, or transmitted in any form or by any means, electronic, mechanical, photocopying, recording, or otherwise, without express written permission of the publisher.

Published by Montlake Romance, Seattle
www.apub.com

Amazon, the Amazon logo, and Montlake Romance are trademarks of Amazon.com, Inc., or its affiliates.

ISBN-13: 9781503953185
ISBN-10: 1503953181

Cover design by Erin Dameron Hill

Printed in the United States of America

To all my friends who make me laugh wine out my nose. You know who you are . . .

CHAPTER ONE

Addy Collins stood near the edge of the hillside overlooking the town and took a deep breath. Haven, Montana.

She closed her eyes as the clear, crisp mountain air hit her lungs. She loved it. Loved the feel of the sun on her face, the bite of the remnants of winter in the air. She heard a bird cry and, when she finally spotted it, smiled at the eagle as it flew overhead.

This is what she lived for. She'd never felt freer than standing in nature by herself.

When she heard a twig snap behind her, she frowned. Who would dare ruin this moment for her? She guessed it was another one of her eco-warriors who, no doubt, had the same idea. To be alone.

When she turned to see who it was, she had to shield her eyes against the sunlight.

All she could see was an outline of a man, but that's all it took. She knew instantly who it was.

Trent McGowan.

Shit.

Shit, shit.

He was one of the reasons she hadn't wanted to return to Haven. She'd come into town with the sole purpose of protesting his family's oil business. She'd tried to stay focused on her goals. But the McGowan brothers had always been a very handsome distraction. So far this trip, there had been plenty of disturbances from the brothers.

With Trent being the biggest diversion of them all.

She squared her shoulders and raised her other hand to deflect the rest of the sunlight.

"Morning." Even his voice was too sexy for this early in the day. Instantly her body reacted.

Triple shit.

"What are you doing here?" She frowned again, wishing she'd thought before she'd spoken. She wanted to blame it on the lack of coffee, but the fact was she'd given up the sugary black goodness almost a year ago—after some of her team members had traveled to Brazil to protest coffee growers cutting down rain forest.

Instead of answering her, Trent just smiled. He didn't move closer or get out of the path of the bright sun. So she stood there, both hands shielding her eyes, trying to get a better look at the sexiest man alive.

At least in her book.

His hair was always a little longer than his brothers'. Currently it was long enough that thick, dark chunks of it fell into his eyes. Those pools of deep mahogany drowned her in memories of the years she'd spent fantasizing about him. His six-foot-plus height forced her to crane her neck to look up the length of his long, lean body to reach those eyes. He must have forgotten to shave that morning, as his face was sprinkled with dark stubble. An even more dangerous look.

"Same as you," he said, finally breaking into her assessment of him.

"What?" She blinked a few times, unable to remember what it was that she'd said. Thoughts of her Haven mission flashed through her mind. If her friends had their way, his company would suffer. Any entity that made millions off destroying land and the environment for oil or any other natural resources should be put out of business. Vaguely she wondered if he'd still stop on the side of a mountain to talk to her if that happened.

Just looking at him made her go all gooey. How was she supposed to do her job when he looked so damn sexy?

His chuckle broke her from the spell. Squaring her shoulders, Addy dropped her hands and turned around to look out over the view. Closing her eyes, she took two quick breaths to clear her mind of Trent.

"I bet it's nice to be back," he said from directly behind her. Which meant he'd moved closer.

"Not really," she said under her breath. But outwardly she shrugged her shoulders.

She'd been back in Haven for a few weeks. Except for a quick trip to North Dakota, she'd been stuck here, back in her small hometown.

Not that she was being forced to stay. She could leave whenever she wanted. But duty and pride had won out. She would remain in town as long as she was needed.

"Why are you back if you don't want to be here?" Trent asked.

She glanced at him and sighed. He was beautiful. Something deep in her heart sank. Sure, if they were the only two people on the side of a mountain, he'd stop and talk to her. But other than that . . .

She shrugged her shoulders again. "I go where I'm needed." She noticed the signs of their small town waking up. Cars could now be seen hurrying around the empty streets, and smoke was coming out of a few chimneys.

"Do you like it?" Trent asked. The question threw her off. She gave him a quizzical look. "Do you like what you do?"

"I love it." She smiled and nodded as she thought more deeply. "It's what I was made to do."

He stepped up next to her, his wide shoulders blocking the view of the mountains. "What exactly do you do?" He shuffled his feet, which he'd done since grade school when he was frustrated at himself. "I mean, besides make signs and block our property."

She chuckled. "There is more to protesting than signs and standing around."

"Like what?" His hands were shoved deep into the pockets of his jeans.

"Organizing where more than a hundred people are going to live during cold winter days and nights. What they're going to eat and drink. Where they're going to shower, go to the bathroom. Gathering the materials and seeking out sponsors to help pay for it all. Setting up interviews so we can reach out to the public. Deciding what to say during those interviews. Attending town hall, county, and state meetings, and getting on the dockets at those meetings so our voices and concerns can be heard. Researching the businesses we're protesting and digging deeper into their practices. Looking at companies for future efforts. Reaching out to companies and voicing our concerns before we would begin protesting them, all while raising more money and organizing for more protests—"

"Okay," he interrupted with a smile, raising his hands to stop her. "I get it." He took a deep breath. "I was thinking about your job the way I used to think about my dad's." He turned back to the view. "I mean, all our lives we believed Dad just went to work." She watched as sadness flooded his eyes. "But after losing him, we discovered exactly what it was he did. He wore so many hats, working in the oil fields, laying pipe, managing all the workers, not to mention running the business and a family."

"I was sorry to hear about his passing." She paused. "Do you love what you do?"

He looked over at her and nodded. "You know what the kicker is?"

"What?"

"The fact that it takes three of us to fill our father's shoes. I mean, we've come a long way in the past six months. Tyler's finally gotten his shit together, Trey is . . . well, Trey." He shook his head.

"What about you? You've changed too."

He nodded, looking out over the town. "You have to. If you don't, you're likely to get stomped on. Then how would you take care of your family?"

"You're a better person than I remember," she said after a moment of silence.

He turned toward her again. "How so?"

She looked him square in the eyes. "You used to be an ass."

He laughed. "Why do you say that?"

"You were busy chasing every pretty girl around. Too busy to be nice to girls like me."

His chuckles died. "Yeah, I guess we've all changed." He moved around her. She turned, keeping him in front of her. "You've changed a lot too. No more hiding behind thick glasses?"

"Lasik," she supplied after a moment, taken aback that he noticed.

"Or bangs." His gaze moved up to her hair.

Addy was a little surprised he'd remembered the bangs. The awful bangs her mother used to make her wear. Her mother used to pay the local hairdresser tons of money to keep her hair above her shoulders in a very unstylish hairdo. Then, once they made it home, her mother would take her own scissors to Addy's bangs and lop them shorter. Straight across her forehead.

She'd always wondered why her mother had done the last bit herself. One time she'd asked and was rewarded with a long answer of how her mother didn't trust the hairdresser to make the bangs straight enough. Perfection. Her mother had always demanded it in everything.

She'd hated it. One of the first things she'd done when she'd gone to college was to grow her hair out.

How to get him off the topic of her appearance? His deep-brown eyes were evaluating her, almost laughing as they ran over her face.

"Your freckles are still there." His fingertip touched her left cheek and she felt her entire body heat.

It was a gut reaction, the giant step she took backward. What she hadn't calculated was the fact that there was a sheer cliff directly behind her.

Two things happened in the next moments. First, the wind was knocked out of her when Trent's arms wrapped around her waist. Second, she overcorrected her position, causing them to go tumbling violently away from the precipice.

She felt every inch of that godlike chest against her as his backside hit the gravel on the trail. She landed hard, directly on top of him. She heard and felt the air knocked from his lungs, then the groan that followed.

Addy was so preoccupied with the feeling of his arms around her that she didn't realize quickly enough that her knee had landed in a very inconvenient place. For him.

As she tried to move, a louder moan escaped his lips, and she watched his eyes close with pain.

"Don't," he warned her in a husky voice, his arms tightening around her. But she was too concerned that she was damaging his balls, and she continued to struggle against his hold so she could remove her weight from him. "Addy, you're killing me," he finally groaned. "Let me."

Hearing the plea in his voice caused her to still. Her breath was coming out in tiny puffs and her heart was racing so quickly she couldn't count the beats.

She looked down into his eyes to see the pain had been replaced with humor. He was actually laughing at her.

Her eyes narrowed. She gripped his shoulders, taking just a moment to enjoy the feel of them under her hands, and met his eyes.

"What. Is. So. Funny?"

A chuckle escaped his lips and he relaxed his hold. "You. You haven't changed that much. You're still a klutz."

"I am not." She pushed herself off him, no longer caring where her knee landed.

Once free, she sat in the dirt next to him, breathing hard.

"I take it back," she said between breaths.

"What?" he said from his position next to her. He still had that damn smile on his face, causing her teeth to clench.

She turned slightly toward him. "You're still an ass," she said, then got up, dusted off her jeans, and started walking back down the trail as his laughter echoed behind her.

◆　◆　◆

Trent couldn't help it. He picked himself up off the ground with a groan and followed her back down the hillside. He'd lucked out earlier when he spotted her white Jeep parked at the base of the trail.

Addy had been back in Haven for almost a full month, docking her small travel trailer at the state park and only moving it when she took small trips to North Dakota.

He'd bumped into her a few times. Once at the grocery store and a few times at the diner. But so far, this had been his only time to actually talk to her. Alone.

Her hips swayed as she made her way down the jagged path. With hiking boots almost as worn as his, she dodged rocks like a pro. Watching her walk away in those tight jeans she was wearing sent his libido into overdrive.

He stumbled on a rock and thankfully caught himself before he took a header down the path. His gaze only returned to her once he was on more stable ground.

She reached the mouth of the trail seconds before he did. Which he'd planned.

"Heading into town?" he asked, catching up with her and leaning against her Jeep.

She glared at him, that chin of hers jutted in defiance.

"What's it to you?"

He laughed. "Addy, I thought we were making headway." He nodded back toward the top of the trail.

He watched her take a couple of deep breaths and noticed her blue eyes soften.

"How about I make it up to you by buying breakfast?"

She shook her head. "Can't. I have four dozen mouths to feed." She glanced down at her watch. "And a meeting after that."

"Lunch?" he asked, unsure of why he felt the need to persist.

Her eyes moved back up to his. "I'm heading out to North Dakota again."

"Oh?" he said, still leaning against her Jeep. "Why?"

She rolled her eyes. "You have heard about the planned oil pipeline." It wasn't a question.

"Yeah." He shrugged. "So why do you have to go there?"

"I don't have to," she said.

"Then don't," he suggested before she could continue. "Are you done here in town, then?" A strange sensation of panic filled his chest and he had to lean forward until it passed.

"No, I just have . . ." She dropped off and looked over his shoulder. He heard a vehicle drive up but didn't glance over. "I have to go." She pushed him away to open her Jeep door.

"Dinner?" he asked with a grin.

When she looked at him and smiled, he knew she'd forgiven him.

"Maybe someday, McGowan." She shut the Jeep door and drove off.

"Having a hard time getting a date?" From just the sound of the work truck's engine, Trent had known that it was his brother who had driven up.

Glancing over, he saw Tyler resting against the truck.

"Screw off," he said with a smile. "Don't you have a woman to keep you warm and out of my hair?"

His brother's grin was quick. "She's resting."

Trent knew Kristen had been through a lot in recent weeks. Her mother, Trisha, was still staying at his own mother's place, making the house a little too crowded for his liking.

Now that he knew he was sticking around Haven, he figured it was time to find somewhere more permanent to sleep than in his childhood bedroom.

Tyler was currently clearing his plot of land adjacent to the family acreage with high hopes of starting construction on his home this summer. Trent had been thinking about following his brother's lead since all three of them had been given an equal share of the land in their father's will.

Having Kristen's mother there was giving him the nudge he needed to get moving on doing something of his own. For the past few days, he'd been house-plan hunting. But instead of building his own place, he was looking at hiring a crew to put together one of those log home kits.

So he'd driven into Helena the other day and had walked through a couple of model homes. He was leaning toward the three-thousand-square-foot place. It had massive log beams crossing the lofty ceilings, a two-story stone fireplace, hardwood floors throughout, large glass windows, and a full wraparound porch.

Not to mention the five bedrooms, three and a half bathrooms, and an impressively sized kitchen.

Plus it could be set up and delivered within five to eight months. Assuming he could get his land and a driveway cleared. Which meant more backbreaking work.

Trent had been helping Tyler clear his land for the past few weeks. They'd made huge progress and he really enjoyed driving the backhoe. The wood chopping he could live without.

Now, however, his brother's work on his place had stopped so that Tyler could spend all his time with Kristen. They were about to embark on moving her and her mother's belongings out from New York.

"How's she doing?" Trent asked.

"She says she's fine." Trent could see the worry in Tyler's eyes. "But she still wakes up screaming every night."

"It'll take time." He leaned against the truck next to his brother. "Not that I would know what it was like to be kidnapped."

It still got to him.

"I wish I could have been the one to . . ." His brother's statement dropped off. Trent watched him sigh and roll his shoulders.

He figured a change of subject was in order. "How's the investigation into the accident going? Heard anything new yet?"

Tyler sighed again and shook his head. "No, other than it was sabotage, nothing more. Our new security cameras seem to have scared off whoever was messing with us. At least nothing else has happened since. I'm starting to lean toward the possibility that it was someone who tagged along with the protesters. A lot of them have come and gone lately. Maybe whoever did the damage has already moved on."

"Yeah," Trent said after a moment. "Or maybe they're just lying low? I kind of wish something else would happen. You know, so we can catch whoever was screwing with us in the act."

"When they destroyed my office," Tyler said, "I had a feeling it was Brian Laster. It just seemed personal."

"Ditto," Trent said, thinking of all the times Brian had been a burden in his life, starting in grade school. The man had returned to town a few weeks ago with the protesters. "Part of me thinks it's him or Darla." Darla was sex in heels and rotten to the core. She worked at the local strip club and seemed to have her claws in a lot of men in town.

"She was acting up there for a while when you and Kristen started . . . you know."

Tyler chuckled. "Seeing one another?"

Trent glanced down the road that Addy's white Jeep had taken.

"It's still hard to take it all in at once," Tyler continued. "First, Dad dies, then when things start going well, Kristen comes in, then all the funny stuff starts, like the destruction of my office and our equipment, and then, to top it off, there was all she was forced to go through."

"Yeah," Trent agreed.

"Well, I guess I'd better go on my damn walk." Tyler nodded to the trail. "Clears the mind."

"And gets some of that pent-up anger out as well." Trent nodded. "Why do you think I'm here?"

Tyler smiled. "Well, I thought you were chasing tail." He nodded in the direction Addy had driven.

"Take your damn walk." Trent moved to his truck as his brother laughed.

"Maybe you need another hike . . . you know, to release some of the pent-up sexual frustration."

Trent turned like he was going to go back and kick his brother's ass, but Tyler jogged up the head of the trail, laughing the entire time.

"Ass," he called after him.

"Love you too," Tyler called back.

CHAPTER
TWO

The drive from Haven to North Dakota was one that Addy had taken several times now. Trent had been correct; there wasn't really a reason for her to go again so soon. Other than her desire to get out of town.

In the past two years, she'd gotten used to traveling. She actually enjoyed it. She had her small travel trailer hooked up to the back of her Jeep and that was all she needed.

Since returning to Haven, she'd only seen her parents for half an hour, twenty-nine minutes of which she'd spent listening to her mother explain how many different ways Addy was ruining her parents' lives and her own. She'd quickly excused herself and hadn't returned to their massive house along the river since.

Addy was truly on her own. What her mother thought of her didn't matter, nor did the disappointed look in her father's blue eyes. One of the only physical traits she'd inherited from him.

Yet her parents were only part of why Haven was now in her rearview mirror.

It took almost eight hours, but she finally pulled into the massive parking area where small groups of people milled around. She knew there were well over a thousand people gathered there, but on a night like this, most were tucked inside their tents trying to stay warm. Snow had started to fall, which had made the last hour of the drive seem to go slower than the first seven.

It had taken her a while to get used to the kinds of people she usually saw when arriving at a location. This time, since it was still snowing, most were layered with thick, heavy jackets, hats, and blankets.

Two summers ago, she'd gone to a location to protest the sale of a lot of land by the beach in California. The buyer was a large company known for getting around laws prohibiting toxic dumping. They'd snatched up land directly next to a huge plot dedicated to California condor mating. Most of those protesters had been half-clothed or only covered in fake feathers.

The rest ran the spectrum—from shady characters to your average family person. Still, she'd learned not to let her guard down while on location. She'd heard a few protest horror stories about rapes, stabbings, theft, and even once, back in the eighties, a murder.

As Addy parked, a short, very thin, redheaded woman waved and started making her way toward her Jeep.

"What are you doing here? I thought Beau had you tied to Montana for the next few weeks," Joy Garrett said as Addy opened the Jeep door.

"No, he told me I could come here," she said, not looking at Joy directly in the eyes. She hated stretching the truth, but she didn't feel like explaining that she had needed to get out of Haven. If for no other reason to prove to herself that she could.

"Addy, Beau isn't going to be happy. He was going to call you later tonight."

"About?" Addy climbed out of her Jeep.

When she'd first met Joy, who was a few years older than she was, Addy had assumed that she and Beau were an item, since Joy waited on the director of Friends Respecting Everything Environmental, FREE for short, hand and foot.

Addy had been hired on as program organizer almost two years ago, shortly after, completely against her parents' wishes, dropping out of college. She'd tried school for a couple of years before finally walking away from her parents' control.

To date, it had been the best decision she'd ever made.

"What's up?" she finally said when Joy bit her bottom lip and remained silent.

"He's gotten wind that there is a large land purchase in the works."

"From?" Addy took a deep breath and tried not to get frustrated as Joy took her time relaying the news. She'd learned early on that she had to handle Joy with a delicate touch.

"Well, he's heard that McGowan Enterprises, that company we went up to Montana in the first place for . . ." She paused and took a few breaths as she glanced around. Probably keeping an eye out for Beau. "They are purchasing over a hundred acres."

"What?" Addy's voice rose. "What for?"

"Well, we've heard that they're going to start fracking for oil."

"Where?"

"Just outside of Haven."

Addy didn't think the McGowan brothers could afford that much land. Sure, she knew that things had been going well for them since they had taken over the family business after their father's death, but she didn't know how well.

"Where did he hear this?" she asked, now gazing around for Beau herself. Perhaps she could corner him and get the information from the man directly.

"Well," Joy sighed. "I'm not a hundred percent sure, but last week when we were there he talked to a man who'd told him about the purchase."

Seeing the back of Beau's dark, curly head down by the frozen water, Addy decided to forgo the rest of the slow conversation with Joy.

"I'm sorry, Joy, I have to . . ." She trailed off when Joy nodded in agreement.

"It's good to see you again," Joy called out as Addy made her way through the snow.

Beau was the skinniest, tallest, and hairiest man she'd ever met. The fact that he'd walked around all summer in California without a shirt and sun rays still never made it down to his pale skin said everything. Still, he had a heart of gold and really, truly cared about people and the earth.

Which, in her book, bumped him up several notches.

"Hey," she said, a little breathless when she finally reached him.

"Addy?" He frowned over at her. "What are you doing here? I thought I . . ."

"Joy told me that you heard the McGowans are buying some land."

He fell silent for a while, scanning the crowd before turning back to her. "Yeah." He took her arm gently and drew her a few steps away from the nearest clump of people. "Not just any land, the land directly east of the Flathead Reservation."

Addy sighed and tried to brace herself for what she knew was coming.

"We'll need you back there as soon as possible. We've got our hands full with everything here." He looked around the campsite, temporary home to the thousands of protesters braving the snow to fight against the pipeline. "I'm really hoping you'll take the lead on this since you know the place and the people involved there. Kind of like an insider . . ." He shoved his hands in his pockets as Joy walked over to them.

"Did you tell her?" Joy asked.

"Not yet." Beau's eyes dropped from Addy's.

"What?" Addy steadied for another blow, but then Joy smiled.

"We're getting married." Joy held out her small hand, and Addy noticed the freshly inked tattoo. Green vines wrapped around her ring finger, and Addy could see an outline of a large flower near the top knuckle. "We'll get it finished on our honeymoon." Joy smiled.

"Wow!" Addy couldn't think of anything more to say. She knew they were both against mining, so it made sense that tattoos were their preferred way to show their dedication to one another.

She watched Beau wrap his arms around Joy, who was almost half his size but fit perfectly next to him.

"Congratulations," Addy said, almost stammering it out.

Personality wise, they were a perfect match. Joy was soft-spoken, sweet, and extremely smart. Beau was everything any normal woman would dream of. Yet . . .

Addy wasn't a shallow person. Really, she wasn't. She'd spent most of her childhood being made fun of since she'd been skinny and taller than most girls and hadn't grown boobs until . . . she stopped herself from looking down at her barely B cups. All that, plus the ugly glasses and the haircut Trent had ever-so-thoughtfully brought up. She'd been teased so many times she'd lost count.

But just looking between Joy and Beau, no matter how antima-terialistic you were, you couldn't miss their size differences. He was six seven, rail thin. She was five one and very petite. She knew that others in camp talked about the pair behind their back. She also knew that neither of them cared what others thought. Something Addy still struggled with personally.

Addy wondered how it would work physically between them. Then she realized she was thinking about their sex life in front of them and her face heated. She had to turn away before they noticed her pink cheeks.

"We're hoping to get married this fall." Joy gleamed at Beau.

Addy could see the love in their eyes, and she knew that any physical differences between them fell away once they looked at each other.

"I'm so happy for you both," she said with heartfelt honesty.

Then Beau turned back to her. "I'm sorry that you just got here, but I really do need you back in Montana."

Addy sighed heavily. "I'll get a few hours of sleep and head back." She turned and started walking toward her Jeep and trailer.

"Hey, Adrianna." The use of her full name made her jaw tense—and the fact that she knew who had said it doubled the force of her clenching.

"Hi, Brian. I thought you were still in Montana." She'd been avoiding him there recently.

"Nope, came down here a few days ago after those McGowans almost killed me."

"They didn't lay a finger on you," she started to say, only to have him interrupt her.

"I'm thinking of hiring a lawyer and suing their asses. Breaking and entering. They tore up my stuff, not to mention had me arrested . . . twice." His blue eyes narrowed. "We have to protect our own." It was a statement he used all the time. She doubted he even knew what it meant.

"What do you want, Brian? I need a few hours of sleep. I've been on the road—"

Once again he interrupted her.

"Oh, man. You just got in? Yeah, sorry, I won't keep you long. I was just wondering if I could catch a ride with you back to Haven when you go? I caught a ride with Reed out here since my car had been acting up."

"I don't know, Brian. I'll probably need—"

"It's just a ride." His tone instantly turned and she knew it would get even worse if she didn't just agree. The man constantly interrupted her. It was one of his patterns. One that always had her on edge whenever she was around him.

"Sure," she sighed. Visions of a nice, quiet, peaceful drive back to Montana fled her mind. "I'll probably get a few hours of sleep, then head back first thing in the morning." She started walking again toward her trailer.

"That's cool. So I was talking with Ricky, anyway, um, he's hooking up with Kitty tonight and . . . I'm kind of out of a place to . . ."

"No," she said, continuing to walk. "We've been over this." She sighed again when he fell into step next to her.

He reached out and grabbed her arm, stopping her. She glanced down at his hand. "Listen, I don't mind giving you a ride, but I don't let anyone stay with me. Is that clear?" She tried to jerk her arm free, but his fingers tightened.

"I'm not asking to fuck you, just to bunk with you. You've got that big trailer all to yourself."

Addy glared at him. "If you don't let go of my arm, I'm going to have to report you." Before she could get her phone out, his hand had dropped. "Now as I've stated on many occasions, I don't bunk up. Go ask Beau, he'll arrange for you to bunk with another man for the night."

Without giving him a chance to respond, she turned on her heel and headed back to her trailer.

Home sweet home, she thought as she climbed in and locked the door behind her. A massive king-size bed occupied the entire back of the trailer. Bookshelves lined both sides of the cozy nook, filled with books of all shapes and sizes. Most of which she'd read at least three times.

The bathroom and kitchen were near the front. A small, one-person dining area connected the kitchen and the bed area.

Pulling off her boots, she set them on the drying rack she had built herself. Hanging her coat on one hook, she pulled off her hat and hung it on another. There was a place for everything she had, and she was meticulous about keeping her space, no matter how tiny, tidy.

Being organized was something she had found out she loved early on in life. It had nothing to do with her mother or the drive the woman had to run Addy's life. Instead, she found great pleasure in knowing exactly where everything was.

When she climbed into the overly soft, expensive mattress she'd splurged on, she sighed and closed her eyes. Instantly Trent's brown eyes came to mind.

Turning over, she tried once more to fall asleep. This time, she heard his chuckle, which jolted her body to full sexual alert. Damn that man for consuming her thoughts. Then she heard the soft chuckle again.

Her eyes opened and she frowned. Turning once more, she punched her pillow and closed her eyes. Only now she heard what she could have sworn was Trent's low voice.

This time, she sat up and glared at her front door. There was no way she was really hearing him outside her trailer.

She sat still for almost a complete minute and, when everything was silent outside, decided she needed more sleep than she'd thought. However, the second she closed her eyes, that voice returned.

She jumped from her bed and swung her door open, almost knocking Trent over as he reached up to knock. His smile bloomed.

"There you are. I was just—"

"What in the hell are you doing here?" she said through gritted teeth. The fact that her knees went weak at the sight of him standing in the parking lot, fresh snow dusting his eyelashes and the long, curly hair that peeked out from under his hat, didn't matter. She tried to ignore what the man's presence was doing to her body as she glared down at him.

Instead of being offended at her sharp tone, Trent just smiled more widely.

◆ ◆ ◆

Okay, so Trent supposed he could see how this looked from Addy's point of view. The word *stalker* popped into his mind. Still, he doubted she'd give him time to explain exactly why he was in North Dakota, in the same town, in the same parking lot as her and more than a thousand other people who some would describe as his enemies. Seeing as he was from an oil family, and everyone here was . . . well, against his kind.

Her blue eyes narrowed at him, and her hands were firmly placed on those trim hips of hers.

"Would you believe me if I said I came here to see a man about a moose?" he said.

Her faced turned a sexy shade of pink, then before he could say anything more, she stepped back and slammed the door on him. He couldn't help it. He laughed.

Less than a second later, her door flew open again. "Why are you here?" Addy asked. "The truth."

"I really am here to see a man about a moose . . . it's a kind of tractor." Trent nodded toward the parking lot, where a large semi sat a few yards away. On the back of the flatbed trailer was a massive blue tractor. What he didn't share was that he'd selected the meeting place. To be fair, Joe, the man with the tractor for sale, had suggested North Dakota, about a hundred miles from their current location, but that town didn't have a runway for Trent's Cessna. So Trent had picked this place himself.

He turned away from her and smiled at the tractor. "I'm going to call her Bessy. I think I might be in love." He sighed as he looked at the machine.

This time Addy was the one who laughed. He turned back around. Something close to an electric feeling flooded his body. The light from inside her trailer cast a halo around her long hair. It wasn't in the braid she'd had it in every other time he'd seen her lately. Now it fell over her shoulders, and she looked even more beautiful than before.

"How did you get here?" She crossed her arms.

"I flew." He moved a little closer as a strong wind blew up his back. "Landed about an hour ago at the airport. Any chance I could come in for a minute?" He looked around her into the trailer.

"No." She blocked his way and closed the door slightly.

"Why? Aren't you alone?" His smile fell slightly.

Her eyes narrowed again. "It's none of your—"

"Addy, it's freezing out here, and I need to talk to you about something I overheard." He glanced around, not wanting to say more.

"About?" She drew the word out.

"Something you've just been told." He really hated being out in the open. Not to mention he was freezing. He'd stood outside for the past hour, waiting for the truck with Bessy on it.

She was silent for a moment.

"Are you afraid of me?" Trent asked, not sure of what he'd do if she said yes. There was one thing you could say about the McGowan brothers: they may be known for chasing women, but they respected every single one of them.

He watched her chin rise slightly. "Of course not."

"Then . . ." He nodded to the inside of her trailer as another burst of cold air hit them both. He shivered noticeably.

Addy stepped back and held the door open. "Five minutes," she warned as he entered.

His mother hadn't raised a fool. To his credit, when he saw how tidy her small space was, he removed his boots and set them on the drying rack next to hers. He hung his jacket next to hers, then moved farther into the small space, ducking his head since the ceiling of the trailer was about six inches too short for him. He noticed her head cleared easily as she shut and latched the door behind them.

She stood back and frowned as she watched him.

"Do you have anything to drink?" He looked around. "I spent the last few hours in the air, then an hour out in the open trying to . . ." He took a deep breath. "Never mind." He shook his head, remembering how the negotiations to get Bessy home had gone.

"I have tea." She moved, and when she bumped into him, nodded to the small table. "Sit."

He edged around her slowly, his head tilted at an odd angle to avoid the low ceiling. He smiled when he heard her breath hitch as he brushed against her. When he sat down, he rolled his shoulders and enjoyed the warmth of the trailer.

He watched her handle the small space like it was the biggest kitchen. She took two coffee mugs down from hooks, filled a small glass container with water and set it down on a black disk, then hit the button to start the warmer.

"That's pretty cool," he said about the glass kettle.

She smiled as she pulled two packets of tea down from a cupboard. "It heats water up in under a minute."

He could tell she was trying to stay busy until the water was hot. She got out some crackers and put a slab of cheese on a plate and set it in front of him.

Instantly his stomach growled. The sound echoed in the small area, causing Addy to look over at him. She frowned again, and he could tell she was debating what to do with him.

"Like I said, I had to rush here to meet Joe." He took a cracker and shoved it into his mouth.

"I can heat up some soup, if you'd like," she said, watching him take another cracker.

"I don't want to put you out," he said automatically.

"It's not a problem, actually. I'm kind of hungry myself."

He nodded and nibbled on the crackers as she went to work on her new task.

"Why do you need . . . Betsy?" she asked as she glanced over her shoulder.

"Bessy," he corrected.

22

She shook her head and turned back around. "Why do men always name their machines?"

He chuckled. "Because we can."

"Why do you need such a big tractor?"

"I'm clearing my land, and since I still have the blisters from helping Tyler clear his land for his house, I figured I'd be smarter than he was. Besides, I found out I love driving one."

Addy set a bowl of tomato soup in front of him along with a chunk of French bread.

"Why did you have to pick it up here?" she asked, sitting next to him with her own soup.

"I'm not picking it up. I'm flying back home. I just came out here to inspect it and sign off on it so he could drive it out to me," Trent said between spoonfuls of hot soup.

"You flew all the way out to North Dakota to buy a tractor?" she asked.

He nodded.

"In a snowstorm?"

"Well, it wasn't snowing when I left Montana."

She peered out of the windows next to the table. "You should probably fly out tomorrow. It's really starting to come down out there."

He looked out too and held in a curse. "Can't. I have a meeting tomorrow morning." He sighed and finished off his soup. "Besides, I've flown in worse."

"You've . . ." She turned and looked at him, then shook her head. She set her spoon down. "What did you want to tell me?"

Trent took a deep breath. "I know that your boss . . ."

"Beau," she supplied, and he nodded.

"I know he's gotten wind of my family's plan to purchase the Lenz family's land."

Her eyes narrowed at him. "How did you . . ."

"It's not what it seems," he added when she didn't finish her sentence. "I overheard him telling you about it."

"Okay," she said slowly. "What is it, then?"

He shifted his feet under the table. "I can't tell you anything about it yet."

She pushed her half-empty bowl away. "Then why say anything to me at all?"

"Because I don't want you to get all worked up about something that's . . . nothing." He smiled again when he noticed her brows arch. "You don't believe me?" he asked.

"I don't believe half the stuff you say to me," Addy said with a smile.

"Why?" He leaned closer. "What did I ever do to you that would give you the impression that I am anything but trustworthy?"

She laughed, and he realized he enjoyed the sound. Soft, yet caressing. The way her eyes changed when she was enjoying herself was mesmerizing. What would they look like in the heat of pleasure?

She stood up. "It isn't what you did to me, more like . . . I've seen every smooth move that you've used over the years with all those other women."

CHAPTER THREE

How was it possible that Trent made the area she'd lived in the past two years seem like a shoe box? He filled the space almost completely. Even the scent of him, woodsy and fresh, wove through every inch of air.

Addy kept herself busy by putting their bowls in the sink and then turned around. Without her knowing, he had moved directly behind her, and she almost bumped into him. His arms came up, covering her shoulders so she couldn't fall back into the sink.

Just the feeling of his hands had her body responding. Her knees almost buckled as his eyes met hers. She'd always believed that Trent's eyes were just brown; however, this close, she realized there was hazel mixed in, giving them an almost lighter hue. His hair had fallen in front of his eyes and he automatically flicked it away, almost bumping his head on the top of her trailer.

"Sorry," he said under his breath. She watched that dimple next to his mouth appear, her eyes drawn to the spot like a magnet. She'd always wondered what those lips would feel like next to hers, under hers, against her skin. Again, her body tried to take over, and she felt herself sway toward him. His hands moved up to her arms, holding her steady even as he drew her nearer.

She realized instantly that she'd seen this move from him before. Many times, with many other women.

"No, you're not." She moved to the side, needing the moment to breathe through her attraction to him. "You forgot one thing," she continued, after taking a moment to compose herself. "I've known you for too long. You and your brothers. I've seen almost every move you guys have used on other women, like I said." She picked up the mugs from the table and put them in the sink with the bowls. The fact that her hands and knees shook with want didn't escape her notice. She just hoped he didn't see them as well. "I don't know why you'd try them on me." She turned back around, and he was in her way again. She easily sidestepped him one more time. "Now if we're done . . ." She cocked her head toward the door.

Trent shook his head slightly, his dark eyes searching hers. "I'm sorry," he said. "Honestly I only wanted you to know that there's no reason to be worried about our purchasing the land."

"Unless you can tell me that your family business won't be drilling for oil on the land directly next to the reservation, there's nothing more to talk about." She walked over to her door and waited.

She could tell he was thinking about what to say next. After a moment of silence, he walked over and slipped on his boots. "You won't have to worry about Brian," he said as he pulled on his jacket.

"Oh?" She stiffened. "Why is that?"

"I've arranged for him to ride with the truck driver." He pulled on his beanie, tucking that wonderfully dark hair underneath the cotton.

"Why did you . . ." She stopped herself. "Thank you."

His smile caused that damn dimple to flash again. She needed him out of her trailer and fast.

"Have a safe trip home," he said, then let himself out of her trailer and disappeared into the night.

It took forever for Addy to fall asleep after that. When she finally did drift off, her dreams were filled with chocolaty eyes and hot lips running all over her body.

She woke with the sun and headed back out on the road after a quick meeting with Beau and Joy. It was official; she was now in charge of everything at the Haven location.

It was up to her to find out what exactly the McGowans wanted with the Lenz land, if they were indeed going to be fracking, who they were working with, and most importantly how to stop them.

When she finally pulled into town that evening, exhaustion had begun to fray her focus. She didn't waste any time and headed directly to the state park, where they had set up camp almost a full month ago.

When she pulled into her designated spot, she groaned when she noticed Brian, back already, step out of the shadows. It had been wonderful not having to spend almost nine hours trapped with the guy.

She was surprised he hadn't chosen to stay in North Dakota instead of coming back to Haven. His mother, Rea, still had a restraining order out against him.

She knew his past, one of the reasons she tried to steer clear of him. He was the kid that, for as far back as she remembered, had bullied or picked on the weaker kids. Some of the kids back in junior high had gossiped about him decapitating cats and other small animals, but she knew how rumors were in small towns and chose to not believe half of what she heard.

He'd been a loner for the most part until he joined the protest group. Now he had a few guys to hang out with, shadier people she also stayed away from. But now that she was in charge of the operation, she knew she'd have to deal with Brian and his followers.

"I didn't think you were coming back until late next weekend," he said as soon as she stepped out.

"No." She frowned. "Who . . ." She let her question fall short since she knew exactly who had said that to give her a quiet drive home. "My plans changed," she added as she unhooked her trailer. She needed to run into town and restock her kitchen, and she knew that it would likely take her longer than she thought.

"I saw Trent McGowan go into your trailer in North Dakota," Brian said, leaning against her Jeep, blocking her from unhooking the power cables. "Fraternizing with the enemy?"

The statement from anyone else would have been a tease, but from Brian it sounded more like a threat.

"Brian, I'm exhausted and I have to get into town before the store closes." She nodded to her hitch.

He leaned closer to her, and she stopped herself from taking a step back away from him.

"I'll be watching. And I have a direct line to Beau." He glanced around. "Don't think you're above all this. Remember, I know people."

She felt her skin crawl and raised her chin. "Oh?" She refused to let the man get to her.

"I know people." He smiled and took a step back. "You think you know what's going on around here? You don't know shit," he said, and turned and walked away, laughing.

As Addy drove back into town, her frustration surged. She'd gone all her life without so much as a flirt from the opposite sex. Then suddenly Brian, Haven's notorious bully, and Trent McGowan, Haven's hottest hunk, were both trying to get into her camper. Why?

She parked her Jeep in front of the grocery store and when she got out, she noticed Kristen Howell.

"Oh." Kristen was still a little pale from her kidnapping ordeal a few weeks back. Addy could still see the worry and fear behind the woman's eyes.

The last Addy had heard, Dennis Rodgers, the former project manager at NewField, was up at a state facility awaiting trial for the kidnapping. The man had not confessed to taking Kristen, but had admitted to siphoning funds from the McGowans' business.

"I'm sorry." Kristen smiled at her. Then stopped. "Addy, right?"

"Yes, Kristen, how are you feeling?" Addy instantly regretted the question when Kristen's green eyes filled with sadness.

"Fine." She looked down. "I'm getting used to . . . things." Addy noticed the sadness retreat as a smile covered Kristen's face. "The movers just arrived with my stuff from New York."

"You're moving here for good, then?" Addy asked, knowing she'd never consider a permanent move back herself.

"Yes, my mother is as well. We'll start looking for a more permanent place for her." She waved to someone over Addy's shoulder.

Addy turned and noticed a woman approaching them.

"Hello." The woman smiled at her. Kristen looked so much like her mother that Addy almost did a double take.

"Hi." Addy held out her hand and shook the older woman's hand. "I'm Addy Collins."

"Hi, I'm Kristen's mother, Trisha." The woman shifted a cart full of groceries toward the back of the truck. She smiled at her daughter. "Well, I think we bought enough groceries to last a month."

"You don't know the McGowan boys," Kristen said.

"That might last you a week." Addy chuckled and Kristen smiled.

"I'd better get going." Kristen gestured to where her mother was loading the truck with the bags. "Are you staying in town long?"

Addy sighed. "Until I'm needed elsewhere."

"Like Mary Poppins." Kristen grinned. "Tyler told me what you did to help when I was . . ."

Addy watched the woman shiver and wrap her arms around herself. She stepped closer and put a hand on her arm. "Anytime," she said warmly. "I'm glad you're okay. I'll see you around."

"We're having a small get-together tomorrow night, for everyone who helped look . . ." Kristen took a deep breath. "Tomorrow night at the McGowans'. My mother is staying there until she finds her own place."

"Sounds good. Can I bring anything?"

"Just yourself." Kristen waved as she got into the truck. "See you around six."

Addy nodded and as she watched the mother-daughter duo leave, she thought about if she'd ever felt that close to her mother. Once again, the answer was no.

◆　◆　◆

Trent was muddy, tired, and hungry by the time he let himself into his mother's place. They'd gotten Bessy unloaded from the truck, and he'd spent a good five hours on her, hauling muck, rocks, and tree stumps from the site he planned for his home.

He'd walked from his land to the main house and up the rear stairs to let himself into the utility hallway. After shedding his boots at the door, he looked down at his clothes and made sure to step directly on the doormat. Better to strip here than track in all that dark mud.

He left his socks and boxers on since Kristen's mother was staying in the guest room—Tyler's old bedroom. After tossing his soiled clothes into the washing machine in the hallway, he started the laundry and headed for his room, then stopped dead in his tracks in the kitchen at the sound of laughter.

"Forgot something, McGowan?" Just hearing Addy's sexy chuckle had him reaching to cover himself. "Shy too." She laughed at his move.

"What the hell?" He took a step back and realized the kitchen was full of people. "Damn it, Mom, couldn't you have warned me?"

His mother was all smiles as she leaned against the kitchen counter with a glass of wine in her hand. "Watch your language." She motioned to the phone in his hands. "I did text you over an hour ago."

Trent groaned as he remembered her telling him about the party a few days ago. He'd gotten so caught up in his new toy that he'd lost track of the days. He made a quick retreat into his bedroom. Would he survive the next few months until his new home could be delivered and set up? Thoughts of renting his brother's old apartment above the Wet Spot went quickly through his head.

After showering and pulling on a fresh shirt and jeans, he made his way back out to the room full of guests.

He'd moved too quickly to register anyone other than Addy and his mother; now, however, his face heated with embarrassment as he realized how big his audience had been.

"Enjoying yourself?" he asked Addy, shoving a carrot stick into his mouth.

"So far I've enjoyed the show," she teased.

"Really?" He leaned closer to her and savored her soft scent.

"I'd say you were the highlight of the party so far," Addy said just under her breath.

He held in a chuckle, but groaned in spite of himself as her eyes moved over him.

"If you want . . ." He trailed off when Addy's gaze moved across the room. He watched concern flood in as she looked at Kristen standing near the fireplace.

"She's still struggling with everything." Addy nodded toward Kristen.

His brother Tyler had his arm wrapped around Kristen's waist, holding her against him with tenderness.

"Yeah, they both are." Trent's good attitude took a dive when he noticed the dark circles under Kristen's eyes. "Being with him helps, though."

"I suppose," Addy said and took another drink.

"You suppose?" He turned to her and took another carrot.

"I mean, he is the one who found her, and it seems like he loves her." She shrugged a little.

"But?" he asked.

"Depending on someone else to heal your pain . . ." She shook her head and glanced back across the room. "Only time and distance from those who hurt you can do that."

His eyebrows shot up. "Who's hurt you?" He took a step closer to her.

Just then, his mother interrupted by tapping her spoon against her wine glass to get the room to quiet down.

"We'd like to thank everyone for coming tonight," she said, as she joined Kristen, Tyler, and Trisha by the fireplace. "I believe Kristen and Trisha have a few words for everyone."

His mother stepped back and gave them the room.

Trisha spoke first. "No words could ever convey how lucky we are to know everyone in this room. For the longest time, it's just been Kristen and me. We've been through a lot together." She reached for her daughter's hand, and Trent heard a sniffle somewhere in the room. Immediately he tried to take a step backward. He hated seeing women cry, especially a whole room full of them.

"Scared of a few tears?" Addy mocked lightly, causing him to relax back against the bar next to her.

"Just wish I had a beer," he said under his breath.

"But," Trisha's voice broke in again, "over the years, we learned to rely on one another. We never for a moment believed that we'd ever feel part of something bigger than us. The McGowan family and you, the good people of Haven, have changed our minds." She raised her glass and everyone in the room followed suit. "Not only did every one of you in this room help find and save my daughter, but you've welcomed us with open arms and hearts. We're both very proud to now be part of this wonderful community and hope that someday, somehow, we can repay your kindness."

There were a few shouts of "hear, hear," and "welcome aboard," then everyone drank.

Kristen's smile was so bright, Trent felt the heat from across the room. His brother had lucked out in finding her, the woman Trent would call sister-in-law soon enough.

"My mother sure does have a way with words," Kristen said, getting a few giggles and sniffles from the room. Her smile dipped slightly, and she reached for Tyler's hand and clasped it together with her mother's. "But I know in my heart that without everyone in this room, I wouldn't be standing here today." She took a deep breath, and Trent watched Kristen's eyes move to Addy, standing next to him. A tear slid down Addy's cheek. "So thank you." Kristen raised her glass.

Trent saw Addy quickly dash the tear away and take a sip of her drink.

"Going soft?" he said when the room filled with noise again.

She glanced over at him. "You're one to talk." She nodded to his damp cheeks.

"I'm allowed to be emotional. I was there when we found her." He rubbed his face dry. "No one should ever have to go through that kind of abuse."

"No," Addy sighed. "They shouldn't." She waved to someone across the room. "Excuse me."

He watched her walk across the room. Somehow, he doubted she'd been talking about Kristen and wondered again who had hurt her.

Trent circulated, chatting with everyone, snacking on fried chicken and his mother's herb-mashed potatoes, and finally got that beer he'd been wanting.

He spent almost fifteen minutes talking to the mayor of Haven, Ms. Martha Brown. The woman was a ball of energy. She filled him in on the new elementary school plans. The building site was just on the outskirts of town. He'd been on the committee who'd voted for the location.

He'd even seen the first run of building plans and had liked what he'd seen. But Martha went on about some of the challenges they would be facing in the future. He was beginning to wonder if she had a point somewhere when she finally got to it.

"So I was talking to your brother." She waved a hand at Tyler, who was busy talking to someone else across the room. Kristen was still leaning against him. "He hinted that you'd be the person to talk to about looking at the landscaping plans for the school. Where to put the playground equipment, what kind of trees and bushes should go in, where it should all go. You know, all that stuff." She waited as he looked down at her. "Basically everything you're now doing for your own business. But for the town and kids."

His heartstrings were sufficiently tugged. He sighed and took a sip of his beer. "I'll swing by your office later this week."

The mayor's smile bloomed bright and big. "Thank you." She reached up on her toes and placed a loud, smacking kiss directly on his lips, much like his mother did. Once she walked away, Addy came back.

"First you give a room full of people a show, and now you're hitting on women older than you by half your age." She tsked as she edged past him. She was heading to the hallway and the front door, so he followed.

CHAPTER FOUR

Addy stepped outside of the McGowan home and hugged her jacket closer to her as the crisp mountain air hit her.

Her mind was already flooded with tomorrow's list of things to do. Since returning to town, she'd barely had enough time to research what Beau had asked her to. She had a trip to city hall scheduled for first thing tomorrow morning.

She was leaning on the front screen door when it opened behind her, nudging her a few steps forward.

Strong hands wrapped around her shoulders and held her.

"Sorry," Trent's deep voice sounded from directly behind her.

She closed her eyes and took a moment to enjoy the feeling of being held by him again.

Then, as quickly as he'd caught her, his hands were gone, his warm touch replaced by the cool air.

She shifted a foot away from the top edge of the porch until she knew she was out of the way of the screen door. He'd been correct earlier; part of her was and would always be a klutz.

"You've forgotten your jacket," she said absentmindedly.

She watched as he shrugged and walked over to the porch railing. "It's warmed up finally."

She moved closer to him, almost as if she were in a trance. The memory of him rushing out of the kitchen, dressed only in a dark pair of socks and tight—very tight—boxer briefs, had her mind swirling.

He had been everything she'd dreamed about. His body had actually been better than her imagination had conjured up over the years.

"Did your . . . Bessy get here safe?" she asked, not sure what to say. The night seemed so quiet. Even with the muffled sounds of the party still going on just a few feet away inside the house, the night air was too quiet.

He glanced over at her, and his smile caused her breath to stick in her chest.

"Yeah, she's a beauty. Spent the entire day on her. Cleared more land in a single day than in a week of backbreaking work between the three of us at Tyler's place. He's already begging me to drive it up to his place and finish the job there."

She couldn't help it; his smile was contagious. She leaned against the railing next to him and lost herself in his eyes for just a moment.

"Why are you clearing your land?"

"I'm having a log home kit delivered in a few months." He turned slightly and his body brushed against hers. She straightened and stiffened. Her chin rose.

"Why do you do that?" he asked, his hand reaching out slowly as he brushed a finger down the arm of her jacket.

"What?" She took a slow breath.

"Tense every time I get near?" A small crease formed between his dark eyebrows.

"Why wouldn't I?" She looked away into the darkness beyond the light from the porch. The yard was too dark to see, but she knew that Gail, Trent's mother, kept her plants and yard as tidy as her house. In a few weeks, the front area would probably be full of blooms. Something she missed living in a small travel trailer. Not having dirt to play with, not being able to help things grow.

His voice broke into her daydreams of planting a garden of her own. "Someday you'll open up and tell me who has hurt you."

"What makes you think I've been hurt?" Her face went blank. She'd gotten good at that.

His head tilted and his eyes bore deeper into hers until she had to blink and glance away. She hadn't realized his arm had remained on hers until he removed it when the front door opened, flooding the front porch with light.

"There you are."

They both turned to see the mayor of Haven walk out onto the front porch.

Addy had seen the woman talking with Trent and half the people at the party. Figuring that she hadn't finished her conversation with Trent, Addy took a step back, expecting to make her retreat. But then the mayor walked over to her and took her arm. "I hope you're not leaving already," she said to Addy, surprising her.

Addy had known Martha Brown her entire life. The woman had been one of her mother's friends. Then again, the mayor of Haven was friends with almost everyone. One of the reasons she was the most popular public official Haven had ever seen.

"I . . . I was about to go. I need to be . . ."

"Nonsense," Martha said, patting Addy's hand. "We were just talking about your little group and could use some help in explaining some things."

Addy glanced over her shoulder at Trent as the mayor tugged her back into the house.

Trent's frown caused her to be very grateful for the interruption. She knew that once he or his brothers got their mind set on finding answers, they were as determined to get to the bottom of things as she was.

There was no way she was ready to open up about her problems to a playboy who at one point or another had dated every girl in town. Every girl except her.

For the next hour, she stood and explained what her "little group" was actually doing in Haven. She felt like she had to repeat herself more than a half dozen times, but in the end, she at least knew that the mayor had really listened to her concerns.

"Of course, I care very much about what goes on in and around my town. I'd like to set up a time when we can meet in my office," Martha said. "Maybe we can have a private meeting with the McGowans as well to talk through everyone's concerns."

"That would be wonderful." Addy smiled. *Score one for me.* Man, would Beau be proud.

"Why don't I check with their schedules and mine and get back to you?" Martha jotted something down. "Give me a call later this week."

She handed Addy a business card; on the back was her private cell phone number.

"Thank you." Addy felt a huge weight lift from her shoulders.

"Don't mention it." Martha smiled. "Now how are your parents doing? I haven't seen them in a while."

Addy blinked and felt her heart kick. "They're traveling," she said between clenched teeth. "For the past few years, they have spent the first month of spring in the Caribbean."

"Oh, that's right." Martha made a tsk sound. "Who would spend the best part of the year away from all this? Watching the last snow melt away, the flowers bloom." She took a drink as her gaze hopped around the room. "We have a good group here," she said, and Addy could see pride and love in the woman's eyes. "I'm happy things didn't end in a tragic way for Kristen and Tyler."

"Yes," Addy agreed. "It must have been terrible."

"That's a strong woman there." She nodded to Kristen. "She deserves to be happy." Martha turned to her and laid a soft hand on her elbow. "So do you."

Addy didn't know what to say. Her throat closed up and suddenly she felt her eyes sting.

"I . . . I am happy," she said. Her voice sounded faraway and hollow.

"Yes," Martha said, drawing the word out. "I can see you are." The tone of the older woman's voice said it all. "Maybe you should take a page from Kristen's book."

Addy's eyebrows shot up in question.

"Let someone unexpected into your life." She patted her arm. "Don't forget to call later this week," she said over her shoulder as she moved across the room.

Addy stood by the kitchen bar and watched as the crowd of people slowly thinned.

She'd meant to leave too, but her feet felt rooted to the spot. Even though most of the people in the room weren't technically related, they acted as if they were closer than most families.

Then again, it didn't take too much to outstrip her own family.

When there was only a handful of guests left, she made her way over to Kristen and Tyler, said her good-byes, and once again stepped out onto the front porch. Taking a deep breath of the crisp night air, she slowly made her way down the steps.

"Leaving so soon?" Trent's voice caused her to jump.

She hadn't seen him sitting on the front porch in the dark.

"Sorry." He chuckled. "It got a little too crowded in there and I needed some fresh air. Again." He stood up and approached her.

"Yeah," she added, looking back toward the almost-empty house. "Still, it was nice of them to include me."

"From what Tyler has told us, you really helped out. Going into the Wet Spot. I heard you took a few cat scratches from Darla." He shoved his hands deep into his pockets.

She grinned at him. "I gave her a black eye."

He nodded. "Yeah, I saw it myself."

"Oh?" She crossed her arms. "Still frequenting the Wet Spot?"

His chuckle echoed again. "They do have the best steak dinners in town."

She dropped her arms and shrugged. "Right," she said, turning away from him. She didn't want him to see her disappointed look. She knew she could never compare to the half-dressed busty women at the local strip club. Darla, as ugly as the woman was on the inside, was wrapped in a very sensual, exotic package that made most men drool.

Compared to her old best friend from junior high, Addy had always been the invisible girl. She couldn't even remember why or how they had become friends back then. Maybe it was because they had both come from damaged families? Maybe it was just dumb luck?

She took a few steps toward her Jeep.

"So what about that dinner I owe you?" Trent caught up to her.

Her eyes flashed to his in question. "Dinner?"

His smile was quick. "Sure, remember?" He had to slow his pace down to match hers.

She stopped just short of her Jeep as she remembered his words on the trail the other morning. "Oh." She shook her head. "How about we call it even since I gave you soup the other night?"

He shook his head. "No, that was you feeding me. I owe you. Not the other way around. Although technically now I owe you two meals." He leaned closer until he was just a breath away. His smile slowly spread, causing that sexy dimple to flash. "How about dinner and then . . . breakfast?" he said in a husky voice.

She couldn't help it. A burst of laughter escaped her lips. Any other woman would have melted at his feet. But she knew him too well.

"What?" He stepped back with an offended look. "What's so funny? The prospect of dinner or the idea of spending a night with me?"

"Both," she said between laughs. She shook her head. "Good night, Trent." She opened her Jeep door and slammed it behind her.

As she drove away, she could still sense the confusion in Trent's eyes, even though it was too dark to see them clearly.

Did he really think that a line he'd used a dozen times on her friends would work on her? She chuckled about his repeat moves until she pulled in next to her trailer.

Then her smile fell away as she saw a small group of people, led by Brian, standing outside her camper.

"What now?" she groaned as she got out of her Jeep.

◆　◆　◆

The following evening, Trent let himself into his mother's house. Once again, he stripped off his muddy clothes, but this time, he was prepared. He'd stacked a pair of old jeans and a shirt by the door, and he slipped them on before stepping into the main part of the house.

His mother and Trisha sat in the living room, drinking coffee.

His mother looked over. "There you are. We were just thinking of heading into town for dinner since neither of us feels like cooking after yesterday. Would you care to join us?"

He thought about it. "Sure, can I take a quick shower and change first?"

Both women nodded. "We'll wait," his mother said, turning back to her coffee.

Once in the shower, his mind spun with the long day of work and the few hours he'd spent on Bessy clearing his land. He'd handled the entire section that the house would sit on in under a week. Now he had the long driveway to clear—almost a quarter of a mile's worth. He'd talked to the local contractor about laying gravel before the house was set to be delivered in three months. His permits had finally come in, which meant that the electric, gas lines, and well drilling could all move forward.

Things were moving along smoothly. At least as far as his house and land were concerned.

He was thankful he'd planned ahead and would be moving into his house long before Tyler and Kristen.

That was assuming everything went as planned.

After drying off and dressing, he drove his mother and Trisha into town and parked outside of the Dancing Moose Diner.

When they walked into the diner, the typical crowd of townspeople looked over. Some waved, others nodded a greeting as Trent, Gail, and Trisha took their seats in a booth in the back.

They had just ordered when a group of loud men entered, led by Brian.

Trent immediately wondered if he should text Tony Whayne, one of the local cops and a family friend.

"Let's wait and see," his mother said in a low tone, reading his mind and putting a hand over his as he reached for his phone.

"It never hurts to be proactive," he murmured as the men made their way to the booth next to theirs. It wasn't the only empty spot in the diner, but he knew Brian had picked it for a reason. Which had him punching a text out to both Tony and Mike Taters, the chief of police.

"Trent." His mother shook her head and sighed.

"What?" He set his phone down. Less than ten minutes later, Tony, Mike, and Tom walked into the diner and took an empty booth across from Brian and his gang.

Tony was the tallest of the three—he had a full head of gray hair, while Mike had shaved his head bald years ago, which had the effect of making everyone in town respect him even more. Of course, being chief of police hadn't hurt either. Tom, for his part, was the only officer who had never looked threatening. The man looked like someone's goofy brother.

So far, Brian's group hadn't done anything but flirt with the waitress, who flirted back with obvious pleasure.

When Trent's table's food was delivered, another group of people came in, this time led by Addy. He'd seen the types before, most of them dressed like hikers and campers. However, there were a few in the group that went all out. He'd seen a bunch of them with painted faces and costumes as they had picketed outside his business, holding signs about how his family was single-handedly killing the earth.

She took in the room, and he watched her eyes flit to him, then away. Her group made their way to a larger table at the other end of the diner. They sat, laughing and joking as the once-quiet diner grew louder.

Trent couldn't seem to tear his gaze from Addy as she enjoyed the company of her group. His mother and Trisha continued their conversation as if he wasn't even there, and he was thankful for it.

Then, a few minutes after he was done eating, the radios and cell phones from the booth across the aisle all squawked at the same time.

Mike glanced over at Trent as he and the rest of the cops jumped up and hurried past the waitress as she brought them their food. "Keep it warm for us," Mike said as they rushed from the building.

"Wonder what that was all about?" Trisha asked.

Trent exchanged a look with his mother. "I'll go see."

She nodded at him as he made his way out of the diner.

"Tom." He caught up with the man just before he got into his patrol car. "What's up?"

"There's a fire at the NewField offices," he said, then slammed his door. Trent watched him drive off. The McGowans had been working with NewField since their father had started his company. The McGowans depended on them to stay in business. The McGowans might drill for the oil, but NewField pumped it and maintained the pipelines for DW Petroleum Industries—the real owner of most of the oil in Montana.

"What's up?" his mother said from directly behind him. "We closed out."

"Fire at NewField. Let's swing by and see if we can help," Trent said, reaching for her keys.

He noticed Brian's group heading out the front door of the diner as he pulled out of the parking lot.

They made it to the building just as the fire hoses began to blast. One thing Trent could say about Haven: the town knew how to come together in a time of crisis.

More than a dozen people out in the street helped where they could as the brick building, similar in design to the McGowans' own office a few blocks away, was totally engulfed in flames. Glass shattered and everyone was pushed back an entire block by the police. Trent and a few others helped make sure everyone was well beyond the safety zones.

They all stood back as the fire department fought the flames shooting from the broken windows.

Two hours later, when there were only wisps of smoke coming from the pile of rubble, everyone began speculating about what started the blaze.

"We won't know anything—" Matt, the battalion chief of the local fire department, was drowned out for a moment by the questions coming from the growing crowd.

Matt held up his hands, waiting for everyone to quiet down. "Like I was saying, we won't know anything until the fire inspector goes through the rubble and discovers the cause. People!" He raised his voice when everyone started talking again. "It could take days to determine the cause. For now, no one was harmed. Everyone has been accounted for. So there is nothing further to see here tonight. You might as well all go home, warm up, and get some sleep."

Matt turned away and made his way back toward his firefighters.

"You heard the man." The mayor's voice rose over the crowd. "I'll be holding a special town hall meeting this Friday to discuss what we've found." She waved everyone away and when Trent turned to go, he almost bumped right into Addy. His hands gripped her shoulders to steady her before he tipped her over.

"Sorry," he murmured.

"You seem to be saying that to me a lot lately." She smiled up at him. "Either you're bumping into me on purpose or you're the klutz instead of me."

He smiled. "I have never been described as such before." He tucked his hands into his pockets, avoiding his near-constant desire to reach out and touch her. He knew when he did, it made her uncomfortable. He could see it deep in those blue eyes of hers.

Her head tilted as she looked up at him. "Was anyone hurt?" she said, then glanced around him at the smoking rubble.

"No." He shook his head. "Just lost a building, some furniture, and a bunch of paperwork . . ." He trailed off as his mind snapped into gear. Suddenly he looked around urgently to find Mike. "Sorry, I have to . . ."

He left Addy standing by his mother and Trisha as he made his way through the crowd to find the chief of police. He had a theory about why NewField's local office was now a pile of rubble.

CHAPTER
FIVE

The fire was all anyone could talk about over the next few days. Addy had called to set a meeting with the mayor and the McGowans, but since Martha had been busy meeting with the fire chief and inspector, their conversation had been pushed off until later next week.

Addy attended the special town hall meeting on Friday night with her old friends from school. Two of them, Becki and Missy, were already married with kids in Haven, whereas Harmony was still single and working at the local elementary school as a teacher.

Addy felt relieved that she wasn't the only one from her class who was currently unwed.

She wasn't surprised to see Tyler sitting at the front next to the mayor. She'd heard that over the last few weeks, he'd filled Dennis Rodgers's place on the city board as city controller. That man had influenced the city with nothing but corruption and deceit.

Addy had heard that Martha had placed Tyler in that position until an election could be had, but everyone in town was pleased with the move.

Now, as the meeting was called to order and the crowded room grew quiet, Addy shifted in her seat and felt the back of her neck tingle. Without looking, she knew Trent must be directly behind her.

Why did that man have so much control over her body? She shifted in her seat again as the mayor started talking.

For the next hour, she tried to listen to the findings on the fire. Really, she did. But it was just like sitting in classes. She'd heard what she wanted to hear—that the cause of the fire was still under investigation and that the authorities weren't releasing any further information yet. After that, her mind drifted off and suddenly she found herself daydreaming about a pair of lips roaming over every inch of her body. Her body heated as her mind sank further into the vision.

She'd felt his hands on her now a few times, but she'd always been covered in layers. What would they feel like skin to skin?

She'd dreamed about him for years. So, as her mind dove deeper into the visions, she was surprised at the new images her mind conjured up. Images, flashbacks really, of how he'd looked standing in his mother's kitchen in his tight boxer briefs. The play of muscles up his arms, over his broad shoulders, down his impressive chest and further down his stomach toward a very sexy, hard six-pack. Not even those half-dressed men on billboards in California or Vegas had come close to his perfection.

Her mind snapped from her dream as she realized every eye in the room was on her. The entire crowd was silently looking at her.

She wondered if she'd made any noises out loud. Her face turned a bright shade of red, and she coughed a few times to cover the fact that her throat had closed up.

"Um." She glanced around. Suddenly a low voice from behind her whispered.

"Fill them in on how long you'll be staying," Trent said in her ear.

"Oh." She took a deep breath, then stood up. "I'm sorry." She coughed again. "I think I'm coming down with something." She searched her mind for an answer as her coughs continued. Her eyes moved over everyone, then landed on the mayor, who waved an encouraging hand at her.

When the woman mouthed *You have the floor*, Addy's shoulders straightened and her chin went up slightly.

"As many of you have heard, my group, FREE—Friends Respecting Everything Environmental—has set up camp on the north side of town at the state park. We're here on a number of environmental concerns. The foremost being the rumor that fracking might be allowed just outside of Haven. Since we first arrived, we've been reassured that this rumor is false. However . . ." She paused as several people whispered amongst themselves. She began again and regained everyone's attention. "However, we have yet to see the local city council take any further measures to ban this destructive process of pulling crude oil from our precious lands." Her eyes met Martha's. "The mayor has assured me of a meeting later next week with several of the local oil drilling companies and the city council themselves. My organization eagerly awaits this meeting and hopes that we can come to some agreements that will protect the land and people living in and near Haven. I would further like to address the purchase of land next to the Flathead Reservation, where I'm sure local businesses will be eager to work with the reservation officials on filling them in on exactly what this land will be used for." She thought over her statement, then added, "Until these items are dealt with, my team will remain in Haven to save not only this beautiful land but to ensure the health and well-being of the people in it."

There was a moment of silence as she sat, then the entire room burst into chaos. Most of the locals shouted at the main table, some of them at her. She heard the words *global warming, fake news, oil haters, tree huggers*, and worse.

Her shoulders remained solid and her chin rose. Even the friends she'd been sitting with looked at her as if she'd grown an extra head. One of them actually scooted her chair farther away from Addy.

"Now you've done it," Trent said directly behind her.

Suddenly there was a loud whistle. The sound bounced around the large room and caused everyone to quiet down instantly.

Tyler stood next to the mayor, his fingers dropping from his lips as his whistle echoed in everyone's ears.

Trent chuckled. "Knew that would come in handy someday." He leaned closer until she felt his warm breath on her neck. "I taught him that."

"Good for you," she said, tapping her ears until they stopped ringing from the whistle.

"Thank you, Tyler," Martha said. "Now I am fully aware of Ms. Collins's group's intentions and my office will fully cooperate." She glanced down at her council. "We are very concerned about what happens in Haven. None of us wants to see our little town turned into a circus show." She glared around the room and Addy watched as a few men shifted uncomfortably in their seats. "Or a wasteland that is environmentally unsafe and full of pollution and earth tremors. I understand Haven was built on gold and oil. But I think we can all come to an agreement that we would hate for our children or our families to start getting sick because we didn't look at all our options and protect ourselves. None of us here want the water table to be flooded with chemicals. We all know about Flint, Michigan." A low rumble filled the room as everyone quietly agreed. "Sure, that wasn't due to fracking, but still, water quality is a high priority for all of us, wouldn't you agree?"

It was amazing. Just a few moments ago, Addy believed the room was on the verge of rioting, but now, every head nodded in silent agreement.

"You can close your mouth now," Trent said.

She realized her mouth was hanging open, so she quickly shut it.

"Impressive, isn't she?" he added.

Addy just nodded in agreement.

The meeting finished up with several questions about the new school structure, and Addy was surprised to hear that Trent had filled the position of landscape project manager for the job. He stood up and waved to the room when the mayor pointed this out.

When the meeting ended, Addy tried to exit the room but was inundated with people asking her questions. Most were individuals who wanted to help; others just wanted to tell her things designed to make her feel small, like that she couldn't get a "real" job.

She was thankful to see that Trent remained by her side during it all. When a few men approached her, she knew there was going to be trouble, but when Trent stepped closer to her and glared at the group, they moved off without a single word.

Finally a path to the door cleared, and she made her way out into the cool night air. She hadn't realized how stuffy the giant room in the city hall had gotten, but after taking a few cleansing breaths, she was relieved to be out of there.

Trent took her arm as they walked toward her Jeep; she felt her body brush against his and tried not to focus on what it did to her own. She looked over at him, her eyebrows raising.

He smiled down at her. "Just making sure you get to your car safely."

"I think I can manage . . ." Her voice dropped off as she noticed one of her tires was flat. She stopped in her tracks. "Damn it." She rushed toward her Jeep. "These were brand-new. Less than two thousand miles on them." She kicked the flat tire as Trent leaned down to get a better look.

When he stood up, she knew what he'd seen. "Slashed?"

"Yeah." He glanced around, then waved to his friend. "Tom's here."

Addy watched as Tom and Rea walked slowly toward him. She hadn't seen the two of them together before, and it kind of shocked her to see that Tom's arm was around Rea's shoulders. They looked good together. Everyone in town knew that Tom had lost his wife a few years back, and Rea's husband . . . well, everyone in town knew that story as well.

"What seems to be the problem?" Tom dropped his arm and leaned down. "Slashed. Looks like someone didn't care too much for what you had to say in there." He sighed. "I'll fill out the paperwork. You can have the vehicle towed in. I'm sure Larry and John can have a new tire put on in no time." He pulled out his phone and started to punch a few numbers.

"I have a spare." She headed to the rear of her Jeep to start the work herself.

"Let us," Trent said, and he and Tom stepped in. She knew she could easily change her own tires, since she'd had to before, but because they were working so quickly, she let them continue.

Addy and Rea stood back as the men rotated her spare to the front. Rea looked just as Addy remembered her. Her golden-brown skin glowed in the dim light from the parking lot. She wore a dark-green and gold blouse with bright-red feathers running down the length of the material. Her thick jet-black hair fell softly over her shoulders in a style she'd worn for as long as Addy could remember.

"I wanted to thank you," Rea said. "I know there are a lot of upset people." She looked around the empty parking lot as if she worried some were still lingering. "And this may seem strange coming from me, someone who's made a living off the oil business, but I'm first and foremost a Native American. I'm proud of my Kootenai heritage." The older woman's shoulders raised slightly. "I may not live on the reservation anymore, but I know how important land is." She reached over and patted Addy's arm. "If you need anything, count me in."

"Thanks." Addy grinned. She'd always liked Rea. There had been a time when the entire town had gossiped about the woman. How she'd married a white man and had a bastard son, then how she'd driven her husband to kill himself and how Brian had turned into a psychopath. Addy knew that her mother had taken part in most of that gossip. Still, Rea had been nothing but kind to Addy and everyone else. Addy had grown up knowing that most of what her mother gossiped about wasn't true. After all, hadn't her mother said as many terrible things about her?

♦ ♦ ♦

Trent rubbed the dirt and grease from his hands and straightened up. "All done. But just to be safe, I'll follow you back to your place."

He heard a soft chuckle from Tom and glanced over in time to see the man turn away.

"That won't be necessary," Addy said, walking to her Jeep and getting in. "Thank you both."

"If you'll stop by the station tomorrow, you can fill out and sign the paperwork for your insurance claim," Tom told her.

"Thank you," she said again, then shut the door.

"You'll have to work harder for that one," Rea said, patting Trent's shoulder lightly as Addy drove away. "You know I've always thought of you boys as my own." Her brow crooked as she looked at him. "So I'll be frank. She'll be worth it. Women like that only come around once in a lifetime. If you're lucky enough to catch her, never let go." Rea had always been there in the office when they needed her. If their folks had been busy, Rea had always had time for them. She gave his face a soft pat before she walked away, holding Tom's hand in her own.

Trent made his way to his truck and, on a whim, decided to follow Addy home anyway to make sure nothing was wrong at her trailer. If someone went to the trouble of puncturing her Jeep tires, a feat impressive on its own, he wondered just how far someone would go to prove to her that she wasn't wanted.

When he arrived, her Jeep was parked next to her trailer and the lights were on inside her small home. He sat across from her spot for a few minutes until he noticed her lights go dark, then pulled away slowly, keeping an eye out for anything that seemed out of the ordinary.

As he drove back to his mother's house, he thought about the private meeting he'd had the day before. It appeared that the case against Dennis Rodgers was halted, due to the fact that all the evidence was now lying in a pile of black ash in the NewField building.

He'd been told that there were only a handful of invoices left after the fire and that most of the proof against Dennis had gone up in smoke.

It appeared that NewField's computer systems had been hacked about a month ago and most of their data for the past few years had been wiped clean. Even the corporate office was relying on paper copies at this point.

Rea had hard copies of the invoices that were due, but the proof that Dennis had embezzled money was gone. There *was* proof that Dennis was a partner in a business called R&R, which had made an offer for McGowan Enterprises. But that wasn't enough to lock him up. After all, it wasn't against the law to start a business and try to buy another.

They had the keys from Dennis's key ring that matched the padlock which had been used to keep Kristen locked up in the cave. Mike had informed them that Dennis was claiming that they coerced a confession from him. He was recanting everything, claiming his confession was beaten from him.

The whole ordeal made Trent sick to his stomach. Kristen and Tyler were taking it better than he would have thought. Especially after they found out that Dennis could be out on bail in less than a month.

Trent parked his truck behind his mother's sedan, making sure to leave plenty of room for his brother's truck to leave.

Somehow, he had known that there would be a family powwow after the town hall meeting.

"Well?" Trey said the second Trent stepped inside.

"Well?" he responded, hanging his jacket up and placing his shoes on the rack he'd made in seventh-grade shop class. "What?" He turned to Trey.

His younger brother crossed his arms. "You're not getting past me until you tell me . . ." The rest of his words were drowned out as Trent tried to push his way past his little brother.

Okay, so they were pretty equally matched now as far as size went, but the fact that he would always be the older brother gave him the upper hand. Once they wrestled their way into the living area, both of them felt the sting of having their ears pulled until they separated.

"Enough." Their mother glared down at them as she held their ears in either hand. "If I remember correctly, I set a rule when Trey was eleven that there would be no more wrestling in this house ever again."

She released their ears and they fell apart.

"Sorry," they said in unison.

"Now, if you're done pretending to be eleven, why don't you both sit down so we can talk about our next move?" She narrowed her eyes at them.

"Move?" Tyler chuckled from his spot across the room. "Why do we have to . . ." His words dropped away with one look from their mother.

"Okay," Gail said after she finally sat down. "Now I saw you change Addy's tire tonight, Trent. Was it slashed?"

He glanced over at Trey and knew that's what his brother had wanted to know before everyone else.

"Yes ma'am." He leaned back in the chair. "Whoever did it didn't have time to finish the job . . . they left her spare and the three other tires alone." His voice trailed off and he sighed. "I made sure she got home okay." His mother nodded with approval.

"I can ask Mike to add a few more drive-bys this week at the park where she's staying." Tyler leaned forward.

"Okay, now that that is handled, how did word get out about our deal with the Lenz land?" Gail looked around the room as if she were looking for the leaker.

"When I went to North Dakota to pick up Bessy, I overheard Addy's boss, Beau, talking about it with her. Apparently he'd been approached by a few men here in Haven who passed the information on to him."

The room was silent. Then their mother spoke again. "Did she mention who it was that told her boss?"

"No," Trent sighed.

"Okay, who knew about the deal?" Gail asked.

For the next hour, they went through a list until they had it narrowed down to a handful of workers. Then they talked about the fire at NewField and speculated who could be behind it. Everything circled back to Dennis and his goons.

"It is important to our plans that this purchase fly under the radar as much as possible so nothing goes wrong. Thankfully Addy was enough distraction that no one focused too much on it. But you can guarantee that someone will put two and two together and start asking questions."

"Until we know something further, maybe Trent should keep a better watch on what's going on in the camp?" Trey rubbed a suspiciously smirking lip. "Besides, he doesn't seem to mind too much hanging around Addy."

This earned Trey an elbow in the ribs from his mother.

"Hush," she scolded and turned to Trent. "As I was about to suggest, I know you've been doing your part to keep an eye out, but is there any way you can get some more information from Addy on who the leak would have come from? We need to know exactly how much they know and their source."

A chance to hang out with Addy more? And all under the guise of doing his job? Hell yes.

"Sure," Trent said, as if it were no big deal. "If we're done, I have an early-morning meeting with a moose." He stood up.

"What would it take for you to bring that beast over my way?" Tyler asked as Trent started for the door.

"A case of beer," Trent called back. "And your firstborn named after me."

As he left the room, he heard Tyler chuckle and Trey respond, "That price is too high."

CHAPTER SIX

Addy stayed busy the following few days. She had arranged her team and divided them into groups, appointing heads to each department.

Minnie, a retired schoolteacher turned activist, organized meals. Helen, another retiree who had been an RN, took charge of lodging, making sure everyone had a place and enough blankets and wood for fires.

Addy figured Helen could keep everyone in line as far as making sure the men and women weren't bouncing between tents. Helen had a strong view that "her camp" not turn into one big orgy. Addy knew she'd chosen wisely.

She'd put Estelle, a young former legal assistant, in charge of banners and signs and organizing events.

Doug would handle the men's housing needs since most of them seemed to bunk together.

Having this small team lightened Addy's own load so she could spend more of her time doing research.

Early Monday morning, she stopped off at city hall, an old faded-pink building that had once boasted a public swimming pool, playground, and a small library. Now, however, the building was in disrepair, and the pool had been filled to make a giant parking lot. A new public library had been one of Martha's first achievements. The new building sat only two blocks away and was a beautiful sight to see with its massive two-story walls of dark glass and rows and rows of books. Addy wished it had been there when she'd been in school. She would have spent most of her evenings there instead of locked in her own room, trying to avoid her parents.

She knew there were plans to redo the old city hall building as soon as the new elementary school was finished. But where was the town suddenly getting new funds from?

She spent almost three hours locked in a back room at the city building, scouring files until her eyes hurt. She pulled out her reading glasses, which she only used when her eyes grew tired, and continued to go through the financials of several businesses in town. Including McGowan Enterprises. The city only had tax information for the past year, before the brothers took over. They were set to file this year in the coming month. But she could glean some information to build her case.

She knew that Thurston McGowan, Trent's father, had been a good businessman. It was evident with the profit noted on the taxes he'd filed that last year.

Still, with the rumors floating around town that the brothers had easily doubled their father's prior-year profits since taking over, she wanted to get her hands on the most recent documents. She knew that they had purchased one local competitor's business and forced another out of business.

The McGowans were okay guys—she'd trust them with most things—but something just wasn't feeling right. They had some big secret they were keeping from the population of Haven. And Addy was determined to figure it out.

"Doing some homework?"

She jerked her head up and peered over her reading glasses at Trent, standing in the doorway of the tiny room. His arms were crossed, stretching his crisp white T-shirt tight over his chest and shoulders. His longest layer of hair now barely brushed his collar and the shortest hung just below his dark eyebrows. He must have gotten it cut. He was wearing a pair of jeans that should have been illegal in their worn, snug fit. He still looked dangerous, but . . . not as much as before.

"No." She glanced back down at the stack of papers and shifted them so he wouldn't see she'd been looking into his business.

"What are you doing, then?" He walked over and took the folder before she could tuck it away. "Oh, that's what. Snooping." He tapped the oaktag against his hand.

"I am not!" she said indignantly. "I'm doing my job." She watched his smile grow as she shook her head. Her eyes moved to that sexy dimple, and she noticed it was deeper when his face was clean-shaven.

"Your job requires you to snoop on my family's business?" He leaned against the desk beside her.

"Yes and no." She pressed her forehead. How was it possible her mind turned to jelly when he was close to her? "I'm not snooping."

"Right." He drew the word out and set the folder down in front of her. "If not snooping, then . . ." He waited.

"Research." She crossed her arms.

His eyes stayed glued to hers. When he finally shifted, he tapped her glasses lightly with his fingertip.

"You're sexy as hell in these." This threw her completely off-balance. She reached to remove her glasses, but he stopped her.

"Why the fear?" he asked, and this time, he hooked her glasses with his finger and pulled them from her nose. "Every time I compliment you, I see it deep behind those crystal-blue pools." He leaned closer until they were almost nose to nose. "See, there it is again," he said, almost under his breath.

"I'm not . . . I don't . . ." She blinked a few times. He was too close. Too big . . . Too . . . perfect.

"I wonder . . ." He dropped off and his eyes traveled down to her lips. "What would replace the fear if I kissed you?"

Her breath locked in her lungs, and she was thankful she was still sitting down, because she doubted her legs would have held her up.

Her eyes slid closed and she leaned closer to him, only to be left waiting. When her eyes snapped open, she saw that he had moved back a few inches and his eyes were roaming her face.

"When I kiss you, I want to watch your eyes fill with passion," he said softly. "Another time." He stood up and flicked the folder. "If you want to know more about our company, come in and talk to Rea. She'll be happy to give you some updated info." He turned to go but stopped at the door. "Addy." He looked over his shoulder at her. "Don't be fooled. I will get that passion from you. Soon." He left the room, leaving the door open behind him.

She sat there for almost a full five minutes until she could get her heartbeat back to normal. *Wow,* her mind kept saying over and over. *Just wow.*

After she left city hall on still-shaky legs, she made her way to the grocery store. She was running low on supplies again and desperately wanted a gallon of mint–chocolate chip ice cream.

Addy had her cart almost full when she bumped solidly into Darla. She was pretty sure Darla had swerved her cart toward hers, but didn't have the energy to fight her old best friend. She knew way too much about Darla. What kind of person she was and what she'd do to gain attention. Addy could tell that her old friend wanted to cause a scene.

"Adrianna." Darla's smile told Addy she used her full name just to get under her skin.

"Darleen," Addy replied and watched the heat behind her former friend's eyes. "I see your eye is better."

Addy smiled when Darla reached up and touched the spot she'd blackened. "If I had a witness, I would have sued you. You and your parents." Darla's smile unfurled further. "It's not as if your daddy doesn't visit the Spot enough when he's in town. That is, when your tight-ass mother isn't running him ragged."

Addy eyes narrowed at the woman. "There is nothing you can say to me about my parents that would ever hurt me." She moved her cart around Darla's easily. "You should know that about me by now."

"Oh." Darla turned her almost-empty cart around and followed her. "I guess that's true, seeing as they don't think you are good enough for them. Tsk, tsk."

Addy knew better than to take the bait, but she was curious to find out how far Darla would go to get at her.

"Good enough?" She glanced over her shoulder as she picked up a carton of ice cream from the freezer.

"Yup—that rich out-of-towner took Tyler right from you. Not good enough there either. I heard they're getting married."

Addy smiled, remembering that she'd made Darla believe she'd been interested in Tyler only to help find out what had happened to Kristen when she'd been kidnapped. It was funny, but in all her years of dealing with the McGowan brothers, Trent had been the only one she'd had eyes for. "Yes, I'm very happy for them." She placed her favorite ice cream into her cart and moved down to the frozen veggie section.

"And Trent." Darla made a tsk noise again.

"What's wrong with Trent?" Addy asked, placing a few bags of frozen broccoli into her cart.

Darla leaned closer and, with a stage whisper loud enough for the whole store to hear, said, "Oh, just that he was telling me the other night that he's moving out of his mother's house." She rattled her cart for emphasis. "I think he's going to move into the apartment above the Spot. You know, to be closer to me."

Addy chuckled as she thought about Trent having to deal with Darla every day as he went home. "Have fun with that," she said and pushed her full cart to the front counter.

"You don't believe me?" Darla followed her. "You never did believe anything I had to say." She jogged in front of Addy, leaving her cart in the aisle. "You won't believe me when I tell you that I'm pregnant either." Her loud statement caused several eyes to pivot their way.

Addy looked deep into her old friend's eyes and saw the truth. "No, I do believe that. Congratulations." She almost patted Darla's shoulder but caught herself. "I wish nothing but the best for you."

That seemed to stop Darla in her tracks, but if there was one thing you could say about the woman, she recovered quickly. "It's a McGowan."

Several gasps sounded behind Addy. "Now that I don't believe." Addy turned back to the checkout. "You should have stuck to the truth." She started unloading her items to be scanned.

"You're right. It's actually your father's," Darla hissed, but not so low that others couldn't hear.

Addy jerked her head around and searched the woman's face. Suddenly her stomach rolled and her vision grayed. Her hands went boneless against the soup she'd been holding. The heavy metal can hit her square in the toe as it fell, but she didn't feel the pain. Her father's? Her parents weren't perfect, but her father cheating on her mother? Never! But the certainty in Darla's eyes . . . she felt her world tilt.

Turning back to the clerk, she shook her head as her vision blurred. "I . . . I'm sorry, I have to . . ." She rushed past the group of people who had gathered to watch Darla's show. When the fresh air hit her face, she bent over the nearest bush and lost her lunch.

"Hey." Someone ran over to her and started rubbing her back. "Are you okay, sweetie?"

"I . . ." She shook her head. "I'm sorry." She wiped her mouth on her jacket and looked up through blurry eyes at Gail McGowan.

♦ ♦ ♦

Trent had spent almost two hours locked away in a stuffy conference room at city hall with a group of people planning the landscaping for the new school. He was beginning to think he'd been swindled into doing a job that was much harder than first described to him.

At his own company, he didn't have to answer to anyone, just do what he pleased with the trees and bushes. Period. Simple.

But for the school, every tree, bush, shrub, and piece of playground equipment was debated over. He had drawn a quick sketch of the layout, which was quickly shot down by the committee—a committee made up of school staff, a few concerned parents, and the mayor herself. He'd never had a more frustrating meeting in his life.

At the end of the meeting, the mayor filled everyone in informally on the progress of the NewField fire investigation. The word was out: a pile of old rags and several gas cans were the origin. It appeared there had been some sort of timer, but the investigators weren't saying much more. The authorities were still looking for clues as to why the fire was started.

Since all he had were his own conspiracy theories, Trent kept quiet.

By the end of the meeting, he was dog-tired and desperately wanted a cold beer and a burger.

He made his way toward the diner, but then spotted his mother's sedan in front of the grocery store and pulled in next to it in hopes she'd join him for a meal.

Instead, he found his mother helping Addy toward her Jeep. He hurried forward, concern flooding him as he noticed her face was red and blotchy.

"What happened?" He scoured the parking lot for an unseen assailant.

"Nothing." Addy shook her head. "Someone just said something to upset me." She shook her head and wiped her eyes again. "Thank you, Mrs.—"

"Gail, sweetie." His mother gave Addy a pat on her back. "Just call me Gail."

"Thank you, Gail."

"Why don't you let Trent drive you home? You're too upset to drive yourself."

Addy started to object, but Gail gave her a look that said it hadn't really been a request. Addy was smart enough to shut her mouth and nod.

"Thank you," she said.

"Anytime, sweetie. Let me know if there's anything I can do to help." Gail placed a hand on Addy's shoulder.

Trent watched his mother's gaze move to the grocery store. When he looked, he saw Darla standing inside the large windows, smiling. His eyes narrowed with anger. As he helped Addy into his truck, he saw his mother march into the store right toward Darla.

He shivered at the thought. He almost wished someone would get the entire incident on video. His mother would walk away the victor.

"Do you want to tell me what has you so upset? Surely nothing Darla says or does can still get to you," he said to Addy.

She rested her head back against the seat and sighed. "I wouldn't have thought so, but . . ." She shrugged and closed her eyes.

He started the truck and pulled out of the parking lot but instead of turning right, Trent turned left. "I was just about to go grab some food." Her eyes remained closed and she sighed. "Care to join me?"

"Whatever," she said. "I doubt I could eat."

"Then you can watch me eat." He pointed the car out of town. He had been in the mood for burgers, but now that Addy was along for the ride, he decided Italian was better. There was only one place within a hundred miles that served Italian, and he headed there, knowing the longer drive would be worth it. Besides, it would give Addy some time to settle herself.

"I'm sure my mother has put Darla in her place by now." He chuckled. "I just wish I had stuck around to see it." He looked over at Addy; she didn't move. He turned back to the road. "I remember one time when Tyler and I got into it, we must have been about ten and eight. Anyway, we were fighting over the last cookie in the cookie jar. We rolled around the house for almost half an hour before we heard the crunch." He glanced again in her direction.

This time, her focus was on him, eager to hear the rest of his story. He wiggled the fingers on his left hand. "Broke three of them." He glanced down at the row of perfectly straight digits. "Of course, being the dumb kids we were, we tried to hide it. Tyler tried to set the fingers by tying a rope around them and yanking real hard, which only made them turn a nasty shade of purple." He laughed at the memory. "So that night at dinner, I wore a pair of Dad's work gloves to hide my twisted and bruised fingers."

"What did your mother do?" she asked.

"Well, first she whooped our butts, then she hauled me down to the ER and watched as they set each finger." Addy frowned, and he smiled in response. "Then she took me out for the largest chocolate-chip milkshake I'd ever had and hugged me until I fell asleep that night."

Addy sighed and looked out the window. "It must have been nice."

"What?" he asked.

"Growing up with parents who loved you no matter what."

He frowned for a moment and was silent. "Your folks love you?" It came out more as a question than a statement.

"No they don't. That is, they don't love the way I turned out. I'm a disappointment." She closed her eyes. "Have been all my life."

"What makes you say that?" he asked.

An odd burst of laughter escaped her. "Oh, I don't know, maybe the hundred or so times they have told me to my face."

"I've met your folks. They didn't seem . . ."

"What?" She shifted to look at him. "That bad? Do you realize that most people who know a psychopathic killer can be quoted as saying they seemed 'so nice and normal'?"

"You don't think that your folks—"

Her chuckle stopped him. "No, I'm pretty sure they haven't chopped up any small children." She took a deep breath and glanced out the window again. "But it didn't stop them from breaking one's spirit." Her voice turned distant. "And now they have become the embarrassment they have always accused me of being."

"How? How have they done that?" he asked.

She turned back to him, and he wished he wasn't driving because he wanted to look deeper into her eyes.

"I'm sure it will be all over town soon enough." She took another deep breath. "It appears that my father is going to be a father again."

His eyebrows rose. "That's not unheard of. After all, your folks are only in their mid-sixties—"

"Not with my mother," she interrupted him, causing him to almost jerk the truck off the road.

"Oh?" he said slowly and felt his stomach twirl as he remembered Darla's smirk.

"Yeah." She looked back out the window. "It's as bad as you think."

CHAPTER SEVEN

The rest of the trip to the restaurant they remained silent. But when Trent parked and shut off the truck engine, he turned to Addy.

"Listen, you know Darla will say anything to get at people. Maybe, hopefully, this is just one of her lies."

"I can always tell when she's lying. Call it my superpower." She rolled her eyes. "She wasn't lying. She's pregnant, and as far as she believes, my father is the father. Which means—" Addy shivered.

"Don't," he warned. "Don't even think about it."

"Too late." She sighed.

"Yeah." He made a funny face and she chuckled. "Me too."

"Okay, enough grossness, I'm actually hungry now." She reached for the door handle. "By the way." She stopped and looked over at him. "Thanks."

"Anytime," he said, then rushed to help her out of the high truck.

The fact that she'd lost her lunch earlier caused Addy to overorder. When her massive lasagna arrived, her eyes grew wide at the sheer size of the meal.

"Don't worry. If you can't eat it all, I'll finish it off for you," Trent said, scooping up some of his spaghetti. "I love lasagna."

"You McGowans can sure pack the food away," she joked.

He laughed between bites. "My mother used to accuse us of having black holes for stomachs."

Addy nodded as she chewed, then took a sip of her wine. "I could totally see that. I bet Carl Sagan would have loved to discover the hidden wonders of the McGowan brothers' stomachs."

He laughed. "The eighth wonder of the world."

"Someone could make a documentary."

His eyebrows shot up. "I'd forgotten you were such a nerd," he said, still smiling.

Her smile faltered slightly. "Yes, one of the reasons I was never on a McGowan radar."

"Would you have wanted to be?" he asked.

Addy thought about how she'd been back then. She shook her head and took another sip of her wine. "No, I suppose not. Still, it would have been a boost to the self-esteem. I always brushed it off that I was too smart for all that stuff."

"I don't know." He sat back and studied her. "Smart women are sexy as hell."

"Oh?" She leaned closer, enjoying what her second glass of wine was doing to her. Empowering her, making her feel like she could conquer the art of flirting. "Then why did you never try to put your moves on me?" she asked.

His smile dropped away. "Because you were too . . ." He shook his head and avoided her eyes.

"Too?" she teased and took another sip of her wine. "Too smart? Too nerdy? Too skinny? What?"

His eyes met hers, and she felt her toes tingle at the heat radiating from those dark hazel-brown eyes of his.

"Too fragile, too smart, too pretty. Too good for someone like me." She watched him swallow and felt the entire room shrink from her view. Suddenly they were the only living creatures on the face of the planet. The cheesy Italian music playing in the background faded away, along with the voices and sounds from the busy restaurant.

The only thing left was Trent.

Then, slowly, everything came back to normal as she took several deep breaths. His hand reached out and touched hers. "I didn't mean to . . ." He shook his head and rolled his eyes. "I've never . . . had to work this hard."

Her smile was instant and something shifted inside her chest. "I'm glad."

He closed his eyes. "Now I'm the one that feels . . ."

"Stupid?" She leaned back and took her wine with her. "Don't. I believe for the first time I've finally scratched the surface of Trent McGowan."

He glanced around and pushed his empty plate away. "So." His eyes moved to her half-empty plate. "There was a mention of a shared lasagna?"

She chuckled and pushed her plate toward him.

"You owe me an ice cream," she said, feeling a little more settled as he finished off her lasagna. "Actually Darla owes me a gallon of it, but I'll settle for a shake at CC's on the way back to town."

Trent looked at her and nodded. "Deal," he said between bites.

They enjoyed their shakes on an old park bench outside of CC's, a small trailer that sat on the outskirts of town and had been selling ice cream for as long as either of them could remember.

"Why is it the drive back always seems to take half the time?" he said when they pulled in next to her Jeep in the grocery store parking lot.

Her entire body had relaxed under the spell of the lasagna, wine, and mint–chocolate chip shake. She felt like she could sleep for days.

Of course, she always felt like that after a powerful cry and a lot of food.

She turned slightly toward him. "I believe that's a compliment," she teased.

His right hand came up and brushed a strand of her hair away from her eyes. She hadn't bothered to braid it today and had worn it down instead.

"It is." He leaned closer, his eyes on hers. "Addy, I'd like to kiss you."

She watched the hunger and felt her own building. Hadn't she dreamed of this for years? She'd wondered what it would be like to have his lips and hands on her.

She moved closer as her body hummed with the possibility. "Okay."

His lips had just had a moment to touch hers when there was a loud knock on his door, making them both jump.

He peered over and groaned. "Shit," she heard him whisper and then chuckle. "It's the fuzz."

He rolled his window down and looked over at Mike.

"Sorry." Mike waved at her. "I was just doing a drive-by and spotted Addy's Jeep. Is everything okay?"

"Peachy," Trent said. "Other than a spoiled moment." He noticed Addy's cheeks heat.

Mike smiled and took a step back. "I'll let you go. Night." He tipped the front of his hat and then disappeared.

Trent leaned back in the seat and looked over at her again. "How about we try this again, say, Friday?"

"What? Dinner or the kiss?"

He chuckled. "Both. I'll cook."

Her eyebrows shot up in question.

"At your mother's house?"

He groaned. "Okay, you'll cook."

She laughed. "How about I make a picnic and we do lunch on the mountain? I think we can find a good spot and enjoy some warm weather." She reached for the door handle.

"Perfect, I'll pick you—"

"No." She stopped him. "I'll meet you at the base of the trail."

Now it was his turn to raise his dark eyebrows. "Afraid of being seen with me?"

She tilted her head and smiled. "You are the enemy." She slid out of the truck, then leaned back in. "Eleven thirty sharp."

He nodded, then she felt him watch her unlock her Jeep and get in.

◆ ◆ ◆

The rest of the week seemed to crawl by. Maybe because Trent's mind was focused on the lunch on Friday. Everything and everyone seemed to have only one purpose: to get in his way and slow him down.

Bessy had blown a hose, which caused almost a day's worth of work to be delayed. The second meeting about the school grounds had eaten up another two hours of his Wednesday evening, and then to top it off, his mother scheduled a family meeting on Friday night. A bad omen.

Especially since he knew that she would ask him for an update. Which meant lunch with Addy would have to turn from pleasurable to fact-finding. How could he get information from her without making it look like that's what he was doing?

Trent knew he had to keep his family as far away from Addy as possible. It wouldn't do to have his brothers trying to interfere or, worse, to have her interrogate and upset his brothers or mother.

He woke Friday with a massive headache and a sour attitude. But when he walked into the kitchen, his mother stood at the stove, dressed in the long red robe that he'd bought her one Christmas, making banana-pecan pancakes, bacon, and scrambled eggs. The smell was pure heaven, filling the house with memories of their childhood. He walked up behind her and kissed her cheek as he swiped a piece of bacon.

"For me?" he asked.

She smiled and slapped his hand away from a second piece. "Maybe, if you think you can set the table."

He rushed to set three places. He poured orange juice and coffee for his mother, then handed her the mug and took over scooping the eggs into the chipped bowl she always served them in.

"We need a new bowl," he said, frowning down at the massive chip.

"No we don't." His mother frowned at him. "Your father gave me that bowl on our second anniversary."

Trent leaned against the counter. The place still felt empty without the old man. There were times he swore he could hear his father's voice in the next room. Not a day went by that he didn't think of the man who would have done anything for him and his brothers. Looking around the house at the small heirlooms around the place always brought up a flood of memories.

"What's all this?" Trisha walked in, freshly showered and dressed. The woman was an early riser just like his mother. He figured that was one of the reasons the two of them got along so well. It was nice knowing his mother had such a good friend after his father's death. The pair had become close in the aftermath of Kristen's kidnapping.

"Something's been bothering my son, so I figured I'd make his favorite breakfast and wiggle what it is out of him." His mother smiled into her mug.

"Oh?" Trisha turned from pouring herself a cup of coffee and looked at him. "Is it a girl?"

Trent's eyes narrowed slightly.

"Oh, it is." Trisha smiled. "Good, I could use a juicy story." Gail and Trisha walked over and sat down at the table, obviously waiting for him to follow.

"This"—he sat down—"is exactly why I'm trying to hurry up and get my own place."

His mother chuckled and patted his hand. "Now, now, don't be cruel, and don't leave out any details." She leaned on her elbows and watched him.

He gave in. While enjoying his mother's delicious breakfast, Trent filled the ladies in on what Darla had told Addy.

"No wonder she was sick," his mother said. "That poor girl. To think that her father was . . ." She shook her head. "Of course, I don't believe it for a moment. I've known Darla since she was this high." His mother's hand hovered just below the tabletop. "That girl's words don't add up because she's never included the truth in her equations."

He rolled his eyes at his mother's old joke. "Yeah, we all know she had it in for Addy after—"

"She clocked her?" His mother's eyes sparkled over her coffee mug.

"You're just full of spunk this morning."

His mother's smile brightened. "Why don't you go on, sweetie?" Trent filled them in on everything he knew.

"So that's all very touching and disturbing, but it doesn't explain why you've been in a sour mood all week." His mother pushed her empty plate away.

"I'm having lunch with Addy today," he said.

The room went silent.

"And?" his mother finally asked.

"Gail," Trisha broke in. "I think he was hoping to spend some 'time'"—the woman actually made air quotes with her fingers—"with Addy instead of grilling her for information."

His mother looked him. "Oh, honey, that isn't what tonight's . . ." She trailed off and shook her head. "Go, have fun. Don't worry about the meeting. I didn't intend . . ."

To Trent's horror, he actually watched his mother tear up.

"Shit," he said under his breath, causing her tears to turn to anger. "Sorry." He rose and wrapped his arms around her. "What's all this about?" he asked as he handed her a tissue.

"It's just—" She sniffled.

"We're having a baby," Trisha broke in.

His eyebrows rose as he looked between the two women.

"Not us, stupid." Trisha giggled. "We're going to be grandmothers."

"What?" Trent almost fell backward. His mother reached out and steadied him.

"They wanted to spring the news on everyone tonight," Trisha added.

"But . . ." He felt like he was stammering. "So soon?"

The two women laughed. "It only takes once to get it right," Trisha said.

"What about the wedding?" Trent blinked. His brother had just been talking about putting the wedding off until next spring.

"We've convinced them to move it ahead," Gail said. "I want our last name on the birth certificate."

"I don't care what name she has, as long as she has ten toes and fingers," Trisha added.

"True, but . . ." His mother stopped. "She?"

Trisha waved her hand and laughed. "Whichever sex, I agree with you. Remember, I'm on your side."

"So?" Trent broke into their chatter.

His mother smiled. "So the wedding will be the first Saturday next month."

"Wow." He shook his head. Suddenly the idea of his brother getting married was heavier than it had been. It had been a thing far in the future, now it was looming right in front of them.

Addy's face flashed before his eyes quickly as he thought about his own future.

His mother's voice broke into his thoughts. "Yes, and that means we need you to make the backyard look as presentable as possible for about two hundred guests."

He groaned. *With what time?*

CHAPTER EIGHT

Addy added the last item to the picnic basket she'd bought a few years back at an antique shop in Maine. She glanced quickly at the mirror and made sure everything was perfect before loading up the Jeep.

"Got a hot date?" Brian's voice had her wishing she'd left to meet Trent five minutes earlier.

"Just a relaxing lunch." She climbed into her Jeep, but he stood just at the edge of her door, preventing her from closing it.

"Then maybe you'd care to invite me along?" He moved closer, and she cursed herself for allowing him to sneak in under her radar.

"Sorry, I'm meeting a friend," she said, silently hoping that her voice was casual enough that Brian would think it wasn't a male friend.

But the look in his eyes told her that he'd guessed anyway.

"It wouldn't be a McGowan, would it?"

"I don't see how that's any . . ."

He moved closer and she tried to inch away from him. She was almost sitting on her gearshift when he spoke again.

"I've warned you, the McGowans are the enemy. If certain people found out about this, you'd lose your job." His hand snaked out and gripped her elbow.

She wished there was enough room to jerk it free, but instead, she narrowed her eyes and raised her chin.

"What I do on my own time is none of your concern." She reached in and turned on her Jeep. "Now if you'll excuse me, I'm going to be late." She looked pointedly down at his hand still holding her elbow.

"You're nothing but a slut, and soon enough you'll be out." He leaned closer to her when he said this, causing his breath to hit her full force.

"Have you been drinking?" she asked. "You know there's no drinking on the premises."

"I had a beer at the diner with lunch." He dropped his hand. "Like you said, what we do on our own time . . ." He stepped back. "That's the last warning you'll get."

As he walked away, she tried to put the entire situation behind her.

It was strange, she thought as she checked in the rearview mirror when she drove away. Brian and Trent were a lot alike, physically. They were both over six feet, built about the same, but where Trent had dark hazel-brown eyes and dark-brown hair, Brian's eyes were an eerie blue, while his hair was jet-black like Rea's, his mother.

As she drove, vague memories surfaced of what Brian's father had looked like. The blue-eyed man had died years ago: suicide. The scandal had rocked the small town. Especially after he'd been found hanging from the local bridge by a couple fishermen. At first there had been speculation that Rea or even Brian had something to do with it, but those rumors died down quickly after the police stepped in and confirmed there was no foul play.

After his father had died, Brian went from being a closet bully to a full-fledged one. There wasn't anyone in school or town that he wouldn't pick a fight with. Including his mother.

Addy had heard that Rea had filed a restraining order a few years back. She hadn't been in town—her family had been on one of their many exotic trips during the incident—but Addy had heard the rumors of how Brian had pulled a knife on Rea simply because she wouldn't give him money for beer.

The entire incident got her thinking about her family. She hadn't heard from her parents since they left town a few weeks back. Nor did she expect to until at least the end of the month.

Just the idea of their next family conversation had her head splitting as she pulled up next to Trent's truck.

He was there instantly, opening her door for her. He looked so sexy in his light flannel jacket.

"I was beginning to think that you wouldn't come," he said.

Just seeing the apprehension in his eyes sent her into his arms.

"Hey," he said as he wrapped his arms around her in response. "Is everything okay?" His arms tightened slightly.

"Yeah." She took a deep breath and inhaled his comforting, spicy scent. "But let's get this out of the way first." She reached up on her toes and placed her lips softly over his.

Addy didn't know what had caused her to make such a bold move, but she wasn't prepared for the flood of electricity that spread throughout her entire body, heating every nerve ending. She felt his arms loosen, then tighten again as his mouth took over. Rubbing against hers gently, his lips moved slowly until she opened hers and felt his tongue dip inside her mouth for a taste.

It was beyond everything she'd ever imagined it would be. Kissing Trent. Her head did a slow spin. She was thankful that he had such a good hold on her—she would have slid to the dirt without his support.

His hand slid to the nape of her neck, holding her as the kiss deepened.

All of a sudden he released her, causing her to blink and look up at him.

"There is nothing I want to do more than stand here and kiss you all day." Trent sighed and looked around. Almost half a dozen cars littered the parking area; this wasn't the time or place.

He dropped his hands and took hers. "Let's go for our hike."

She started following him, then stopped. "The lunch." She rushed back to the Jeep and opened her door to get out the basket, but before she could reach it, Trent was there, hoisting it out of the passenger seat for her.

She locked her Jeep and tucked her keys in her pocket. "Ready."

They walked hand in hand for a few minutes in silence. She could tell he was deep in thought. She wondered why the silence between them felt so good. Still, she felt something else. The sexual tension was almost overwhelming. It was so powerful she found it hard to focus on where they were going.

"So," he finally said when they reached a fork in the trail. "Which way?"

She tugged on his hand until they set foot on her favorite path. It was the least used, and there were several tricky spots that most hikers didn't care for. Especially since during the spring it meant getting your feet wet.

"Excellent choice." He pressed on, only dropping her hand occasionally to push a low branch away.

When they reached the highest point in the hike, Trent set the basket down on a small patch of tall grass and turned to her.

"So." He cleared his throat. "I have to ask."

She could see his cheeks turn a light shade of pink.

"What?" Her curiosity was piqued.

"Something set you off."

Taking a deep breath, Addy answered, "I had a slight run-in with Brian."

His gaze ran over her. "Are you okay?"

Nodding, she bent down to pull out the small blanket from the basket.

"What happened?" he asked as he helped her lay it out near the edge of the hill so they could overlook the mountains as they ate.

"He told me to stay away from you and your family." She sat down. "Needless to say, I didn't listen to him. I know how to handle bullies."

He sat next to her. "Are you sure you're okay?"

She nodded. "You seemed upset yourself." She had wondered about bringing up her questions for him, but now, seeing the dark look in his eyes, she knew she should hold off, at least for now.

"Not upset—distracted, busy, overwhelmed." He sighed. "Any of those would fit."

"What's overwhelming you?" she asked as she started to pull out the food.

"Well, it turns out I have less than a month to prepare for a wedding in my mother's backyard."

"Wait, what?" Addy turned to him. "They moved up the date?"

He nodded and looked out at the view. "They're having a kid."

"So soon?" she blurted before thinking.

"That's what I said. I guess . . ." He shook his head. "I don't know, I guess I just thought . . ."

"Marriage first, then kids?"

"No, I'm not that old-fashioned. If it's right, it's right. But at least I thought they'd want some time . . . you know."

"To themselves?" she asked, handing him a plate.

"Yeah. I mean, I guess I'd be a little more selfish. Not that I don't want kids, hell, I want at least three of the little buggers myself." He chuckled. "Someday."

"I think that's why my parents had such a tough time with me," she said as she opened a bag of chips.

He looked over at her as he put a sandwich onto his plate.

"Why is that?" he asked.

"They had me so soon after getting married. They didn't have any time to discover who they were together. If they fit."

"Some people should never have kids," he said, piling chips on his plate.

She glanced over at him, and he quickly repaired his statement.

"Not that I'm saying—uh, I'm very thankful your parents had you."

She laughed. "I know what you mean." She'd never seen Trent so flustered before. He was usually so smooth that everyone fell at his feet. But now, she saw a side of him that most people didn't get—vulnerable, less of a player. Maybe it was the setting, maybe the boldness of her kiss, but she felt her reservations starting to loosen.

◆　◆　◆

Could I get any dumber? Trent thought as he chewed his food. She'd put him off his game with that kiss.

Just the memory of those lush lips on his had his mind doing somersaults.

"What about you?" he finally asked.

Addy tilted her head toward him and raised her eyebrows in question.

"Kids?" he asked.

She smiled. "If I do, I'll make sure to have at least two. Being an only child was . . . tricky. I think that if there had been someone else, maybe things wouldn't have been so hard."

"Were they that bad?" he asked, shifting so he could look directly at her. He watched her eyes turn to the mountain view and fill with sadness.

"There were times it wasn't so bad. But for the most part, I retreated into my books."

"Now there's something we have in common." He smiled.

She laughed, a full-body laugh that almost had him reaching to cover that sound with his lips. "You read?"

"Why so shocked?" He narrowed his eyes at her. "Men can read."

"Yes, but . . ." She shook her head. "I've never seen you with a book."

"And I've never seen you in a dress. It doesn't mean that you're not a woman." Parts of her body begged to differ. He reached for another sandwich to distract himself. "So I'm being a complete ass *and* a huge sexist."

She shook her head with a grin. "Okay, all sexism aside, what kind of books do you enjoy?"

"Most anything." He looked at her. "I noticed copies of Orwell's *1984*, H. G. Wells's *The Time Machine*, and a few other of my favorites in your trailer when we were in North Dakota."

She nodded. "I have a first edition of *Do Androids Dream of Electric Sheep?* too."

"No way!" He sat up a little, intrigued and impressed. "Any chance I can borrow it?"

She narrowed her eyes at him. "I don't know, are you the kind of reader who folds the pages or uses a bookmark?"

He gasped. "I don't get a person who would damage a book just to hold their spot."

"You have passed the first test." She nodded regally.

"What's the second?" He leaned back on his elbow again.

"Do you own a copy of *The Hobbit?*"

He rolled his eyes. "Who doesn't? My father gave me one for my thirteenth birthday."

She smiled. "You are free to borrow any of my books."

From there, the conversation turned to movies and food. They must have enjoyed the sunshine for almost an hour before her cell phone chimed.

"Sorry." She reached into her pocket and pulled out her phone. "It's Beau." She raised her finger and, standing and walking away, answered the call from her boss.

Trent listened to her talk as much as he could without snooping. By the time she hung up, she'd reached the edge of the hill, looking down into the valley that held Haven.

He approached her. "Is everything okay?"

She turned slightly toward him. "What are your intentions with the land you're purchasing from the Lenz family?"

He sighed. "I suppose work was going to come up sooner or later."

"Well?" She turned to fully face him.

"I can't tell you," he said. And before she could interject, he continued. "Not that I don't want to, but I'm under strict legal orders not to."

He watched Addy's eyes narrow. "Can you tell me if you plan on drilling on the land?"

He thought about it. "No."

"No, you're not drilling or no, you can't tell me?"

He sighed and nodded.

"Ugh!" She threw up her hands.

"Tell me how you found out about the purchase," he said. "Who told Beau?"

"I don't know," she said almost defensively.

"You don't know? Can you find out?" he asked.

"Why?"

"Because it's obvious we have a leak that needs to be plugged."

"Trent, FREE benefits from leaks like this all the time. Information in small towns travels, especially when people know their way of life could be in jeopardy. Why all the secrecy now?" she asked.

He shook his head. He couldn't get into that with her here, not when it had been going so well. He knew she was getting more frustrated.

"It has nothing to do with . . ." Trent stopped himself and took a deep breath. "I can promise you this—whatever my family has planned, it will not affect the reservation."

"That's not good enough."

"Why?" he asked.

Addy shrugged her shoulders, then walked over and started cleaning up.

"Why can't you just take my word for it?" He bent down and helped her place the plates into the basket.

"Because." She glanced up at him, then stopped her cleanup. "I have to answer to my boss. I have to let everyone know what your plans are. My staying in Haven depends on it."

He tilted his head. "So if you find out what we're doing with the land, you'll leave Haven?"

She nodded. "If I find no cause for us to stick around, I'll move on to the next site. Which, at this point, might be back to North Dakota."

Trent felt his heart kick up a notch. "Then I hope you don't find out anytime soon." He took her by the shoulders with a kiss that melted his fears away. When he released her, her smile flashed. Then, leaning forward and wrapping her arms around his neck, she knocked him on his ass as her lips covered his.

CHAPTER NINE

Addy looked down at Trent pinned underneath her. Her head spun as he nudged her lips apart. She'd had romantic encounters before but had never wanted them to progress very far. With Trent, she knew it wouldn't stop like the others. She didn't want it to.

His hands roamed slowly over her body, tugging her button-up flannel loose from her jeans until his fingertips brushed her bare skin.

She moaned as the pressure of his touch heated her skin and his mouth set fires down her neck. Her fingers dug into his hair, holding him to her body, demanding more. He flipped them over until she was immobilized beneath his broad shoulders.

"My god," he said between kisses. He'd unbuttoned her shirt and pulled back to look down at her. She wore a sheer white spaghetti-strap tank top underneath; she could feel that it was pushed up to expose her stomach.

His eyes took her in as his hand shifted slowly over her bare skin. "You're so beautiful." His voice roughened as his gaze ran over her.

When he tugged on her tank top and pulled it up higher, she moved to give him better access. Instead of pushing it all the way up, he nudged the soft material to just under her bra, then began to play his finger over her belly.

"Appendix?" he asked, fingering a small scar.

She nodded. They had both shed their jackets after sitting in the sun for over an hour. Now she leaned up and tugged his shirt over his head. Then ran her fingertips over all those sexy muscles.

Even though it was early spring in Montana, his skin was tan. A lot tanner than her own.

"You work with your shirt off?" She watched his dark hazel-brown eyes lighten as she touched him.

"When I'm clearing my land." He closed his eyes, and she knew he was enjoying her touch. She leaned up and placed her lips where the warmth of her touch lingered. His fingers dug into her hair, holding her to his chest.

"My god," Trent repeated, then tugged her head back, laying her on the soft blanket, until their lips met again. This time the kisses grew deeper, causing her entire body to respond.

Her legs wrapped around his jean-clad hips, pulling him closer until she felt his desire pressed up against her core. His hands moved, pulling her flannel off and tugging her tank top fully over her head until she lay underneath him clad only in her new pale-pink lace bra.

His mouth moved down to brush against a spot just above the light material. Addy groaned and tightened her grip in his hair. While his fingers brushed the top of her jeans, his tongue plunged under the lacy material and had her hips rising off the blanket.

It was a move designed to loosen the last strings of her hold. Trent had somehow undone the top button of her jeans without her knowing. His fingers dipped underneath and found her soft folds just as his mouth closed over one taut nipple and began a soft torture.

Her nails dug into his skin as he slowly loved her, giving her more pleasure than she'd ever experienced in her life. His mouth touched first one nipple then the other as his fingers worked, getting her closer to the edge.

When she cried out, he moved up and covered her lips with his own and kissed her until she felt her entire body vibrate under his touch.

"My god." She sighed and wrapped her arms around him.

"Yeah." She could tell he was smiling as he pulled her closer to his chest. "Definitely on the list."

"List?" She chanced opening one eye and looking up at him.

He looked down at her with a grin. "Top ten moments of my life."

"Oh?" She smiled and opened both eyes. "But we haven't even . . ." She reached for him, only for him to grab her wrist and hold it down next to her hair on the blanket. She had never known it could feel like this, wanting someone so much.

"Next time." He leaned down and placed a soft kiss on her lips. "I'll want a soft bed and an entire night to watch those blue eyes of yours darken."

"Your eyes turn a lighter shade of hazel," she blurted out and instantly felt stupid.

"They do?" He leaned down until they were eye to eye, nose to nose. "Yours are the same color as the South Pacific."

"Really?" She smiled up at him. "That's got to be better than most coasts I've protested."

He chuckled. "I've only been to one place and"—he leaned down and placed another kiss on her lips—"it didn't come close to your beauty."

They both heard voices coming closer and moved at the same time. She felt and heard the smack as her head hit his chin.

"Damn," she cursed and rubbed the spot, then looked over at him doing the same to his chin.

"I'll get your shirt." He gestured for her to stay put, then leaned over and deposited her tank over her head. She pulled her flannel shirt on the rest of the way as he tossed his T-shirt over his head.

She sighed as those sexy muscles disappeared from her view.

By the time the hiking group hit their spot, Trent and Addy had their picnic all packed up and were heading back down the trail as if nothing had happened.

She felt like they were in a stalemate on the issue of what his family had in store, but personally they had just taken a giant step forward.

Of course, her heart rate took until they reached the bottom of the hill to return to normal. Her mind kept flashing to what he'd done to her. How he'd made her feel.

By the time they reached her Jeep, she was pretty sure that she was falling for Trent McGowan.

She was screwed.

♦　♦　♦

Trent sat in his mother's living room and tried to act surprised when Tyler and Kristen sprang the news. It helped that his mind kept wandering to Addy.

They had parted without setting any further plans. She'd agreed to try and find out who had talked to Beau if Trent would ask his family if he could share their plans with her.

He'd hesitantly agreed but wanted to postpone asking the family for as long as he could. He knew where his loyalty lay, but it wasn't as if his family was going to kick him out if he didn't get the information that they wanted from Addy.

Not that he was trying to trick her, just keep her around town for a little longer. Hell, to be honest, he'd keep her here as long as he could.

She was different than any woman he'd dated before. Different in so many ways. It wasn't just that she was smart—in being with her, he could be himself.

He'd never talked about his love for books with anyone else. Like his brothers, Trent had a reputation around town, and in the past he hadn't wanted to do anything to shake himself from that because it had tended to benefit him with the ladies. Maybe that was changing.

Once congratulations had poured out for Tyler and Kristen and plans had been preliminarily discussed, the family gathered around another homemade dinner.

"So have you found a place of your own?" Kristen asked her mother.

"Well, Gail and I have been talking."

"Once Trent moves out . . ." His mother's eyes met his.

"Hopefully in three months," he supplied.

"Once he moves into his own place, we were thinking she'd just remain here. It's not like there isn't enough room."

"That's a wonderful idea." Kristen reached over and took her mother's hand. "To have two grandmothers in one place and so close by."

"That was what we thought too," Trisha said. "That is, the plan will work until either of us finds a new man."

"What?" Trent and his brothers all sat up a little. "Who's finding a new man?"

"No one is," their mother said. "For now. But your father and I always talked about what would happen if one of us passed on before the other. Your father wouldn't want me to be lonely."

"You're not," Tyler said. "You have Trisha. Besides, the two of you walk around here as if you are half of the *Golden Girls* quartet."

Gail rolled her eyes. "Don't make me remind you that even women our age need another kind of companionship."

"Gross," Trey said and plugged his ears. "I don't want to hear any more." He turned to Trent. "Make her stop."

Trent laughed. "So what about all your things?" he asked Trisha.

"I've sold most of it. The rest we figured we could go through and decide what we can incorporate here."

"God knows I have enough stuff I could toss out," Gail added.

"Like the chipped egg bowl?" Trent took a sip of his tea.

"Some things I'll hold on to." She smiled.

"How did your lunch with Addy go?" Trisha asked. Suddenly every eye was on him, waiting.

"Fine." Trent set his drink down and made a point to push the last pea across the plate as if he were playing hockey.

"Just fine?" his mother asked.

"Yeah." He avoided eye contact.

"Did you ask her?" she prodded.

Trent shrugged. "She is going to look into who told Beau about the purchase."

He watched his mother's gaze sharpen. He could tell she was thinking. "How are our plans going?" She turned to Tyler.

"Fine," he said. "We've got the lawyers' go-ahead. That is, after May first. We'll be legally free then to do what we want with Dad's methods."

"What about your Uncle Carl?" Kristen asked.

"He signed away his rights long ago," Trent said. He felt something roil in the bottom of his gut. His father's brother was a sore subject in their family.

"I mean, does he know? Shouldn't you tell him?"

Trent didn't really care what the old man thought about their deal, but he did know the guy didn't deserve to be blindsided.

Everyone looked at each other in silence.

"Should we take a vote?" their mother said.

Suddenly four fists were in the air, and at the count of three, four thumbs rose up.

"Okay," Kristen laughed. "What the heck was that?"

"How we McGowans vote." Tyler smiled and took her hand.

"What does it mean?"

"If the thumbs had turned down, the answer was no. But when the thumbs are up, it's a yes. Which means we tell my uncle ahead of time." He winked at her. "Want to see how we decide who gets to tell him?"

Trey and Trent groaned at the same time.

An hour later and sporting a bruised ego, Trent made his way into his room. Now, on top of his very long list of things to do, he also had to make time to tell his uncle of their plans for the Lenzes' property and the future of McGowan Enterprises.

When he crawled into bed, he pulled out his cell phone and called Addy.

"So you're a caller, not a texter," she said, answering the phone.

"I can't hit those tiny buttons fast enough." He smiled and settled into the pillow. "Are you in bed?" he asked.

"Just about to get there. I was reading."

"What?" he asked, glancing over at his own stack of books he'd borrowed from the library earlier in the week. He'd been too busy to even crack one open yet.

"You wouldn't know this one," she said, and he could hear her shift around.

"Is it a romance book?" he asked, chuckling at the memory of the ending to their earlier conversation.

"So?" He heard the defiance in her voice. "What if it is? People read all kinds of things."

"Nothing wrong with that," he said. "I've read a few of those myself."

"Oh?" she said slowly. "Which ones?"

For the next forty minutes, they compared book lists and talked about good plots and characters versus bad ones. The only thing they disagreed on was horror books. Addy loved scary books, while he stayed clear of them.

"I love a book that keeps me up at night." She sighed, and he could tell she was growing tired.

"I could keep you up all night," he said softly and smiled when he heard her breath hitch. "Addy . . ." He waited a beat.

"Hmm?" she said.

"Dream of me," he whispered.

"I already am."

CHAPTER
TEN

Addy did dream of Trent that night, and the next. With each night, the dreams grew more detailed and her desire for him stronger.

She kept busy, even as the numbers of her group dwindled. Most had moved on to North Dakota and only about a dozen people remained. Even Helen and Minnie had gone on.

Since Estelle had decided to stay in town, Addy had put her in charge of as much as she could to allow herself time to continue her research.

She'd finally had a quick meeting with the mayor and Tyler, Trent, and Trey. They had discussed current oil drilling plans and future ones, but nothing concerning the new land or their plans for it. Basically the meeting had been less productive than just talking to Trent. He'd hurried out of the meeting, claiming the brothers were late for another meeting, and she hadn't even gotten a few minutes alone with him.

She had ended up talking to Martha for another half hour, learning about rumors that had been floating around. Addy told the woman more about the dangers of fracking and other issues with dangerous drilling methods, which was all more concrete information than anything Martha told her.

She'd spent another few hours scouring the web for anything about Trent's family's business and the land purchase, but she was beginning to feel like there was nothing real she could discover. Not without the help of the McGowans.

On Tuesday morning, she dressed in her newest black slacks and added a silk top and low heels. She took extra time fixing her hair and applying the slightest makeup to finish the look.

When she parked near the building that housed McGowan Enterprises, Addy's palms felt damp, and she wished she'd worn her hair up since it had rained that morning. Now her well-placed hair would become a rat's nest. She tied it up in the Jeep before making a dash to the front door, her small, broken umbrella over her head.

She shook the umbrella off and sat it just inside the doorway.

Rea, sitting behind a massive wood desk, watched her as she walked across the glossy wood floor.

"Hello, dear. I hope your Jeep tire got all fixed up."

"Yes, thank you. My insurance paid for everything."

"Oh, good." Rea shifted. "Trent mentioned that you might be stopping by. I've got a few things ready for you." She stood up and moved over to a file cabinet. "Here." She pulled out a thick folder.

"You didn't have to . . ."

"Nonsense." Rea smiled and handed the folder to her. "If I could, I'd be camped out there with your group." She walked back over to her desk. "You have a look through that and if you still have questions, let me know." She winked at Addy. "Now I was given strict orders, if Trent was in the office when you stopped by, to show you in."

Addy swallowed and wished she'd spent a few more minutes fixing her hair.

"But since he's not here . . ." Rea trailed off as the door opened.

"I'm here." Trent walked in and almost tripped on Addy's umbrella.

"Sorry." She watched him move her umbrella aside. Their picnic encounter surfaced in her mind, causing her face to flush.

"Hmm." He smiled. "Don't know what I did to deserve the blush, but I'll take it." He walked toward them. "Thanks, Rea." He took Addy's free hand, and she followed him back down a long hallway. She hadn't registered Trent holding her hand until she glanced back at Rea and noticed the woman's smile. When she tried to tug her hand free, Trent shifted, bringing her closer to him.

They walked past two impressive conference rooms until they came to a tall door with his name etched in the smoked glass.

She wondered just what she had gotten herself into. Could she really spy on Trent's family's business while trying to have a relationship with him? Because that's what it was. Spying. Or was it the idea of the relationship that bothered her the most?

When he shut the door behind her, he pulled her close. The folder Rea had given her crumpled between them as his mouth covered her lips.

"There." He pulled his mouth away. "Much better."

"Speak for yourself. Now I can't walk," she joked.

His arms remained wrapped around her and he nuzzled her neck. "I could always carry . . ."

"No." She took a step back and shook her head, causing him to chuckle.

"I'm glad you stopped by," he said, moving to his desk. But instead of sitting behind it, he motioned for her to sit in one of the brown leather chairs.

She did as he suggested, thankful to be off her feet.

"I like this." He touched the shiny material of her silk shirt. The shirt hung low over her chest, showing off more cleavage than she was used to but not enough to make it inappropriate business attire.

"Thanks," she said, then bit her bottom lip. She could still taste him and smell his aftershave. She had to admit, part of her wished he'd carried her to his desk and . . . her face flushed again.

"There it is again." He leaned closer. "Did you miss me?"

"No." She raised her chin. "Did *you* miss *me*?" she asked after a moment of silence. She wanted to hear him say it first.

"Very much." His gaze moved back to her lips. "The feel, the smell, the taste of you." A low growl radiated from his chest.

She swallowed slowly, and he watched her chest rise and fall.

This time, the growl came from deeper.

"Addy, you're killing me." He shifted slightly and she couldn't help it. Her eyes tracked his motion. Her mouth went dry when she noticed he was hard, very hard.

Closing her eyes, she took several deep breaths and licked her lips. Which didn't end up helping, since she could still taste him on them.

Just then, his office phone chimed and Rea's voice came over the intercom in a soft whisper. "Trent, your uncle just walked in. Shall I have him wait?"

Addy's eyes had flown open and were glued to his as Rea spoke. Without breaking eye contact, he reached back and pressed a button on his phone.

"Yes, thank you." He stood and walked over to the large windows behind his desk.

Addy remained still, unsure of what to say or do.

"How about dinner tonight?" Trent asked, looking out the window.

"I . . ." She shook her head and took another deep breath. "I can't tonight." She held in a groan when she thought about why she couldn't be with him. She'd rather spend the evening anywhere than with her parents.

He turned around and finally met her eyes. "Tomorrow?"

She thought about it for a moment.

"Don't make me beg." She heard his voice crack slightly.

"Okay, tomorrow." She took a step toward the door. "My place," she said without thinking. "I mean, I'll cook." She turned and left before he could respond. His instant smile had given her the answer she needed.

She walked down the long hallway, past Rea and Trent's uncle, Carl. The man looked a lot like Trent's late father, just with a large beer belly.

Once outside, she dashed to her Jeep, avoiding several puddles as she went. The folder Rea had given her remained tucked tight against her chest to keep it from getting wet.

Addy sat in her car for several minutes before she felt she was under control enough to drive back to her trailer.

She was due at her parents' house promptly at five o'clock that evening. A groan escaped her as she thought about the awkward family dinner that would follow.

She spent almost two hours skimming over what Rea had given her. As a person in a leadership position herself, she was impressed at how the three brothers had strengthened their father's business. The rumors were true; they had easily doubled the last year's profits.

But as an activist, she wondered if they had cut corners to obtain the added profits.

She needed more information than what Rea had provided. She needed inspection logs, invoices for supplies, time sheets, reports on safety. She needed more. She needed answers directly from Trent.

◆ ◆ ◆

It took almost five minutes for Trent to get his body back under control. He could still smell her soft perfume in his office as his uncle walked in.

"Heard you wanted to talk to me." Aside from the passing family resemblance, Carl McGowan was nothing like his brother had been—especially in personality. Carl had gone through a handful of wives, DUIs, and jail sentences—and he had gone through money like it grew on trees. As far as Trent knew, he was currently living in a rundown trailer house at the edge of town.

From the looks of his clothes, he would have guessed that the man slept in a gutter.

"Sit." He motioned to the leather chair. Instead, his uncle remained standing.

"If this is about my money, it's about damn time." Carl didn't beat around the bush. He'd already scanned the room for any liquor, which Trent normally kept on the back table but had locked away before his uncle had arrived.

"No, this isn't about money." Trent motioned again to the chair, not willing to sit before the older man. Though he barely deserved that level of respect.

His uncle's eyes continued to scan the room as they both sat.

"Nice place you have here," Carl said. "This should have been my office."

"What makes you say that?" Trent leaned back in his chair. Tyler had recently ordered new chairs and computers for the entire office. Trent was thankful.

"Your father and I built all this." Carl waved his hands around.

"We know exactly what you contributed to this business, and we believe that you've been fully compensated." Trent kept his cool.

"Your father . . ."

"My father is the one who cut you off. His will clearly states that—"

"Don't bullshit me." Carl stood up slowly. Trent followed suit. "I know what I'm due."

"You're due common courtesy. That is why you're in my office today." He motioned again to the chair. Carl hesitated, then sat down.

Trent joined him. "As you know, you made a deal with my father almost ten years ago. You gave away your half of the business for payments made to you over a decade. In that agreement, any income from new procedures and processes would not continue to you. And this would mark the completion of all obligation McGowan Enterprises and our family has toward you." Trent watched his uncle's face turn a deeper shade of purple than normal.

"Your father was a thief. He stole—"

"My father didn't steal anything, and we have the proof." His uncle shut his mouth, and Trent continued. "The agreed-upon ten years is up, and his procedures have been proven not only extremely productive, but lifesaving and cost-efficient. We've worked up a deal with our lawyers for a method of releasing my dad's knowledge to the general public for free."

"You can't do this!" Carl stood up again, his voice echoing throughout the building. "That knowledge is mine. I could make millions selling that oil-drilling method! You're nothing but thieves." The man started coughing and choking. To Trent's horror, he watched his uncle go from bright purple to sheet white in under thirty seconds.

As Carl went down, Trent dove to catch his head before he cracked his skull on the wood floor.

He yelled to Rea to call 911. By the time she rushed into his office, the phone held up to her ear, he was already performing CPR.

Three hours later, Trent left the hospital and drove his mother back to her house. His brothers had left minutes before they had.

"He'll be okay," she assured him. "The heart attack wasn't your fault. Years of bad eating and drinking habits, combined with the late-night lifestyle . . ."

"Mom." Trent stopped her. "I know. I don't blame myself."

"Good." She nodded. "That's good," she said and looked out the window.

He could tell she was wiping a tear away and wondered why his uncle's bad health was not affecting him the same way. Maybe she was thinking about his father?

His dad had died a little over a year ago from a heart attack while on a job. His father had been in perfect health, but now Trent and his brothers all wondered if the stress of holding down a business and a family had weighed heavier on him than they thought. Guilt over their former partying lifestyles now hung over all three of their heads on a daily basis.

It wasn't as if his uncle's heart attack was a big surprise. After all, his mother was right. His uncle had been a walking time bomb for as long as Trent could remember—one of the reasons they had all been certified in CPR in high school. That and the work they did demanded they knew the basics of first aid.

The doctors had told Trent that his uncle had been lucky he'd been there. Otherwise he'd have been lost. Trent parked the truck in the drive at his mother's house but kept the motor running.

"Are you okay?" his mother asked, reaching out her hand and touching his arm.

"Yeah." He shook his head clear. "There's something I need to do."

Her eyes met his and her smile grew. "Be gentle. Something tells me that girl needs gentle."

He closed his eyes. "Jesus, Mom."

"What?" She giggled. "Just because I don't allow it under my roof unless it's a sealed deal doesn't mean I don't know it goes on." She poked him in the stomach. "I didn't raise any fools." She leaned over and kissed his cheek. "Good night."

"Night." He watched until she shut off the front porch light, then pulled out of the drive and headed across town.

As he drove, he thought about his uncle, looking pale and fragile lying in the ICU with tubes sticking out of him. Regardless of what his mother said, or for that matter what his own brain told him, guilt seeped in.

He compared the situation to his father's. If Trent had been there, performing CPR on his dad, would his father have lived? Hell, if the three brothers had stuck around and had actually helped out, his old man could have retired early and would right now be spending his golden years sitting on the back deck with their mother.

His mind played over and over the conversation he had with his uncle. Asking all the same questions. Could he have done anything differently? Anything?

But as he drove through the dark town, he had to admit there wasn't anything different he could have done to help his uncle or his father. Except not leave town and not have the damn meeting with his uncle in the first place. What he needed was a time machine.

As he passed the many different strip clubs that flooded the small town of Haven, he wondered when he'd changed. The row of clubs had moved in close to ten years ago. They were designed to draw the oil workers in and help them spend all the money they made working long hours. What they did for the town was more than just earning tax money; they helped keep a lot of the men busy and out of fights.

There was a time when he and his brothers would have spent countless hours in any of them. Now, however, the thought of spending time with that weird, sexy activist appealed to him so much more.

Addy was right. He had changed.

CHAPTER ELEVEN

Addy was in hell. She knew it was hell because she was on fire. Not out of embarrassment either—it was anger that consumed her.

She'd arrived at her parents' home, the five-thousand-square-foot ranch spread out over an entire hillside, *exactly* on time. But according to her mother, they had been waiting and waiting for her to arrive.

Then, after Addy had apologized for being late, which she hadn't been, her mother's eyes raked her up and down. She gave a smirk that told Addy her mother wasn't pleased with her hair, which was up in a tight bun at the nape of her neck, or the outfit and shoes she'd worn.

As she followed her mother farther into the immaculate house, through the massive living room, down the two steps into the great room, Addy wondered if she'd ever thought of the space as her father's. She couldn't hear a whisper of him in this place she knew like the back of her hand.

The man was just a visitor and acted as such. Her mother had never made anyone other than herself comfortable in the large house.

Sure, it was gorgeous and deserved to be on the cover of a magazine. But Addy thought of it as tainted. Any home this clean seemed spoiled to her these days.

Sure, she liked knowing where everything was, but there were small things she did in her own space that countered her upbringing. She didn't organize the food in her cabinets. She actually used her towels and didn't just put them out for show. The list went on. Even in her small space, she made sure to go against her mother's training.

"We were beginning to wonder if you'd forgotten about tonight." Her mother perched on the edge of the sofa, then crossed her ankles like she was in front of the queen.

"No." Addy plopped down on the sofa. She knew it drove her mother nuts, but since she'd already been accused of being tardy, she didn't care. She hid a smile as her mother's eyes narrowed at the move. "According to my iPhone, I'm right on time." She held up her phone and showed her mother her phone screen, which showed exactly one minute past five.

"Well." Her mother's eyes darted everywhere except for her phone. "We're disappointed that we had to come back to town because of these nasty rumors you've spread. I don't know what makes you think . . ."

Addy stood up slowly, causing her mother to stop talking.

"I?" Addy repeated her mother's words over and over in her mind until they finally registered. "*I* spread?" She swallowed and felt a sharp tug in her heart. "I didn't spread any rumors."

"No?" Her mother shook her head as her father looked on from the only armchair she let be "his."

Addy had barely noticed the man. Actually she'd been avoiding looking in his direction. Just knowing what he'd done . . . She blocked that thought from her mind.

Her parents were older than most of her friends' parents. It had been her excuse as to why they hadn't been like everyone else's parents.

Her father was pushing his mid-sixties, her mother just two years behind him.

Darla was her age . . . Twenty-three. Her skin felt like it was crawling, and she rubbed her arms.

"No!" Addy knew the raised voice would get her another glare from her mother. "I was the one who stood there, in the middle of the grocery store, and listened to his harlot explain how she's pregnant with my father's baby. A woman my age, almost three times younger than him." She turned to her father and pointed her finger at him. "Are you going to sit there like this woman's puppet and deny that you have slept with Darla?"

Her father just shook his head and began clearing his throat. He'd always been thin, but in the past few years, he'd turned frail. His wiry frame was looking more fragile than ever before.

"Your father has done no such thing. That woman and you have clearly concocted this entire scheme to get money from us." Her mother crossed her hands over her lap and straightened her shoulders. "Well, we brought you here tonight to inform you that your diabolical scheme won't work. We've taken measures to protect us—and our assets—from you."

"Measures?" Addy stood still, feeling her head spin at her parents' stupidity. "What measures?"

"We've gone to our lawyer and blocked you from inheriting a thing from us."

"Okay." She felt like laughing. "Good, I suppose. More for Dad's new child."

Her mother plowed right through that statement as if Addy hadn't even spoken. "No matter what rumors you spread, you'll never see another dime from us."

"I haven't taken a dime of yours for almost two years. What makes you think I'd want anything now?"

"Isn't it obvious?" Her mother's head wagged slightly. "You're living in that tiny trailer, moving around the world with those . . . drifters. Who knows what kind of drugs you're on? Or worse, what kind of diseases you've gotten from your shenanigans. Not to mention the talk that is going around about you and those McGowan boys. I never did like those boys. They've spent most of their lives running wild in this town." Her mother shifted slightly, a look on her face like she'd just passed by a dump. "It's a shame that you don't care about your reputation anymore."

Addy burst out laughing. When she could finally talk, she took a deep breath.

"First, I'm not the one who should be tested." She turned to her father. "Seriously, the rumor last year was Darla has a nasty case of herpes." She watched her father's eyes fill with worry as he crossed his legs. Then she looked at her mother. "I don't now, and haven't ever, used drugs of any kind." She didn't know why she was defending herself. "Second, believe it or not, I'm still a virgin." She took a step closer, but her mother's expression did not waver. "I wouldn't take another penny from you if my life depended on it."

Her parents trailed her as she stomped back to the front door. She stopped with her hand on the doorknob. "Last, what I do or don't do with any of the McGowans is none of your business." Her eyes turned toward her father. "If I were you, I'd get as far away from that"—she nodded toward her mother, who stood with her arms crossed—"as fast as I could. She's nothing more than a cancerous cell, spreading to take everybody else down with her."

Addy opened the door. "I have no parents."

She slammed the front door behind her and smiled when she heard glass break as one of her mother's many perfectly placed pictures fell off the wall.

Addy drove back into town completely and totally pissed. Her entire body shook as the nasty encounter looped in her mind.

She considered dropping by the Wet Spot and laying some of her anger on Darla, but then thought better of it and pulled into the parking lot of the diner instead. She didn't want to end up in a jail cell that night and prove her parents right.

The Dancing Moose was full for a Tuesday night. When she walked in, she ignored all the stares and the whispers about her father's indiscretions and headed to the farthest, darkest booth.

She ordered a large chocolate shake, the biggest burger they had with cheese, and an entire serving of onion rings.

Comfort food, she thought as she dug into her shake. She didn't need parents. Didn't need anyone.

She closed her eyes and rested her head back as the cold shake slid down her throat and hit her stomach. When was that burger going to get here?

Her mind replayed the scene at her parents' house several times. Then, for some reason, Addy remembered all the times her mother had mentioned the McGowan boys while she was growing up.

Her mother had never liked the boys—she'd constantly complained about them, how they were running around town, sleeping with everyone. Addy had been warned so many times to steer clear of the three of them that it had sunk in.

She closed her eyes and felt her heart plummet. Maybe her earlier indifference to Trent was really her mother's doing?

Then again, her mother didn't really get along well with anyone in town. Sure, she was nice to some folks, but she had always steered clear of others, such as Rea and Gail. Addy was grateful that her mother didn't know that Brian, Rea's son, was part of her group.

Almost an hour later, soothed, at least temporarily, by the greasy comfort, she drove back to her place.

She'd been in her trailer less than fifteen minutes before there was a knock on her door. Her mind still roiled from her ordeal.

When she opened the door, Trent stood outside, looking up at her. The anger she had for her mother bubbled to the surface again, and she realized that no matter what she'd believed about this man in the past, she wasn't going to let it affect her now.

Before she got a chance to say anything, he joined her inside and pulled the door shut behind them as his mouth covered hers.

♦　♦　♦

Okay, so it wasn't the smartest thing to do. He knew his mother had been right, Addy deserved gentle. But he wasn't feeling gentle right now. Instead, he was filled with an intense urge to prove to the world that he was alive.

And she was the means of proving it. He carried her, her legs wrapped around him, until the back of her knees hit the front of her massive bed.

"Trent," she said between kisses.

"Let me stay." It almost came out as a plea. "I really need you, need this."

"I overheard someone talking about your uncle," she said, breaking free of him.

The mention of his family made him pull away. "Damn." He rubbed his hands over his face. "Sorry."

"Don't be. It's perfectly . . ." She stopped talking when he gave her a look. "Sorry." She shook her head. "I'm sorry to hear about your uncle. Is he okay?"

"Yeah. We stuck around as long as we could at the hospital until they kicked us out."

She nodded.

"Where did you hear about it?" he asked, moving over and sitting down at her little table. He wasn't in the mood to get a crick in his neck from stooping.

"At the diner. I went there for dinner."

His gaze caught hers. "I thought you had plans?"

She took a deep breath. "I did, but instead of sitting down for a nice family dinner, my parents only wanted to inform me that they've cut me off."

He stood up and went to her, taking her shoulders in his hands. "I'm sorry."

She shook her head. He was thankful he didn't see tears in her eyes, because he didn't think he could deal with seeing her hurt.

"Don't be. I'm not. It was bound to happen sooner or later."

"What? Them cutting you off?" He nudged her over until they sat on the edge of the bed together. She nodded. "Why?"

"The story in our family is that my mother comes from old oil money. My father as well."

He nodded. "Yeah, everyone around here knows about the Collinses. They helped rebuild Haven when they were the first to strike oil."

"Well, both of them were always . . . privileged." Addy exhaled. "Especially my mother. I never knew either of their families, but she's always kept very tight reins on her money. Even my father had to ask her for anything. A few years back, when I left school, they threatened that if I didn't fall in line, I'd be cut off." She shrugged.

"And you've pursued your dreams anyway?"

She nodded, and he reached up and cupped her face in his hands. "Good for you."

She chuckled. "So I live in this tiny trailer that I bought with my college fund and make barely enough to survive each year doing the exact opposite of what my parents wanted."

"Is that why you do it?"

"No, but it helps." She smiled up at him. "I love what I do. What about you?"

"Now I couldn't imagine being anywhere else than here." He leaned closer and kissed her. Her lips were intoxicating. She had a fuller top lip that he enjoyed sucking on until he felt her melt next to him.

"Trent," she said, wrapping her arms around his shoulders. "Tonight, my mother accused me of . . ." She stopped, remembering her mother's words and the hurt it caused her. Then her eyes met his, and she realized just being with him caused the pain in her head and heart to subside. "It doesn't matter. What matters is that I want you to stay with me tonight. I want you to make love to me." Addy leaned up and kissed him again.

"Are you sure?" he asked. He'd cooled down a lot listening to her problems. After his mind had taken over, he'd realized she did deserve better.

She tugged him until he was next to her on the bed, then pulled his head back down to hers and kissed him until his thoughts of leaving vanished.

He took his time, forced himself to go slow. He inched her clothes from her body, making sure to enjoy every part of her that he exposed.

The soft sounds she made almost drove him crazy, but he kept himself in check. Her hips moved as he pulled her soft slacks off.

When he exposed dark-red silk panties that matched the bra she was wearing, he felt himself grow harder than he could remember ever being.

He leaned up on his knees and looked down at her.

His hands had freed her hair from the tight bun. Now it was fanned out on the bed as she looked up at him with her blue eyes.

She reached up and yanked off his shirt, then ran her fingertips over every inch of his chest and arms.

"I've dreamed about you for as long as I can remember," she said, her cheeks turning a slight shade of pink. "Even before I knew . . ." She shook her head.

"What?" he asked, nudging her legs wider as he played with those soft, cherry-red panties.

Her eyes met his. "Before I knew what sex was. I dreamed of touching you."

He smiled. "You know what it is now." He hooked a finger under her panties, but she stopped him by putting her hand over his.

"Not yet," she said. "But after tonight I will."

CHAPTER TWELVE

Addy watched realization flood Trent's expression and fear replace desire. He leaned back and dropped his hands from her like she'd caught fire.

She chuckled. "What? Haven't you ever been with a virgin before?" She leaned up on her elbows and cocked an eyebrow at him.

He swallowed a few times, then shook his head.

"I mean, um . . ."

She giggled and moved up until her almost-bare chest was against his warm skin and toned muscles. "I won't break."

"Yeah, but . . ."

"Trent." She placed a finger over his lips. "This doesn't change anything."

"The hell it doesn't," he said and ran his hands through his hair.

"What?" she asked, trailing kisses along his collarbone.

"I'll think of something in a minute," he said, and she heard a small groan escape his lips.

"I've always thought it was an excuse men used to end things."

"It's no excuse." His fingers wrapped around her wrists as he nudged her back onto the mattress and looked down at her. "Just a reason to go slow and make sure you enjoy yourself."

"Oh?" she asked. "How would you do that?"

He smiled down at her. "There are many different ways to please a newbie. I can do this . . ." He bent down and started raining kisses down her neck. "This." He dipped farther after a moment and trailed his lips just above the red bra, licking the soft material above her nipples until they poked through. "Or this," he said, sliding his finger into the top of her panties.

"Yes, I remember this one." Addy shifted, but instead of continuing with his finger, Trent nudged her legs wider as he settled his shoulders between her legs. When he pushed the silk aside and placed his tongue on her, she squealed and gripped his hair.

He took his time, using every move he'd learned over the years until he found the one she liked best, then enjoyed himself as he pleased her.

When her nails dug into his scalp and he felt her convulse under his tongue, he slid out of his jeans, donned the condom he always carried, and nudged her legs wider.

"That was a new one," she said, softly.

"You ain't seen nothing yet." He leaned in and kissed her softly as he slid into her. When he reached the barrier, he held his breath and jerked his hips.

The same cry came from her lips as when he'd pleasured her. He held still, praying he would be able to last more than five seconds.

Then, when he finally had his breathing under control, he felt her legs wrap around him.

He looked down at her. "You okay?" he asked, hoping she'd say yes.

She nodded, then leaned up and took his mouth in a deep kiss as he started moving with her.

He'd never felt anything as wonderful as Addy. She did more than consume him; she took him body and soul.

By the time he felt her building again, he knew there was no holding himself back any longer.

When he felt her tense, he followed her and could have sworn he saw stars.

It took almost a full five minutes for him to regain any signs of intelligence. Then he realized he was probably crushing her and rolled to the side, taking her with him.

"That was . . ." Her words drifted off into a moan.

"What?" he said after a moment.

"*Amazing* just doesn't fit."

He chuckled. "Surprising? Stunning? Staggering? Astonishing?"

"Breathtaking." She rolled over until she was on top of him. "Can we do that again?"

His eyebrows rose. "Now?"

She smirked. "Maybe after a quick nap."

He nodded and pulled her closer. "Perfect." He reached up and kissed her. Her lips felt so right against his. "Why is it that you're still . . . um, were still a virgin?"

She glanced down at him. "I don't know. I mean, I thought going into college that sex would be one of those things that just happened." She shook her head slightly. "My mother had always been so protective of me. Never allowing me to date. But then I got out on my own and decided I didn't want to rush into something just out of spite." She sighed. "Then, before too long it just became, I don't know, almost like a badge I wore."

"There had to be plenty of guys asking you out," he said, causing her to chuckle.

"No, not really. At least none that I wanted to be with."

"I would have done something to get your attention." He looked down at her; her hair was fanned out, his fingers tangled in the soft tresses. Her blue eyes shone in the dim light. Her lips pouted, swollen from kisses, and all he could think of was what more he could do to keep things just like this.

"You wouldn't have had to do anything to get my attention," she murmured.

They passed a little time in silence, then before he knew it, he was ready and rolling her once more to her back.

"What about that nap?" She kissed him between words.

"I'll sleep when I'm dead," he said as he slid into her heat again. This time, he watched her eyes and knew that he'd never get tired of that blue shimmer as he made love to her.

◆　◆　◆

Light from the lamp over her bed hit her face and woke Addy the next morning. She blinked, then sat up. "What time is it?"

"Sorry," Trent mumbled as he moved around the trailer collecting things. "I've got . . . early meeting. Couldn't see in the dark." He searched around at the foot of the bed. "Stop by to see how my uncle is doing. Couldn't find . . . shoe." He held it up. Then looked up at her and smiled. "Morning."

"Morning." She rolled her shoulders slowly, stretching, and looked at the large numbers on her clock. "It's only four."

He nodded and she noticed his eyes were focused below her chin. Glancing down, she realized she was stark naked.

Instantly she reached to cover herself.

"No, don't." He grinned. "Leave me with the memory of those for the rest of the day."

"You saw them last night."

"Yeah, but that was last night." He leaned over and placed a kiss on her lips. "I really do have to go." He sat down and pulled on his boots. "I was too preoccupied to take these off at the door, sorry."

She shook her head and held in a yawn. "It's okay, I'm not anal about it."

He smiled guiltily. "Good, because I left a mess." He glanced at her floor. "If I had time, I'd clean."

"Go." She waved him away, and her heart softened at the thought of him keeping her place tidy. "Let me sleep some more." She lay back down as he turned off the light, sending the trailer back into darkness.

"We still good for dinner?"

"Sure," she yawned. "See you. Text me and let me know how your uncle is doing."

She felt him place another kiss on her lips, then was fast asleep before he shut the door to her trailer.

After she woke several hours later, Addy thought about her time with Trent as she cooked herself a simple breakfast of eggs and toast. What was she doing? Could she really pull off being with him and doing her job?

As she showered, she tried to come up with a plan of action, but her mind kept wandering back to how it felt when he touched her, how wonderful it felt to be with someone who cared so much.

When she finally stepped outside, she had a list of to-dos to complete that day—stocking her kitchen, filling up her propane tanks, and stopping by to talk to Rea to see if she could get more information from the woman herself. Rea knew everything there was to know about the McGowans personally and professionally. Maybe, just maybe Addy could work around Trent and find out what she needed to know.

After loading her empty tanks into the back of her Jeep, she dropped them off at the refueling station and was told it would take half an hour before they could be filled. She realized she missed the big cities where she could just swap them out with new ones. But she left her tanks there and headed into the McGowan offices to talk to Rea while she waited.

She was surprised to see Kristen sitting behind the counter instead of Rea. Addy thought about making an excuse and coming back later, but Kristen waved her in.

"I was hoping I'd run into you soon." Kristen stood and hugged her. "Did you hear the news?"

"Yes, congratulations. When are you due?"

"Not soon enough, according to my husband-to-be," she said. "We think December. We won't know for sure until I go in next week."

"Wow, only just pregnant." Addy calculated quickly.

"Not even eight weeks yet." Kristen sat back down. "Now you must have also heard about the early wedding."

Addy nodded. "It's coming up."

"Yup. We haven't gotten the printed ones yet, but I'm hoping you'll accept a verbal invitation."

Addy blinked. "Of course. I'd be honored."

"Good." Kristen's smile was contagious. "Now." She put her elbows on the desk. "What can I do for you?"

Addy chuckled. "Rea had given me some data. I was hoping she was around to answer some questions."

"She has the day off, but I can help." Kristen nodded to the chair across from her. "It's always quiet here on Wednesdays, so we should be undisturbed. What kind of information do you need?"

Addy told her what she was looking for while keeping it as generic as possible. She didn't want to come right out and say that she was looking for something to give her boss that could possibly break the company.

While there, she got a text from Trent saying his uncle was out of ICU and in recovery. They were thinking of moving him to a special facility near Helena that would be able to help him recover faster.

Over an hour later, Addy walked out with a small box of papers. Kristen had been completely open with her about everything except what they intended to do with the new land. Again, Addy hit a brick wall. A lot of what Kristen had told her fell in line with what she'd heard from the mayor. More rumors, such as they were planning on expanding their offices or they were going to use it as storage for heavy equipment. Addy's conversation with Kristen had at least confirmed that, in her mind, there was no way the McGowans would start fracking. She knew Kristen had just gone through a traumatic event, so she hadn't pushed her further. She'd heard all the issues Kristen and the McGowans were going through in their legal fight with Dennis Rodgers. Jumping through hoops to find enough evidence to prove that the man had almost killed her.

Addy shoved the box of papers, no doubt more invoices and spreadsheets that would lead to nowhere, into her back seat, then went to pick up her full tanks and head to the grocery store. She debated having lunch in town or making something back at her trailer, but the chance of running into someone she knew at the diner sent her to the freezer aisle for a precooked meal.

She'd been in the store less than ten minutes and was just placing another gallon of ice cream in her cart when someone screamed, "Fire!"

She rushed to the front of the store with several other people and looked out the front windows.

Her mind didn't register at first what she was seeing. Then she gasped.

"My Jeep!" Her entire Jeep was engulfed.

She had just made it outside the glass doors when the fire hit the propane tanks. The blast threw her, and everyone else who had been watching, back several steps. Knocked on her ass, Addy landed on the ground as the glass from the front windows shattered and large shards fell around her. She threw her arms up and covered her face as pieces rained down on her. She felt the sting as glass sliced into her skin.

She'd just recovered and was on her hands and knees when the next blast hit. This time, it knocked her face-first into the cement that was now littered with glass. Pain shot up her arms from the glass piercing her hands just as her chin hit the ground and everything went black.

◆ ◆ ◆

Trent rushed into the hospital for the second time in two days. Nothing about the first visit had prepared him for the second—Addy, sitting on a gurney, her chin covered in large white bandages that continued down over her arms, right to her fingertips.

The nurse was working on cleaning Addy's knees, removing shards of glass from her skin with a pair of long tweezers. When the nurse saw him, she tried to shoo him out, but he just glared at her.

"He's fine," Addy said, smiling, which caused the tape on the bandage on her chin to pop loose. He rushed over and gently smoothed it back into place.

"What happened?" he asked her.

"I wish I knew." She shook her head and he watched her wince.

"Have you given her anything for the pain?" he asked the nurse.

"Yes." She did not seem pleased by this intrusion.

"I'm fine." Addy reached for his hand but stopped short when the bandages got in the way. "Really. It was stupid of me to rush out there."

"We're treating several others from the store for cuts as well. She got the worse of it, but from the sound of it, even if she'd stayed inside she would have gotten hurt."

"The entire storefront is destroyed," Addy said. "I had just picked up my propane tanks. They were in the back of my Jeep." Trent watched as sadness filled her eyes. "It's gone."

"It's okay." He wrapped his arm around her gently.

She nodded. "I'm just thankful no one was hurt too severely."

His eyes moved over her. "This isn't severe?"

118

She shook her head, and he watched her eyes cloud as the pain medicine finally took hold.

"No. You should see my Jeep." Addy rested her head back with a sigh.

The nurse broke in. "She'll rest for a while. Then we'll discharge her after the doctor confirms she doesn't have a concussion."

Trent nodded, keeping his eyes on Addy. He wanted to touch her but was too afraid he'd hurt her. Her bandages ranged from the size of his hand to a butterfly bandage.

He sat with her until the doctor walked in and assured them that she didn't have a concussion, just a nasty bump on her chin. He suggested Addy be watched for the night, then come in and get checked again and have the stitches removed in a few days.

Almost two hours later, Trent was wheeling her out when Mike stopped by. The man was covered in soot and looked like he'd fallen headfirst into a campfire.

"What happened to you?" he asked.

Mike looked at him, then wiped a hand over his forehead. "Damn it." He pulled out a handkerchief. He shook his head and continued to clear his face. "Happened to sneeze when I was a few inches away from the pile that used to be Ms. Collins's Jeep."

Addy giggled and covered her mouth then rolled her eyes.

"Don't mind her, she's on some pretty good drugs." Trent waited until Mike's face was clear of soot.

"Well?" he asked finally.

"Addy, you don't smoke, do you?" Mike looked down at her in the wheelchair.

"Nope. Why would I kill the ozone and myself?" She made a face that said she was disgusted at the thought of it. "Never even tried it."

Mike sighed. "Found a cigarette butt in what appeared to be a box of papers in her back seat. It looks like the papers caught quickly, then spread to the two tanks, which caused the gas tank on the Jeep to take out the rest."

"Boom." Addy looked up at Trent. "I stopped by your office first. Kristen printed out some stuff for me to look at."

He glanced over at Mike. "Anyone see who?" The man shook his head. "Any idea what brand?"

"Gold Crest, but the fire inspector will want to double-check that it was the official cause of the blaze," Mike said. Trent thought of a few people he knew who smoked the brand.

"We'll narrow the list down," Mike added. "They would have had to open her door to toss the butt in since she had a hard top on the Jeep. Is she going home with you?"

Trent nodded.

"If I find anything, I'll let you know."

"Thanks." Trent started to walk Addy out, but she stopped him.

"No, I want to see how everyone else is." She tried to turn the wheelchair around but almost fell out of it instead.

"I'll go ask," Mike said, then moved over to the desk.

He came back a few minutes later. "Mrs. Anderson had a cut under her left eye that was bandaged up with a few stitches, Mr. Thompson had cuts on his hands—he pulled Addy into the store after the Jeep blew. The store clerks both have minor cuts, no stitches, but other than that, everyone was just shaken up. They were all released and went home almost an hour ago."

"Thank you." Addy sighed. "I owe Mr. Thompson. He taught me how to play cello." She looked up at Trent. "Did you know that I know how to play the cello?"

"No, but now I do." He pushed his drifty angel out to his truck and helped her in. Instead of waiting as she tried to get her feet on the ground, he picked her up and set her on the seat, kissing her forehead before shutting the door.

She slept during the short trip to his mother's house and was still asleep when he carried her inside.

His mother had prepared his room for her. He'd texted her when he heard that Addy'd been hurt and had filled everyone in on her progress.

Trent's mother, Kristen, and Trisha had wanted to come to the hospital, but he stopped them since the place was too small. And he needed some time alone with Addy to ensure that she was okay.

Now everyone waited as he carried her straight to the living room sofa. He sat down, still holding her in his arms. She snuggled up against him and sighed.

"Well?" his mother whispered.

"She's out. You can talk normally." He shifted slightly, pulling Addy closer.

"What happened? Someone said the entire grocery store blew up." His mother sat across from him. He nodded.

"We just drove by there on the way back. Her Jeep was nothing more than a pile of metal. The whole front of the store is gone, including the sign her Jeep was parked near."

"What caused it?" Kristen asked.

"Someone flicked a cigarette into a box of paperwork she'd gotten from you, then the fire spread to the two full propane tanks she had in the back of her Jeep, which caused the gas tank on the Jeep to blow, taking out most of everything in the front of the store. Three other cars were charred beyond recognition."

"Oh my," his mother said, shaking her head. "Any idea who would have done such a thing?"

"A few," he replied, looking at his brothers.

"Darla smokes," Tyler said.

"Not Gold Crests." Trent shook his head.

"Still, she could have bummed a cigarette off someone."

Trent thought about it and nodded. "It wouldn't hurt to see if she was working at the time."

"I'll swing by tomorrow." Tyler leaned forward.

"Addy's folks cut her out of their will."

"What?" His mother almost gasped the word. "Why would they do such a terrible thing?"

Trent shook his head and looked down at Addy. "Apparently she's a big disappointment to them."

"Well, I never did like those two. Especially her mother. Victoria always acted like she was better than everyone else in town."

The room was silent for a while. "Do you think she will be hungry when she wakes up?" Trisha finally asked.

Trent sighed. "I know I am."

"What about a change of clothes?" Kristen added. "She can't go around in the hospital gown."

Trent looked down at the material she was wrapped in.

"Yeah, I have her keys to her place." He shook the purse he'd carried in with her, knowing the sound meant they were inside the bag.

"I'll swing by." Trey stood.

"We'll go." Kristen tugged Tyler up. "She may want some other things. We can pick up some burgers in town too, so no one has to cook, and I'll pack her a bag."

"Thanks. I'm going to get her to bed." Trent started to stand.

"Son." His mother stopped him. "I know you know my rules, but I have no objection to you staying in your room with her tonight."

He chuckled. "You couldn't have stopped me if you tried." His mother joined in his laughter as he stood up with Addy and carried her down the hallway.

CHAPTER THIRTEEN

Addy woke when Trent laid her down on a soft bed. Her eyelids felt like they were being held shut with glue. When she moved to reach up and wipe them, pain shot through her hands.

"Easy." Trent's voice sounded so close to her ear. "I'll get you a warm washcloth. Give me a minute."

She heard his footsteps retreat, then return less than a minute later. She'd tried several times to open her eyes but was having no luck. They felt too heavy.

"What?" she blurted after the washcloth touched her face. He had started with her scalp, and the warmth felt wonderful. "What happened?" she asked when she finally could open her eyes.

He frowned down at her. "Your Jeep blew up." He stopped washing her face and looked at her. "Do you remember?"

Memories flooded her foggy brain. "Yes," she almost moaned. "Where am I?"

"My room." He went back to wiping her face. "Your hair's still got grit in it." He touched a strand. "Hopefully we can figure out a way to wash it without getting your bandages wet."

She groaned and shut her eyes. She must look horrid.

"Do you think you can eat? You're supposed to take some more of these." She heard a bottle of pills being rattled.

"What are they?"

He glanced down. "Codeine."

She shook her head. "All I need is some Tylenol." She shifted and tried to sit up, but when she put her hands flat on the bed and pushed, she cried out.

"Easy," he said, dropping the pill bottle. "Here." He helped her shift until she was sitting up.

She held up her hands. "Have you seen them?"

"Your hands?" he asked. "Thirty-two stitches overall, mostly in your hands and knees. No nerve damage and no concussion. They gave us some of this stuff to put on your cuts when we change the bandages." He held up a tube. "Antiseptic ointment." He wiggled it. "Fun."

She felt like a mummy when she looked down at her arms and legs. The pain was minimal at this point, but she knew that once all the codeine she'd been given at the hospital wore off, the stinging would increase.

"Can I shower?" She looked up at him.

"No, but you can do sponge baths." He grinned. "I'm looking forward to giving you your first one." Then he glanced at the closed bedroom door. "But don't tell my mom."

She couldn't help it; she laughed, causing more pain to shoot from her chin.

"Ouch!" She reached up.

"Sorry." He held her still. "Let me look at that one. The tape keeps coming off."

She sat still as he gently removed the bandage from her chin. She watched his eyes to see how bad it was, but so far, she didn't see upset behind the dark hazel.

"Well?" she finally asked.

"Not bad." His gaze ran over her slowly. "I'll go get a mirror." He stood up and disappeared into what she assumed was a bathroom.

She looked around at his room. Dark, rich browns and blues. She would have guessed instantly that this was his. A massive bookcase occupied one wall, and she couldn't hide a smile when she noticed that it was full.

He came back with a small mirror and held it out for her.

She carefully took it with her bandaged hand and held it up.

There was a good-sized cut running from one side of her chin to the other. No stitches. However, the area was dark red and appeared to be bruised underneath.

"They used glue instead of stitches here." He sat next to her, pointing as he talked. "Since the cut wasn't too deep, the doctor said it would leave less of a scar too."

"Okay, will it hold?"

He smiled. "The doc said it will hold longer than the stitches. He only stitched up the deep cuts." Trent took the mirror and held her hand up. "These ones were too deep to use glue." He gestured to several spots on her arms and the palms of her hands, then to her left knee.

"I fell on my hands and knees, I think—it's all fuzzy." She closed her eyes as what she could remember played over in her mind.

"You bumped your head pretty good, and the medicine they gave you will mess with your mind."

She nodded just as a knock sounded at the door.

"Come in," Trent called out.

Kristen walked in, holding a large duffle bag. "We went and got you a few of your things. Oh—" She set the bag down and moved closer. "That doesn't look so bad."

"I think we can leave that bandage off your chin for a while." Trent tossed the wadded-up bandage he'd been holding into a trash can across the room.

"Do you want some help cleaning up?" Kristen asked, looking at Trent.

"My mother sent you, didn't she?" He crossed his arms.

"I do what I'm told." Kristen smiled. "I'm not about to mess with either my mother or yours." She winked at Addy.

"I'd like to see if I could do something with this." Addy waved her bandaged hand over her face and hair.

Trent stood up and rummaged through his drawers, pulling out a neatly folded pair of sweats and then a crisp white T-shirt.

"These might be bigger and looser than anything you have. It will be easier to get in and out of, plus give us room to check on your knees later." He set them on the bed. "Feel free to use anything else. I'll go check on . . ." He looked toward his bedroom door. "Things." He rolled his eyes. "Let me know if you need anything," he said before stepping out.

"We're fine." Kristen smiled at him until he shut the door. "Now." She turned to Addy. "Let's get you cleaned up."

It took a lot longer than Addy expected. Almost an hour alone to wash her hair. They decided on using the bathtub instead of the bathroom sink since Trent had one of those removable showerheads everyone dreams of. She sat at the edge of the tub and leaned back as Kristen gently shampooed her hair.

Kristen chatted with her as she took her time trying to get all the tangles out. Sitting there with Kristen working on her hair, Addy closed her eyes and thought that this would be how it felt to have a sister. Someone to help her through a rough spot. Someone else who would care about her, who had been there during the hard times. Her mind flashed to her mother and how she used to cut Addy's bangs. There hadn't been gentleness or kindness like Kristen was showing her. Her eyes started to sting, so she focused on what Kristen was talking about instead.

When Addy's long hair was wrapped up in a towel on the top of her head, Kristen used a washcloth and soap to clean where she could since Addy's hands were out of commission. She even had black soot on the back of her neck. It felt a little awkward, but wonderful to be clean.

"Okay, after that, there should never be any awkwardness between us." Kristen chuckled.

"Right?" Addy laughed. "I could use some food now, and I guess one of those pills."

"Are you hurting?"

"Yup. Every muscle feels like it went through a blender."

"I'm curious." Kristen bit her bottom lip.

"About?" Addy asked as Kristen helped her into Trent's sweats.

"Was it like it is in the movies? The explosion?"

"I don't know. I guess I don't remember much, other than being thrown around." She lifted her arms as Kristen pulled the large T-shirt down over her head. "Was being kidnapped like it is in the movies?"

Kristen shifted, then a slow smile formed. "Guess we've both been through some crazy stuff. I don't think either of us will be signing up as stunt doubles anytime soon." Addy laughed in agreement. "Sit, I'll get your brush." She tugged the towel off Addy's head and pointed to a chair near the bookcase, then disappeared back into the bathroom where she'd left a smaller bag of Addy's toiletries.

Addy sat and reached for a book, but it fell out of her bandaged hands. She bent to try and pick it up.

"Here," Trent said from just inside the doorway. "Let me." He set a tray of food down on the nightstand.

Kristen walked in with a brush.

"I can handle it from here." Trent took the brush from her. "Thanks." He leaned down and placed a soft kiss on Kristen's forehead. "Go home and get some sleep."

Kristen nodded, then turned back to her. "If you need anything . . ."

"Thank you," Addy said.

"Think you can eat while I do this?" Trent held up the brush.

"Yeah, if you open the book and lay it on my lap and flip pages for me."

"*To Kill a Mockingbird*," he said as he retrieved it. "One of the first books I read in high school."

"Me too." She smiled.

It took a few minutes to organize everything. The plate of food sat on the wide arm of the chair, the book sat in her lap, and Trent stood behind her, slowly brushing out the tangles that remained in her hair.

He even helped her eat the fries since they were too small for her fingers to pinch.

"When can the bandages come off?"

"In a few days. Depends on how the cuts look. We can wrap your fingers individually so you don't have mittens."

As he continued to brush her hair and the food filled her stomach, Addy began to get drowsy. Closing her eyes, she let her mind drift through a list of things she had been toiling over. How to get to the bottom of the McGowan plans, for example? But then, suddenly, her thoughts took a different turn. She was floating across a bright-green field; the grass was high and swaying in the light summer breeze. Slowly she drifted toward a small log cabin. On the wide front porch sat two wooden rocking chairs, and in her mind, she knew who she wanted to fill the comfortable seats.

"Here." Trent's voice broke in, and she shook the images from her mind.

He handed her a pill and a glass of water.

"I know you said you wanted Tylenol, but for tonight, maybe take one of these."

She complied with a nod.

"Almost done here," he said. There's just one knot left." He moved back around her. She'd set the book down since her eyes refused to focus anymore.

She leaned her head back as he worked the knot out of her hair. Once he was finished, he picked her up and carried her to the bed.

"Thanks." She nestled down into the covers. "I feel so much better."

"I've been given permission to stay in here tonight." He smiled down. "If you think I won't bother you."

She scooted over slightly and nodded her head to the empty side of the bed. "There's plenty of room."

He pulled off his clothes and crawled in next to her, reaching over to flip off the light before pulling her closer.

"Trent?" she said once her face was settled on his shoulder.

"Hmm?" The sound vibrated against her skin.

"Thanks for being there for me." She sighed as his arms settled around her.

◆　◆　◆

Trent had a hard time sleeping. It wasn't the softness of Addy pushed up against him but the images of her destroyed Jeep and the storefront that kept him awake.

Things could have ended much worse than they had. So many different scenarios ran through his mind. What if Addy had been standing directly next to the Jeep?

When the sunlight started streaming in his window, he edged out of the bed and showered. His brothers had told him last night that they would fill in for him today at the office, but there was some detective work he wanted to do on his own while Addy was still sleeping.

When he came back into the bedroom to gather his clothes, he heard her moan.

"Wow, what a nice view to wake up to." She stretched her arms over her head. He noticed a slight wince, but otherwise she was looking much better than last night.

He glanced down at the towel he'd wrapped around his hips and smiled. "I was thinking you'd sleep in."

"If the sun is up, so am I." She shifted and sat up without using her hands.

"How are you feeling?"

"Better. I'd like to see what's under this mess today." She looked down at her hands. "Maybe see if we can just rebandage the fingers?"

"Sure. How about after breakfast? I'm sure my mom or Trisha have something cooking by now." He smiled. "I smell bacon."

"So do I." Her stomach rumbled audibly. "I haven't had bacon . . ." She shook her head. "In too long."

He walked over and took out a pair of boxers, then quickly tugged them up his legs and shimmied out of the towel. He heard her groan and then whistle.

He turned. "You *are* feeling better."

"Why don't you come over here and . . ."

A knock came at the door. "Breakfast is ready," his mother called out, causing him to roll his eyes.

"Okay, we'll be out in a minute." He waited until he heard his mother's footsteps retreat. "She has a sex radar," he whispered, causing Addy to laugh.

Once he tugged on the rest of his clothes and Addy had climbed out of bed, they made their way out of his room and down the hallway.

"You look more alive today," Trisha said to Addy from her spot at the stove. "How are you feeling?"

"Better, thank you." She sat down when Trent pulled out a chair at the table for her. He busied himself with getting them both full plates of eggs, toast, and bacon.

"Do you drink coffee?" he asked.

She put up a bandaged hand. "Nope, gave the stuff up. But I like orange juice." She nodded to the glass container.

He grabbed a mug for himself, then a glass of juice for her, and finally sat down with their plates.

"I can't eat half of this." She chuckled as he set the plate full of food in front of her.

"I'll finish what you can't." He smiled.

She reached for her fork and frowned when she dropped it and it hit the table.

"Here." Gail walked over and handed her a thick wooden spoon. "This might be easier."

"I feel like a child," Addy said, looking around the table.

"The good thing is you're here, safe, and well," Trisha said. "When I think of what could have been . . ." She shook her head.

"You and me both," Trent said to Trisha.

His mother glanced in his direction. "I thought you had the day off?"

"I do. Just have a few things I wanted to take care of this morning." He looked at Addy.

"We were going to sit out on the back patio for a while this morning. Why don't you go run your errands, and Addy can enjoy the spring sun with us until you get back?" Trisha suggested.

"I don't have to be babysat," Addy chimed in.

"No, but you're under doctor's orders to take it easy, at least for the first forty-eight hours." He finished his plate and reached for hers that she'd pushed away. She'd eaten less than half of her food, but last night, she'd eaten a full burger and half the fries, so he wasn't too concerned.

He left Addy in his mother's and Trisha's very capable hands and headed to the police station. When he drove by the store, he saw that the lot had been cleared of cars, including the remains of Addy's Jeep.

The front windows had been boarded up and a handwritten sign had been posted saying they'd be open tomorrow after some repairs.

He parked in the guest spot at the station and noticed how full the lot was. When he walked in, he knew why. It appeared the entire town had shown up when the doors opened that morning wanting to know what had happened.

He stopped next to Trey and nudged him with his shoulder. "Have they given up anything new yet?"

Trey shook his head. "Not yet. They have a list from the gas station and store of everyone who purchases Gold Crest cigarettes."

"And?" he asked, noticing Tyler walk by. Trent waved him over.

"Well, they're about to start calling people in and finding out where they were yesterday when the fire started."

Trent looked around and sighed. He doubted anyone on the list of possibilities would be standing in the station the morning after setting a fire.

Then he spotted a dark-green cap on a man standing in the corner and he tensed. "What the . . ." He pushed through the people around him. Just as he broke through the crowd less than a foot from Dennis Rodgers, his brother's hands yanked him back.

"Easy," Tyler said next to him. "He was released on bond a few days back."

"Why the hell—" Trent said loudly, glaring at the man who'd kidnapped his soon-to-be sister-in-law.

"Lack of evidence," Dennis interrupted. "It will all come out in the trial." He crossed his arms. "I'll find some proof that you three set me up."

"You son of a—"

"Trent McGowan." His name rang out, causing everyone to turn and look at Mike.

Trent's chin dropped. "What?" He looked at the chief of police.

"You're the first on our list to be interviewed," Mike said.

"Me?"

Mike nodded, causing Trent to laugh. "The hell I am. I don't smoke."

Mike crossed his arms and glared at him. "Are you going to come peacefully?"

Tyler shoved his brother toward Mike and whispered, "He's just doing his job. You're closest to her, and he wants to find whoever did this as much as you do."

Trent's shoulders firmed and he made his way through the crowd once more as people started whispering around him. "Knock it off. I would never hurt Addy." He glared at a few of them.

"Of course you wouldn't," several people said together, causing him to smile as he entered the interview room with Mike and Tony.

He sat down at the table and waited until his two friends sat across from him.

"Where were you yesterday around eleven in the morning?" Tony asked, looking down at his list.

"Work," Trent answered, causing Tony to glance up at him over thick-rimmed reading glasses.

"Which site? The office?"

"The office—my office. Rea can account for me. I was there on a phone call when I got the call from my mother about what had happened."

Tony nodded. "What time did you arrive at your office?"

"Seven in the morning."

"Where were you before?"

"Ho . . ." He backtracked and took a deep breath. "I'd spent the night at Addy's."

Both men's eyebrows shot up. The room remained silent for a while.

"Does your mother know?" Tony asked, causing Trent to laugh.

"Tony, I'm a grown man."

"Course you are, son, just . . ." He shook his head and leaned forward. "You know how she is, about spending the night with a lady before . . . marriage."

Trent leaned forward. "The question is, how do *you* know how she is?" His eyes narrowed as Tony's face turned a shade of red.

"Enough," Mike broke in. "What time did you leave her place?"

"Just after four. I went home, showered, and changed, then was in the office shortly after Rea arrived. I had a conference call with a new supplier for our fir trees. That lasted almost thirty minutes before I had another meeting with . . ."

"Okay." Mike stopped him and jotted a few things down. "At any point in the morning did you leave the office?"

He thought about it. "No. Rea ran over to the diner and grabbed me a breakfast sandwich. I was just about to go to lunch when my mother called." His eyes moved to Tony, who quickly looked down at his paper to avoid his gaze.

"Thank you, you're free to go." Mike stood.

"Not so fast," Trent said, not moving from his seat. "I expect to know . . ."

Mike stopped him by raising his hands. "I've already bent the rules once for your family in the past few months. We're playing this one by the book. I've got the fire inspector coming back into town. He's still looking at the NewField fire, and now he's adding this one to his list. You'll find out the same time everyone else in town does." Mike turned and opened the door.

Trent glanced at Tony, who was still looking down through his glasses at the stack of papers.

When he walked out of the interview room, he was shocked to hear his brothers' names called directly after his.

He kept telling himself that they were just doing their job, but part of him was angry that the officers would call in the McGowans first. What were they looking for?

Later, as the three brothers walked out of the station, Trent pulled out his cell phone and called his mother.

"Want us to pick up some food?" he asked.

"Pizza," she said. "You know what we like. Any news?"

"Nope," he said. "How's she doing?"

"She's resting again."

"Good, see you in a few."

CHAPTER
FOURTEEN

Addy had asked Trisha earlier to help her unwrap her hands. She needed to stretch them, and the bandages were suffocating her. Well, okay, not actually suffocating her, but it was driving her nuts that she couldn't move her fingers individually. She'd expected that she would be able to rewrap any fingers separately that still needed it.

However, when she looked down at her swollen digits, she realized the task was too great for her alone. Gail and Trisha helped her clean and rebandage several fingers.

At least now she could hold a fork and a glass all by herself.

Several of her fingers were . . . gross. Not only were her hands and fingers crisscrossed with large red gashes, but they were swollen. Dark bruises covered most of the skin.

She had seen the stitches on three cuts: one just below her thumb joint, the second near her elbow on the same side, and the third spot, the largest gash, on her right knee, which was the reason she was walking so stiffly.

On the rest of her, the cuts ranged from scratches to glued-up lines that she knew would hardly leave scars.

It was the bruising that turned her skin a nasty dark color and hurt more than most of the cuts. She'd taken a Tylenol after breakfast instead of a codeine, which had allowed her to stay clearheaded.

Shortly after Trent had left that morning, she'd called Beau and filled him in on what had happened. Beau was worried about her, and it took half of the conversation to convince him that she was okay. Then she'd called her insurance and given them the information they needed along with the phone number for the police station so they could work directly with them.

She'd been so tired after all those calls that she'd rested and slept deeply until her phone chimed a message from her parents' number.

She sat up and debated listening to the voice mail for almost five full minutes before swiping her screen and deleting it without listening.

They were done with her. She was done with them. Period.

She knew that a lot of her trust issues with Trent were thanks to her own parents' rough marriage. She couldn't imagine ever wanting anything close to what they had and, since she'd been a child, she'd believed that all marriages fell into that same pattern.

Addy didn't have any more room in her broken heart to ache for them. She knew that whatever her mother had to say would have just upset her, and she'd had enough of that in the past day.

She actually felt better for it.

After stuffing herself with Hawaiian pizza at lunch, she sat in the living room and listened as Trent filled them in on what was going on at the police station. The family then talked about whether they should move their uncle to the specialty facility or not. He didn't have insurance, which meant it would fall to the McGowans to pay for his long-term care.

Gail was looking into further possibilities closer to home.

Then Trent broke in.

"Why was I the last to find out that Dennis is running around a free man?" Trent had Addy tucked next to him, and she jerked when she heard this.

"But I thought . . ." Addy sat up.

"He's out on bond until his trial in a few weeks," Gail said. "We didn't think it would do to have you upset."

Trent huffed. "Yeah, you're right, it was much better seeing him smirking at me across the room in the police station this morning," he said sarcastically.

"Do they think the two fires are related?" Kristen asked.

Addy hadn't thought of that angle but looking around the room, she could tell she was the only one who hadn't made the connection yet.

"I wouldn't cross it off the list of possibilities yet," Tyler said.

"When did Dennis get free?" Trent asked. "Before or after the NewField fire?"

"After," three voices answered together.

"Well, that marks him off that list at least."

"Yeah, but he's got friends—a handful of his workers loyal to him," Trey added.

"Any smoke cigarettes?" Trent asked.

"I can look into it." Trey stood up. "I've got to get back to the grind."

"Me too." Tyler followed him. "Some of us can't afford to take an entire day off." He smacked Trent on the shoulder as he walked by.

"Right," Trent called back. "You just take weeks off instead." He pulled Addy closer to his side.

She'd seen the dark circles under his eyes during breakfast and lunch. She knew that if she could convince him to lie down with her, he'd sleep too.

"I'm feeling tired." She stretched her sore legs and winced when she felt pain.

"Want me to get you another pill?" he asked, eager to get up.

"No, but I could use someone to help replace this bandage." She wiggled her left hand. "I think it's too tight." It wasn't, but she needed an excuse to get him to the bedroom with her.

"Sure." He stood up and helped her to her feet.

"We were going to head into the store, but . . ." His mother sighed.

"The store will open back up tomorrow," he said.

"So soon, I suppose . . ." Gail started to say, then coughed when Trisha looked over at her.

"I guess we'll head over to Avon to the general market there," Trisha said, looking down at her watch. "We should be back just in time for dinner."

"Um, yeah, in time for dinner," Gail repeated.

"Okay," Trent said, then followed Addy back to his room.

Addy held in a chuckle as the two ladies exchanged glances behind them.

Instead of letting him replace her bandage, she tugged him to the bed. "To be honest, I was just looking for a way to get you to lie down with me." They settled on the comforter together. "I wanted to be next to you for a while," she said against his chest, humming. "Mmm, this is what I needed."

She felt him relax as his arms came around her. "Sneaky." He grinned. "I guess I could lie down for a while. I haven't taken a nap in . . . years," he said, his hand going into her hair.

She listened as his breathing shallowed. His heart slowed and she could tell he was fast asleep.

At first her mind refused to settle down. She'd slept plenty, but her body was still too weak to remain awake as her mind raced through things she had to do.

Purchasing a new Jeep or truck was at the top of her list. She had loved her Jeep and only had a few more payments until it was hers. Now she wondered if her insurance would cover enough to get something as nice as that one had been.

The Jeep had been just the right size to pull her small trailer. The thought of getting a truck or van was disappointing.

She'd have to go into Helena to the nearest Jeep dealer and see what she could afford on her salary. Which wasn't much, considering who she worked for.

Suddenly thoughts of getting a different job, a stationary job, popped into her head. Did she even like what she was being forced to do? She wasn't a spy. Especially when there were people she liked and trusted at the other end of the game.

She was no closer to figuring out what they wanted with the land than when she'd started. Which made her think about why she'd started doing what she was doing.

She'd been on the road for almost two years. Would she like staying in one place again? *Where? Here? Hell no,* she thought. But then Trent shifted and pulled her closer, and the thought suddenly didn't scare her as much as it would have weeks, or even days, ago. Despite how her job put a wedge in their relationship, she still felt oddly relaxed about being with him now.

Even the prospect of living in the same town as her parents didn't bother her as much as it had before. She took a deep breath and enjoyed the way Trent's scent drifted into her head, causing her body to react.

She'd dreamed of being with him again earlier; now was no different. She knew her hands were too messed up to enjoy feeling him but still ran her hands over his chest slightly until he stirred.

Reaching up, she laid a soft kiss on his neck. He turned toward her and wrapped his leg over her hip and buried his face into her hair.

"You smell so good," he said softly.

"So do you." She leaned up and kissed him as he looked down at her.

"God, I want you so bad," he said, his voice going husky. His hips started moving against hers and she felt her body react.

"What about your mother?" she asked, enjoying the feeling of him against her.

"She and Trisha have gone to Avon to the store," he said between kisses on her neck. "Remember?"

"Yes, but isn't . . ." She didn't get anything else out because his mouth had covered hers.

She lay there and waited as he gently undressed her, pulling off his sweatshirt that she'd put on earlier that morning. His T-shirt she was wearing was next. Then his eyes roamed over her as he nudged the sweats down her legs, making sure to go slowly over the bandages on her knees.

"You'll let me know if I hurt you."

"You won't." She sighed as his hands roamed over her skin. "I just wish I could . . ." She held up her hands and frowned at them.

"Just lie there and let me take care of you," he said.

His hands drifted over her as his lips raised little bumps all over her skin. He took his time and kissed every bruise as his hands gently massaged her sore muscles.

"Mmm," she moaned. "You could make a living doing this."

He laughed outright. "I think that's still illegal in the States." He'd removed his shirt and was in the process of pulling off his jeans.

"Not that." She smiled up at him, then gasped when he came back down to her, skin to skin.

His lips covered hers again as his fingers found her and sent her hips jerking toward him.

"My god," she said between kisses. She wrapped her arms around his broad shoulders and held on to him as he used all his skills to send her over the edge quickly.

◆　◆　◆

There was nothing sexier than watching Addy lose control.

Her long hair was spread out on his pillows and even that small detail was sexy as hell.

She tended to bite her bottom lip when she was just about to come, so Trent dipped his head down and tasted her lips as she came. Her hips spasmed toward his hand and he felt her slick heat against him.

He reached quickly over to his nightstand and pulled on a condom, then before her eyes could blink open, slid slowly into her heat.

This time, it was him saying, "My god."

She was so tight, so wonderfully ready for him. She felt like home and ecstasy all at once.

Her bandaged hands reached for his shoulders, but he moved until they fell back beside her head on the mattress.

His lips covered hers as his hips moved with her, against her. He tried to be gentle, knowing what she'd been through, how she was hurt, but she was moving, demanding, and he felt his self-control slipping.

When she cried out, he was less than a second behind her.

He woke when he heard the garage door open. Then, just like a thief in the night, he hurried around his room, making sure they were fully dressed. Even though he knew his mother would never barge into his room, he still felt guilty.

Addy chuckled but dressed quickly. "If you keep blushing like that, there's no hiding what we did in here."

He closed his eyes as he took several deep breaths.

"Funny, I never struggled with this before." He moved closer to her and wrapped his arms around her.

"It's because you've never done that"—she nodded toward the bed—"here."

"I've never had you before." He placed a gentle kiss on her lips. "We'd better go out before they make up some excuse to come looking for us."

She nodded.

When they walked out, his mother and Trisha smiled over at them. "You both look like you got some rest," Trisha said, unloading a bag of groceries.

"Yes, I guess I needed that." Trent took over the job for her. "I can't remember the last time I took a nap," he said.

"You were eleven," his mother piped in as she put a carton of milk away in the fridge. "I could probably come up with the exact date and time if I thought about it." She winked at Addy. "He was a very strong-willed child."

"Was?" Addy raised her eyebrows and snorted.

"I like this one," Trisha said. "She's a keeper."

CHAPTER
FIFTEEN

After a dinner of barbecued steak sandwiches, they all sat around the living room. Addy tried to build up enough courage to try to convince Trent to take her back to her place for the night.

Finally, just before dark, she brought it up.

"So." She took a deep breath and looked at Gail. "I'm very thankful for your kindness in allowing me to stay here. I can never repay you."

Gail smiled over at her. "I'm just thankful you're okay."

"We all are," Trisha added.

She stood up and glanced down at Trent. "If it's not too much, I was wondering if you'd mind taking me back to my . . ."

"No." He shook his head. "It's too soon."

"Honey," Gail said in a softer tone. "The girl wants her own bed." A look passed between mother and son. One that Addy had always hoped she'd see in her own mother's eyes one day. Love. "Take her home."

Trent took a deep breath, then stood.

"Thank you," Addy said again. "For everything."

"If you need anything," Gail said, "just let us know."

Addy made her way back to Trent's room. He helped her gather her things in the duffle bag she'd bought at an army surplus store in Colorado. Then he carried her bag to the front door in silence. She followed and stood still as he helped her on with one of his jackets. Which reminded her that she was now out of a coat since hers had been ruined along with her favorite pair of shoes, jeans, and her red sweater.

"You okay?" he asked as he got behind the wheel of his truck.

"Yes, just thinking of everything I have to replace."

"When will your insurance be paying you?" He pulled out of the driveway.

"They said in a day or two. No more than a week."

"You can borrow . . ."

"No." She looked over at him.

"What? You don't even know what I was going to suggest."

Her eyebrows shot up. "You were going to suggest I borrow one of the company's cars."

He frowned. "So? What would be . . ."

"Trent." She paused. "You do know what I do. Who I work for. Why I'm here."

He took a deep breath. "Fine. How about I let you drive my car until we can go to Helena and get a replacement for you?"

"I'll figure something else out." Her gaze shifted out the window. She was sure there were already rumors spreading about her staying at the McGowan place; driving around in Trent's car for the next week would be the icing on the cake and get her fired.

She'd been honest with Beau when she'd talked to him earlier.

"Are you okay?" Beau had asked after she'd filled him in on everything that had happened to her.

"Yes," she'd started to say, but he'd jumped in.

"We're heading there. Just give us—"

"No," she'd broken in. "I'm fine. Really."

Beau had been quiet.

"I just wanted you to know that I was staying with some old family friends, actually it's the McGowans . . ."

"Really?" he'd said, sounding excited. "Any chance you could get a little chummier with them?" It had actually sounded like he'd held his breath while he waited for her answer.

"I . . ." She didn't know what to say. "I guess."

"Good, then it's settled." She could hear him shift and imagined him doing one of the fist pumps he often did when things were going his way. "You'll keep me posted when you find something out?"

"Yes." She'd caved. Completely. Wholly. Why was she so weak?

She hadn't wanted to argue that she'd been too tired and hurt to even focus on trying to play spy.

As it was now, she was thankful she had a full bottle of Tylenol in her cupboard.

Trent parked next to her trailer and helped her out of the truck, then pulled her bag out of the back seat.

She was so busy watching him that she didn't notice Brian and one of his buddies walk up.

"So the rumors are true," he said, his tone causing her to cringe slightly.

"What rumors?" she said as she turned toward the pair. She was trying to act casual, but she knew that if the group found out their relationship, things could get even more complicated.

"That you're shacking up with a McGowan," Brian's friend Gary said.

She felt Trent tense next to her and put a bandaged hand on his arm.

Brian and his little gang had tagged along with the rest of the protesters. She'd gotten the feeling early on that they hadn't really had their hearts in the core of the group's goals, but had rather used their time with the group to benefit themselves by any means possible. They spent half their time flirting and eating free meals and the rest of the time complaining about everything else. She doubted Brian truly cared what FREE's goals were.

She knew what the rest of the group would think. Outside of Beau and Joy, no one else knew that it was their plan for her to get close to Trent. The term *sleeping with the enemy* came to mind and had her cringing inwardly. She wasn't a spy. What made her think she could do this? Still, she felt the need to defend the only people in town who had gone out of their way to help her when she needed it.

"Not that it's any of your business, but I'm not shacking up with anyone. The McGowans were kind enough to help me after my ordeal." She turned as if to go.

"Don't think this is over," Brian said under his breath. The two men chuckled and walked away without a backward glance.

"Damn it," Trent said. "What the hell does that mean?"

"He thinks he's trying to get me fired." Addy shrugged, knowing that Beau was fully behind her methods, and went to open her trailer door.

"Why would he do that?" he asked, stepping in after her.

"Who knows." She sat down on her bed and sighed.

"You really like this place, don't you?" he asked, setting her bag down on the table.

"It's home. My home." She smiled.

"It is small." He glanced around before sitting down.

"Not for me." She sighed again and then remembered something vital. "Damn it," she groaned. "I guess I'll be going without gas for—"

"Tyler and Kristen got you two new tanks and hooked them up yesterday," Trent said.

She had to swallow back the tears that started to burn her eyes.

"Hey." He wrapped his arms around her.

She hadn't allowed herself to cry yet. She was thankful that Trent held on to her as tears began to roll freely. Her chest hurt, her head hurt, and most of all, her heart hurt. Not for the pain or the loss, but for the possibilities that could have been.

Addy had berated herself more than a dozen times for rushing toward the fire instead of away. She'd always believed herself to be smarter than that.

She was just like those silly girls in a horror flick to be killed off first because they'd gone into the basement alone.

"No, you're nothing like that." Trent chuckled.

She hadn't realized she'd spoken the thought out loud.

Leaning back, she reached to wipe her eyes, but he beat her to it and gently used his thumbs to dry her tears.

"Yes, I am," she said, holding in a hiccup.

He smiled. "What doesn't kill you . . ." He tilted his head. "Actually I probably would have done the same if it was Bessy."

She rolled her eyes. "You're a terrible liar."

He pulled her close and wrapped his arms around her one more time.

"I'm just thankful you'll be okay."

"Me too." When he released her, she stood up. "I need to get Mr. Thompson something wonderful. To thank him for pulling me inside."

"He's a sucker for anything with the Coke label on it," Trent said.

She looked at him in surprise.

"How did you know that?" She had been thinking the same thing.

"I helped him build a shed out back of his house one summer. He filled it with his collection so he could go out there and relax. I think Mrs. Thompson forced him to get the last bit of it out of her house after she retired."

Addy giggled. "Yeah, every time I would go over there for lessons, she would complain that it was slowly taking over."

"There are a few antique stores on the way to Helena. I could drive you up there to look for a replacement car and we could stop along the way?"

She thought about it. "I should have my check by Friday, or so they said."

"How about Saturday?" Trent suggested.

She nodded and smiled. "You don't have to."

He brushed a strand of her hair away from her dry face. "I know that." He leaned down and kissed her slowly. "I really want to stay here tonight with you, but . . ."

She nodded and closed her eyes as she rested her forehead against his chest. "Go home."

She felt his chest rise and fall. Then he nudged her chin up with a finger until she met his gaze. "This means something. More than anything I've ever had before."

Her throat had closed up tight, too tight, so she just nodded in agreement.

"If you need anything," he said, before dropping his arms from her.

"I'll let you know." She watched him leave her trailer, and suddenly the emptiness in the small space seemed to make the room grow until it was too big, too empty.

She walked over, flipped the lock on the door, and leaned against it.

♦ ♦ ♦

Trent had a few days' worth of work to catch up on. He hadn't realized before how much paperwork went through his desk. It took him until late Friday evening to finally catch up on the invoices and orders.

He was in charge of making sure the land they were done pumping oil from got back to its beautiful self. Which meant more work than most people realized. Even he didn't understand how his father had handled every aspect of the business himself.

Of course, Trent had a knack for land development. He would have never guessed it until it had been thrust at him. He was even enjoying working on the board for the school.

The mayor had talked about giving him a full-time position on the board, under the title of town development. He'd gracefully declined, given the pace of his own business. Still, part of him was thankful that she had offered.

He had texted and talked on the phone with Addy several times. She'd been getting rides from a coworker, Estelle, who had shuttled her around so she could continue her errands.

He'd asked Kristen to reprint everything she'd given Addy the day of the fire and deliver it to her trailer.

Addy had texted him immediately and thanked him. He asked her to meet him at the diner for dinner, but she'd declined. She had a group meet-up planned.

He remembered everything she'd told him she did for FREE, but still, what was left for them to do in Haven? Sure, there were still signs all over town and outside several of the McGowan sites, but for the most part, the group had been relatively quiet.

Maybe it was the calm before a storm. What exactly was Addy searching for besides their plans for the new land?

Before heading home, he stopped by the police station to see if Mike knew anything further about Addy's car fire. The man told him they had interviewed everyone, including Dennis, Darla, and Brian. So far there wasn't any further information he could or would give him.

"It looks like the investigation has stalled."

"Stalled?" Trent repeated the word. "Like the NewField fire investigation has stalled?"

Mike leaned back in his chair and nodded. "There's nothing more I can tell you."

"Well, at least tell me you know where the three of them were and can confirm they weren't anywhere near her Jeep when all this started."

Mike's head tilted and, after a moment, he nodded. Trent knew that would be all he would get out of him.

He ate dinner at the diner that evening alone. About halfway through his meal, he watched Addy's parents walk in and take the table across from him.

There were a million things he wanted to say to the pair, but he remained silent, observing.

Her mother, Victoria, tore down the establishment, the food, and the waitress. She talked like she was above everything. Addy's father sat by and kept his eyes glued to the table as his wife berated Katy, one of Trent's favorite staffers at the diner. Actually, now all of the staff at the Dancing Moose were nice, since Darla had been fired a few weeks back.

Finally, after the woman had threatened not to pay for anything they had eaten, he stepped in.

"Katy's just doing her job," Trent said, controlling his tone, causing every eye in the establishment to turn toward him. Of course, everyone had been watching the show, and he could tell the crowd was curious as to what he was going to do next. "Pay your bill," he warned. "I'd hate to have to call Mike over here and have him charge you with skipping out on it."

Victoria's eyes narrowed. "I shouldn't be forced to pay for something that wasn't up to my standards." Her chin lifted, a move he'd seen on Addy plenty of times. Even though it was familiar, it had a totally different effect than Addy's.

"You seemed to be enjoying it enough to clean your plates." He nodded to the empty dishes. "If you had a problem, you should have left some evidence for Mike to see." Trent let his words sink in, trying his best to look relaxed.

He watched the woman's eyes heat and happened to chance a glance at Addy's father, Richard.

"What about you?" he asked. "Do you have any complaints about the food?"

Richard glanced toward his wife, who started to speak.

"I wasn't asking you," Trent broke in. "I think the man can speak for himself." He turned. "So?"

"Like my wife said . . ."

"Right." Trent shook his head and took a deep breath. "I bet you just sat back all those years as she tore Addy down too and didn't do shit about it."

"How dare you!" Victoria stood up and tossed her napkin on the table. "We won't sit in this half-rate diner and have some local tell us—"

"You're locals too," Trent pointed out.

The woman pushed Katy aside. She had been standing dumbstruck in the aisle, watching the entire thing.

Now Victoria stood over him, glaring down.

"I don't know who you think you are, but you have no business talking about something you know nothing about. Our daughter is a spoiled child who has been acting out since she was eleven."

Trent's eyes moved once more to Addy's father. He noticed the man's shoulders had hunched, and his eyes were again fixed on a spot on the table.

"We've searched out help for our daughter, but she refuses it. We want nothing but the best for her. I don't know who you think you are," she said again, "but we're not going to sit here and be attacked. This town can go on spreading rumors about us all they like. We're ending all charity to this stupid place—charity we've been giving for more than a decade." Victoria's voice rose as she looked around the room. "I believe in giving where it's earned, and I see nothing here worth it."

"Not even your daughter?" Trent stood up and watched Victoria move back several steps. "You must have heard by now that she was almost killed the other day." He watched for any reaction from the woman but found none, then he turned and saw Richard wipe a tear from his eye before his wife could see it. "If you cared anything about her, you would have at least called her to see how she was." He tossed some bills down on his table, then tossed some on theirs. "If you can't stoop to paying for your food, allow me." He looked over at Katy. "Thanks," he said and winked at her before walking out of the diner.

His temper kept him revved up the entire way out to the state park. He parked in the spot where Addy's Jeep normally sat and switched off his car's engine.

He sat there for almost five minutes trying to calm down. Then he noticed the lights in her trailer were off.

Getting out, he followed the sound of voices to a larger tent where Addy was holding forth with passion to a small group of people. She was a born leader.

Then he heard what she was saying and wondered if he'd made the biggest mistake of his life by trusting her.

CHAPTER SIXTEEN

"There are several possibilities the McGowans have for wanting the land near the reservation. None of them could be described as environmentally safe." Addy showed her next slide. "This land here"—she used her laser pointer to circle the land in question—"sits directly above the water source for the entire Flathead Reservation. If polluted, more than five thousand families would be directly affected. We must gather more information and find out what they intend to do with this land and, if necessary, stop the purchase from going through. I'm going to need volunteers who have legal experience." She squinted in the dark tent as she tried to find Estelle. Instead she noticed a shadowed figure just inside the tent. Her heart skipped, and she had to hide a quick smile at seeing Trent.

Her heart fluttered once, then sank when she realized what he must have heard. How long had he been standing there? The look on his face told her long enough.

She shut the small projector hooked up to her cell phone off and flipped on the portable light. "We'll finish this discussion . . ." She came up with a blank. "Later," she finally said. "The meeting is adjourned." She walked toward the back. Taking Trent's arm, she pulled him outside and as far away from her small group as possible.

"What are you doing here?"

"That was quite a speech back there," he said. She could hear the anger in his voice.

"I'm just doing my job," she said, stopping by a large fallen tree and sitting down, patting a spot next to her. At this point, she didn't trust her legs—they were shaking so much. "What are you doing here, Trent?"

"Well, I was here looking for you." He took a step toward her. His not taking a seat was a bad sign. "I guess I found more than I bargained for."

"You've known why I'm here since I got back to town," she said. She felt her chest constrict when she saw the look he gave her.

"Yes, but . . ."

"What?" She stood to meet his gaze.

"I had hoped that you'd come to trust us." His voice dipped.

"I do." She shook her head, unable to explain more. "It's just I have a . . ."

"Job to do." He sighed.

"Yes, I have to do the best I can, explore every—"

He stopped her by holding up his hand. "I get it, really I do." He nodded back in the direction they'd come from. "But from what I heard back there, you make it sound like we're out to destroy the planet."

"Drilling for oil . . ."

"Don't give me that bull. You drive a gas-fueled car like the rest of us. You use plastics and drive on asphalt."

She sighed. "Yes, but it's my job to make sure you're pulling oil from the ground in the most sustainable way possible."

He was silent for a while. Then his head tilted as he held out his hand to her. "Take a ride with me."

She hesitated for a split second, then acquiesced. Only three bandages remained on her right hand, and when it landed in his, he took a moment to look down at them.

"How are these?"

He threw her for a loop. One minute, she was sure he was so pissed he was about to . . . What? Break up with her? She held in a laugh. She wouldn't describe their relationship as boyfriend/girlfriend. Not that she'd ever had a boyfriend before, but from what she knew, they didn't fit the mold.

"They're fine," she said, trying to tug her hand free, but he held it gently. "Where are we going?" she asked as they made their way across the parking lot.

"Well, I have a quick stop first, then, if all goes well, I'd like to show you something," he said, opening the door to his sedan.

"Not driving the truck?" she asked when he got behind the wheel.

"Trey needed it today," he said. "We'll be switching this out for it." He glanced over as they pulled out of the parking lot. "If it goes the way I hope."

"What?" she asked, but he only shook his head.

"You'll see."

They sat in silence as they drove toward his mother's place. When he parked behind the work truck, she automatically knew his entire family was there.

"We normally have dinners on Friday." He helped her out of the car. "I skipped it tonight because I wasn't in the mood."

He took her hand again and she followed him into the house.

Everyone stopped talking at the table when they walked in.

"Addy, what a pleasant surprise." Gail stood up, but a look from Trent sent her back down.

"I need a family vote," he said, still holding Addy's hand.

"Okay," Gail said slowly. "Go ahead."

"Everyone knows what Addy has gone through in the past week. What you don't know about her family doesn't really matter, but needless to say, we are the closest thing to a family that she has now."

Addy's heart melted as she looked up at Trent, then over at his family as everyone nodded in agreement.

"So I'm proposing a vote to let her in on the McGowan secret." He held his fist up and waited for everyone else to follow.

Addy looked around and noticed that even Trisha and Kristen had their fists up.

Gail counted, and a tear escaped Addy's eye as she realized every thumb was raised high.

"Good," Trent said, then tossed the car keys at Trey. "I need to switch with you." He grabbed her hand and tugged her out of the room.

"Wait," she started to say, looking back at his family. But there wasn't enough time to get out anything beyond a quick thank-you.

He helped her into the truck, and they sat in silence as he drove. When they reached the turnoff for the reservation, she glanced over at him.

"Where are you taking me?"

He smiled. "It might take a visual to explain. Besides, I'm in the mood for a little night hiking."

She sighed and crossed her arms. The man was infuriating. She'd expected anger when she'd seen him in the tent. She hadn't expected this. He was almost . . . excited. Why? What was his game? She hadn't lied; she did trust him and his family. But what was he up to now?

"This? This is how you plan on telling me what your family is going to do with the land?"

He chuckled. "Would you prefer charts and graphs? We have some, but . . ." He shook his head. "I like seeing the real deal."

"Okay." She drew the word out.

She silently watched the darkness out her window as they wove their way around the hills, across bumpy dirt roads, toward the valley where the Lenz land sat directly across the river from the reservation.

He parked at the side of the road, then helped her out.

"There's a jacket somewhere there." He nodded to the back seat. Thank goodness. She still hadn't replaced her heavy coat.

Together they started walking toward the middle of the field, the moonlight giving their path a glow. He stopped in the middle of a large, flat section.

"This"—he took a deep breath—"this is where the main building will go." He indicated the area around them.

"Okay," she said, waiting. Her mind whirled with a million different options. What was he telling her? She hung on his every word.

"Then, over that way, three larger ones for housing." He waved toward the river. "We're debating if they will be apartment-style or more like dorms." He leaned toward her. "My vote is for apartments. Anyway, there will be enough housing for almost five hundred. Then," he continued before she could ask any questions, "over there will be seven more buildings." He motioned into the darkness. "There, the classroom buildings, and this way . . ." He took her hand and walked a few paces away from the river. "Several more, including the hands-on training facilities."

"Okay." She tugged his hand until he stopped. "Trent, what is all this?"

He smiled and pulled her closer, wrapping his arms around her. "This is the Thurston McGowan Flathead Drilling Training Center."

"The . . ." Her head spun.

"The Thurston McGowan Flathead Drilling Training Center," he repeated. "My father's dream for the past few decades." He dropped his arms and motioned around them. "One hundred and three acres. A facility that will teach the safest method of drilling and extracting oil from the earth while doing as little to no permanent harm to the land as possible."

Her chin dropped. "You . . . you're going to teach people how to drill for oil?" Instantly she wondered if she was going to have to fight a bigger battle to get them to stop their new plan. Then she played over his words again, and the words *safest* and *no permanent harm* stuck out.

"No, not exactly," he said. "My family is going to teach my father's technology to others. Businesses will bring their employees here and pay to have them trained in my dad's secret methods."

Her head went through the details as fast as she could. Did she believe him? Why would he lie about their plans to her now? Her eyes scanned over him, and a part of her remembered how he and his brothers had been in the past. She was pretty sure Trent was no longer the same boy-toy he'd been back then, but with all her faults, she questioned if she had the ability to spot the full truth.

"My father's methods will stop fracking globally altogether. Not only are these methods cheaper, it's more environmentally sound."

"Okay," she said, still not able to grasp it all. "But you'll be giving your father's knowledge away?"

His teeth flashed in the moonlight as he grinned. "It's what he wanted."

"Then how will you make a living? What about McGowan Enterprises?"

"Oh, we'll still be in business locally. But we'll shift some of our focus to this. I'll be in charge." He looked around the moonlit field. "It's already been decided."

"You . . ." She blinked. "Will run all this?"

He nodded, then moved closer to her. "And we've been talking about needing someone with your skills. Someone who knows and is concerned about the environment. Someone who can help me maintain the integrity of my father's wishes." He took her hand in his. "Someone we trust."

She felt a mental kick in the gut and almost doubled over from the pain.

"Trent, I can't . . ." She stepped away from him.

"What?" He tried to follow her.

"I'm only here to find out what your family intends to do with this land. Now that I know, I'll report it and—"

"You can't." His voice dropped. "The family voted that they trusted you. We are taking you in our confidence and risking this deal by doing so. Legally, no one can know until the ink is dry."

"Why?" she asked. Her heart felt heavy. Why would his family trust her with such a secret? Especially when they knew she was working for the enemy?

"We have until the end of May before my father's legal obligations are free from my uncle's input. They signed a contract." He sighed and ran his hands through his hair. "We need until the end of May."

She wondered how she'd survive after the secret came out, what she would do. Did she really imagine she could have a normal life in Haven? Something shifted inside her, and she knew exactly what she needed to do. The same thing she'd told herself a million times before.

"Okay, I'll keep your secret until then," she said. "But I can't . . ." She shook her head. "I don't think I can stay in Haven."

◆　◆　◆

He felt the bottom drop out of his stomach.

"Is it because of your folks?" he asked.

"No." It burst from her. "That has nothing to do with it."

"What then?"

"I just . . . I have my job."

He could see the question in her eyes. "Will you stay around until our secret's out?" he asked.

She bit her bottom lip, but then nodded. "I'll have to—if I can't explain why I would leave to anyone."

He moved closer to her. "And . . . what about us?"

At her smile, he pulled her back into his arms.

"Good." He kissed her.

She broke the kiss. "You can't come by the camp like that again." Then she looked up at him. "Why did you stop by? I thought we were going car hunting tomorrow."

"We are still, but . . ." He decided to tell her after all. "I ran into your folks tonight at the diner."

He felt her stiffen. "And?"

"I guess you'll hear it anyway, small towns and all, but I gave them a piece of my mind."

"Was that all?" she asked.

"Yes." He nodded. "I'm afraid your mother isn't happy with me, and I worried she'd take it out on you."

"She isn't happy with me either. You'll get over it." She turned and started walking back to his truck. He followed her. "I did," she said when he caught up with her. "Now if we're going to leave early tomorrow, I need some rest."

"Still set for me to pick you up at six?" he asked.

"Yup," she said. "I've been looking at a few dealerships online."

"And?"

"I picked up my insurance check today." The feeling of relief still hadn't left her. "It should be enough for the Jeep I want."

"Another Jeep?" he asked, opening the truck door for her.

"Yeah, this time, the four-door Wrangler." She waited to finish her thought while he climbed in behind the wheel. "A white one again."

He dropped her off back at her trailer, only having enough time to give her a quick kiss before she got out of the truck.

By the time he pulled into the driveway, the only cars left were his mother's and Trisha's. The house was dark, but when he walked in, his mother was in the kitchen making a grilled cheese sandwich.

"Can't sleep?" Trent asked.

"No. Do you want one too?" she asked, looking over at him.

"Yeah." He could go for one of his mother's grilled cheese sandwiches just then. He needed the comfort food, even if he wasn't hungry.

He sat at the bar and filled his mother in on the entire evening.

"Well, you have until the end of May to change her mind." His mom cleared their dishes and piled them in the dishwasher.

"What if she doesn't change her mind?"

His mother walked over and placed a hand on his face. "If she's as smart as I know her to be, she will." She leaned up and gave him a kiss on his cheek. "Just don't do anything to screw it up." She patted the spot she'd kissed.

"Me?" he laughed.

"You boys, you take after your father—good-looking, smart, and, when the going gets tough, you tend to screw up love."

"Love?" he asked as she walked down the dark hall toward her room. "Who said anything about love?" he called after her.

"Exactly." She waved at him over her shoulder as she disappeared into her room.

CHAPTER
SEVENTEEN

Addy's excitement started to percolate as they drove toward Helena. She knew that she was taking a bigger step than just buying a new car. In her mind, she was coming closer to making a decision about her future.

The car dealerships opened around nine, which gave them plenty of time to get there and stop off for some breakfast.

At the restaurant, she pulled out a local paper and started scanning it for Jeep deals. Some of the smaller dealers weren't online.

"When did you buy your last Jeep?" Trent asked her.

She glanced up from circling a white Jeep. "Three years, two months, and fourteen days ago." She smiled. "You never forget your first."

His eyebrows rose slightly, and her face heated at the realization of what she'd just said. She turned her eyes back to the paper and reached for her blueberry bagel.

"Do you want some help looking?" He looked down at the paper.

"Sure." She handed him the next section. "I circled a few local antique stores too. You can see if they mention anything about having a Coke collection."

She watched him frown, but then he got to work. He even pulled out his cell phone and called a few shops.

"How much?" he asked into the phone, getting her attention. "And how late are you open?" He nodded. "Okay, thank you." When he hung up, she waited.

"Well?" she finally asked.

"How much are you wanting to spend on Mr. Thompson?"

She thought about it. "I guess it depends on how much I can talk these guys down." She turned her cell phone screen around and showed him the Jeep she wanted.

"Let's go make a deal." He picked up their trash and walked over to toss it in the bin, then came back and gathered their stuff.

Something about watching him clear a table had her heart jumping. It was stupid, really. Most people she knew didn't blink twice about leaving a messy table at a diner. Even some of the people she worked with didn't clean up after themselves, but Trent . . . he was different.

"The grocery store is open again," he said as he drove.

"I know, I stopped by the other day." She didn't tell him that it had taken her almost ten minutes before she had the guts to walk in.

Once she had, she was grateful. Everyone there rushed over to see how she was doing. Even the clerks went out of their way to check in with her.

Since she'd arrived, the people of Haven had done nothing but treat her with kindness and were making it harder and harder for her to hate being back in town. Something deep inside her wanted to find faults, but if she had to be honest with herself, there were only a handful of people she had problems with in town. Unfortunately two of them were related to her.

After almost three hours at the dealership, she drove her new white Jeep off the lot, following Trent's truck as they headed toward the antique store.

She had more than five hundred dollars left in her car fund, which, when she pulled into the antique store, she knew she was going to spend entirely on the perfect treat for Mr. Thompson. One vintage Coke-themed restaurant booth later, she and Trent were on their way to deliver the gift to Mr. Thompson.

By the time she made it into her trailer after enjoying a few cold Cokes with the older man who had saved her, she was exhausted. The last thing she wanted to deal with was a phone call from her mother again. But there was the phone, ringing with her parents' phone number.

This time instead of letting it go to voice mail, she answered it.

"What?" she said, allowing her frustration to come out in her voice.

"Addy," her father whispered.

"Dad?" She hugged the phone closer to her ear so she could hear him.

"I wanted . . . I just had to say . . . I'm sorry. I know I disappointed you. I never meant to . . . things got . . . it doesn't matter. I'm sorry. I can't talk too long, but I wanted to tell you that I've always been so very proud of you, and I love you more than I ever could show you. I'm so sorry I never stood up for you."

"Daddy." Tears rolled down her face and she found it hard to breathe.

"I should have been a better father. There are a lot of things I should have done better. Just remember that I love you, sweetie."

Something in her father's voice had the hairs on the back of her neck standing up.

"Dad?" She gripped the phone. "Let me come over."

"No, sweetie. Not tonight. I will always love you." He hung up before she could say anything more.

Without thinking, she grabbed her keys. Gravel and dirt flew out from under her tires as she peeled out of the parking lot.

She punched in her parents' home number and cursed when she got a busy signal. Her mother had never wanted cell phones around, so they still had only the landline. She tried it a few more times with the same results. Next, she dialed Trent.

"Hey." The cheer in his voice sounded almost alien in the situation she was in.

"Trent, something's wrong with my dad," she cried out.

"What?" His tone changed to instant concern.

"He called. It was—it was off." She jerked her wheel as she turned out of town. "I think he's going to do something."

"I'm heading there." She could hear him moving around. "I'll call Mike and meet you there."

After she pulled the Jeep to a quick stop directly behind her mother's sedan, she jumped out while the Jeep was still settling. All the lights were off inside the house.

She found the front door locked, and when no one answered the doorbell she rushed back to the Jeep to get her set of house keys.

By the time she made it back to the door, the front porch light had turned on and her mother stood inside the door, looking at her like she was crazy.

"Mom! Where's Dad?" She rushed into the house.

"What? Adrianna, what on earth is going on?" Her mother tightened the robe around her waist.

"Where's Dad?" she repeated, rushing toward her parents' room.

"He's not here," her mother said, following her.

"Where is he?"

"He's out in his shop." Her mother nodded toward the back building her father had built when Addy was eleven. It had always been his domain. Even her mother never went out there or asked him what he did in the massive two-car garage at the edge of their property.

Addy hit the back door at a sprint just as the shot rang out in the night. Its sound, that instant, shocking crack, would echo in her mind for the rest of her life.

♦ ♦ ♦

Trent held Addy as she looked off into the distance with owl eyes. The fact that her tears had dried up almost an hour earlier scared him. Her breathing was shallow, and he could tell that she had retreated into her own mind. Nothing could get through to her at this point.

He'd arrived at her parents' house less than five minutes after her. Victoria had been on the phone in the living room, looking a little frazzled. When he'd rushed in, she motioned to the back door and he'd followed the sound of screaming to find Addy holding her father's lifeless body, weeping great, wrenching sobs as if her heart would never heal.

Mike and Tony had arrived a few minutes later, and he had helped them remove Addy from the garage, her body limp in their arms.

"Take her inside. Get her cleaned up," Tony had said with kindness. "There's nothing more she can do here."

Trent had taken her back into the house, where her mother had produced a change of clothes for Addy and suggested she go take a shower. Almost as if she'd fallen into a pile of mud instead of being covered in her father's blood.

Addy didn't fight him as he walked with her into the bedroom Victoria had pointed out, saying only "There's fresh towels under the sink."

He tried to find any hint of emotion in the woman whose husband had just taken his own life, but blankness looked back at him.

He didn't even stop to register the tidy bedroom that must have been Addy's growing up. Instead, he ushered her directly to the attached bathroom and started peeling off her soiled clothes, dumping them directly into the sink. Then, after helping her into the shower, he took a washcloth and gently wiped her face and hands free of blood before helping her change into the clean clothes.

"He's gone," she whispered. "I didn't get to tell him . . ." She closed her eyes and tears slid down her face.

He cupped her face in his hands. "Your father knew that you loved him."

She shook her head. "No, not that."

"What?" he asked, pulling her closer to him.

"That I'm sorry." She opened her eyes and raised them to his. "I said—I said terrible things to them. I didn't get to say I'm sorry."

She rested her head against his chest.

"I think he knew." He caressed her back and wondered how he was going to be able to help her through this.

When they returned to the main room of the house, Mike was standing over Victoria as he talked to her, asking questions in a low voice.

"How is she?" Mike asked, pausing in his conversation.

Trent coaxed Addy into a chair nearby, leaving Mike's question unanswered for the moment.

"I was just telling your mother," Mike said to Addy directly, "that we found a note addressed to you." He handed a crisp white piece of paper over to her.

Trent crouched next to her. "Are you up for this?"

She nodded, then closed her eyes and took several deep breaths.

She read it several times in silence as everyone looked on. Then her gaze flitted to her mother as she folded the paper back up and hugged it to her chest.

"I'd like to go home now," Addy said, standing up. "Is there anything more you need from me?" She turned to Mike.

"No." Mike shook his head. "We'll contact you when we release your father's body."

"Thank you." Addy looked at Trent. "Do you think you could drive me back home?"

He nodded. "Mike, can you have Tony take my truck home?"

"Sure," Mike said, and Trent tossed him his keys.

"Thanks."

"Adrianna." Addy's mother looked up at her, but Addy didn't even acknowledge that she'd spoken and continued out the front door.

Trent drove them back to her place in her Jeep. Any other time he would have enjoyed being behind the wheel of a new machine like this, but now, his mind was too occupied with Addy.

When they got back to her trailer, his phone chimed. He glanced down and saw his mother's number. He picked up the call as he parked.

"Hi sweetie," his mother said. "Tony's here and filled us in. My god." He could tell that his mother took a deep breath. "Let us know . . ."

"Yeah," he said, glancing over at Addy, not wanting to upset her further.

"Tell her . . ." His mother's voice broke and he could tell that she felt like him. There were no words that could comfort Addy at this point. "Tell her we love her," she said.

"Will do." When he hung up, he got out and walked around to help Addy out.

"Slumming, McGowan?" Brian's sarcastic voice sounded directly behind them just as they were about to go inside.

"Piss off, Brian, not in the mood." He drew Addy into the trailer without another word to the man.

"I should . . ." Addy said.

Instead of letting her finish, he pulled her into his arms and onto the bed. He held her gently, the small space quiet except for the sound of their breathing.

He held her all through the night, not sure if she slept or not.

When the sun broke in through the blinds, she shifted. "I need to . . ." She sat up, tousle-headed, and looked around blankly. "I don't know what to do next."

"Take one day at a time." He stroked the skin of her arm in long, soft moves.

She glanced over at the piece of paper she'd set on her table.

"Do you want to tell me what the note says?"

She retrieved the note and handed it to him.

"He called me just before. He told me he was sorry." She closed her eyes for a moment and then walked into the small closet that he knew was her bathroom without a word.

He opened the paper and read her father's words twice.

Addy,

> *Nothing I can say would ever come close to telling you how much I've loved you your entire life. I know I didn't always show you the affection you needed, and I won't make excuses other than telling you I was too weak to stand up and fight for what I loved.*

> *My life didn't turn out the way I had hoped. So here's my advice for you. Follow your heart. Don't let anything or anyone stop you from doing and getting what you want. Find someone who loves you for who you are, then never let them go.*

> *I know there's a mess I'm leaving behind. For that I'm sorry.*

> *I've secretly kept my own will. I know your mother never mentioned it, but I'm the one who had the oil family inheritance. Your mother may have cut you off, but I never did. I hope you will look at this as your chance for a fresh start.*

My only regret in life was allowing someone to make me feel less than I was. It made me a weaker person and father. Don't let anyone drag you down.

I love you, Addy. I always have.

I'm sorry,

—Dad

CHAPTER
EIGHTEEN

The next few days flew by so quickly, it felt like Addy blinked and they were gone. The numbness had consumed her, making her feel less than whole.

Everyone in town showed up for her father's funeral. Even Beau and Joy drove back into town to be there for her.

Trent wanted to stay with her every night, but she needed some time alone to think. So instead, he showed up every day and brought food or cooked for her. She knew she was pushing him away, but at this point, it was needed. She had too much on her mind to think about a relationship.

A large dinner at her mother's church followed the funeral services. During the entire process, she didn't speak to her mother once.

Addy stopped looking for wet eyes from the woman after the first ten minutes of the funeral service. After that, her own were too wet for her to care.

She cried more for the lost opportunity of actually having a father. Her mother had robbed any chance of having a normal family life from the both of them.

If only she had . . . she stopped herself from dwelling on the mile-long list of possibilities that threatened to flood her mind.

Trent's hand reached out and took hers, but she nudged it away and walked outside to get some fresh air. He kept his distance, and she wondered if he knew that she just needed the space.

She could tell he was getting frustrated. Yet one thing was clear in her mind: she didn't want to fall into the same trap her father had. Not that Trent was controlling or self-important like her mother, but she just couldn't focus on him at the moment.

No one at the services had questioned why she and her mother weren't sitting next to each other or, for that matter, talking to one another.

Toward the end of the service, she'd looked over and noticed Darla standing at the back of the funeral home. She watched as Gail walked over, took the woman's hand, and led her outside. She knew Gail was trying to shelter the woman from her view, but just seeing Darla stirred anger in her gut.

She hadn't seen Darla since that day in the grocery store. She knew she was still working at the Wet Spot, and the rumor was she was still taking her smoke breaks.

Which caused her to wonder if she was really pregnant. Maybe she'd finally learned how to lie well.

She put that thought out of her mind until she could actually get her mind back into gear. Not that she planned on that happening for a while.

For the next few days, Beau and Joy stuck around to help her out. They were down to a handful of people in the camp. Unfortunately Brian remained one of them.

Addy had let Estelle take over for her and was thankful the woman was a natural. Several thoughts about her future had crossed her mind, but she hadn't been able to verbalize them quite yet. One thing losing her father had done was to make her think even more about her own future. Still, she had doubts.

Every night she read her father's note over and over. The more she did, the more she questioned if she was truly happy.

It was almost a week after her father's passing when she received a call from the lawyer. There were only a small handful of lawyers in Haven, but she'd never met Matt Grengs before. She agreed to meet him at his office the following day.

"Want me to go with you?" Trent asked as he flipped a pancake over in her skillet. He'd continued to show up at her place every morning and acted like nothing was wrong between them. But she knew that it was only a matter of time before he stopped coming by.

The fact that he had his legs spread wide so he didn't have to cock his neck at an odd angle under the trailer's ceiling caused her to smile for the first time in days. He looked like a giraffe trying to drink water.

"No." She looked down at her hands. "I know you probably have tons of work to catch up on. You've taken almost an entire week off for me." She didn't know how to tell him that he could go back to his normal life without her.

"I don't mind." He glanced over at her. "Course my brothers probably do."

"I'm sure you have plenty to—"

"Addy, I remained quiet when you started pushing me away, but I'm where I want to be." He set the pan down after flipping the pancake onto a plate.

She felt her heart sink as she watched him set a large stack of pancakes in front of her. What was it going to be like once he lost interest in her? Could she go back to being alone?

He sat down and took her hand in his.

"It's hard." She shook her head and pulled her hand away. "I know you have your job and I have mine." She took a deep breath. "With everything that's happened . . . recently, I guess I just need . . ."

"I know. After my dad died, I didn't think I'd be able to get back to life," Trent said.

"How did you do it?" she asked. "Get your life back to normal?"

"You don't ever really get back to normal. But you go on every day, remembering the good times, and soon the bad times aren't even a flicker in your memory. I have this drive to end up as close as I can to how great my dad was." His eyes met hers. "I know that it's different for you. Everyone needs to go through their own healing process."

"Your mother coached you, didn't she?"

"Actually it was Trisha. Did you know that she has a sister who is very abusive toward her?"

Addy shook her head and she felt a pang in her heart. Trisha was such a nice person. She couldn't imagine anyone being mean to her.

"You should talk to her about it sometime. She might have a few pointers on how to deal with your mother."

Just then there was a knock on her door. "Come in," Addy called out after checking her watch. She knew that Joy and Beau were supposed to come over for breakfast; she invited them over every time she knew Trent was going to be around, kind of like a buffer.

At first she thought that they would feel awkward around him, but instead, Beau and Trent seemed to get along great. Even Joy had mentioned how impressed she was with his entire family.

"Sorry we're late," Beau said, sitting down.

"You're just in time," Trent said. "I doubt I can eat all this myself."

"Don't lie," Beau joked back. "I bet you could easily put all those away on your own."

It was still weird seeing Trent and Beau get along so well. She'd imagined them as mortal enemies with her in the middle being tugged to either side. But since their arrival, Beau had been nothing but kind to Trent and vice versa.

They chatted about a few lighthearted things as they ate. When the food was gone, Beau stood up and asked to talk to her outside about work.

"So we have to head back to North Dakota tomorrow. Do you think you'll be okay here?" he asked when they stepped outside. Addy could see the concern in her friend's eyes.

"Yes, Estelle has really been such a big help. Actually I was hoping to talk to you about her."

"Oh?" Beau said.

"I think . . ." She took a deep breath. "I believe that it might be time for me to move on to something else in life." She twisted her hands in front of her. "I believe Estelle is a perfect replacement. I'll work with her over the next few weeks until the end of this month." She watched Beau's face and saw the surprise in his eyes. "That should be enough time to bring her up to speed."

Beau fell silent for a moment.

"Is this a personal choice or a professional one?" he asked.

"Both," she said. "My father wanted me to follow my heart, and I'm just not sure my heart is with FREE anymore. I have had another job offer, but I'm still not even sure about taking that one yet. This will give me the opportunity to explore for a few months before I make a choice."

"Of course," he said after a moment. She could tell he was sad but could see that she'd made up her mind. "We want nothing but happiness for you," he added. "You'll keep in contact with us, no matter what?"

"Of course." She felt her breath whoosh out. "I plan on still being invited to your wedding."

"For sure." Beau smiled. "I'll talk to Estelle and see if she's interested in the position." He opened the door and waved for Joy to come out.

Joy hugged her. "We'd better get back out there. Thank you for the breakfast."

"Anytime," Trent said. "Oh, hey—"

Beau stopped and glanced back.

"Addy mentioned that someone told you about our land deal?"

Beau frowned but nodded. "Yeah. I'm not sure I trusted the man completely, given his history, but after looking into it further, it seems some of his information was dead-on." When Trent just waited quietly, Beau continued: "It was Dennis Rodgers."

Trent nodded, and Addy could see the anger fill his eyes. "Yeah. I figured it was him."

♦ ♦ ♦

Trent tried to keep the swirl of questions he had for Addy to himself until after they had finished doing the dishes together. He had texted his brothers the information Beau had told him.

What did it mean? How had Dennis found out about the property? Had it been before or after he'd kidnapped Kristen? Trent knew his family had as many questions about it as he did. But for now, he had other questions he could get answers to, he thought as he looked over at Addy.

He knew some of Beau's thoughts on Dennis, but still, he wondered if Beau believed everything Dennis had told him. And what had Dennis told him exactly? Trent's mind was torn between protecting his family's business and shouting their plans from the rooftops so everyone would just leave them alone.

His eyes met Addy's, and his growing frustration with her taking a giant step back in their relationship surfaced. He'd tried to be patient; after all, she'd just suffered a terrible loss.

But the way she was acting around him, he was getting the hint that she was done with him. Done with wanting to be with him. What would he do if she didn't want a relationship with him anymore?

Suddenly he needed to move. To get some of the frustration out.

"Will you take a walk with me?" Trent held out his hand, knowing the fresh air would do them both good.

He had to get back to work tomorrow, but there was nothing stopping him from enjoying today.

"A walk sounds perfect." Addy gave him a slight smile.

She only had a few small Band-Aids left on two of her fingers. He couldn't even see the scar on her chin or most of the scars on her hands.

They grabbed their light jackets and headed out on one of the popular trails.

"Looks like we might get some more rain later today," Trent said as they began to walk. "Funny, we usually have one more snow in May, but I think we've already seen the last of it for this season."

"Yeah, it's been warmer weather so far this year," she said. "I remember a time when I was about ten, it actually snowed two inches the week before my birthday."

He glanced over at her. "Which is . . ."

She smiled. "June third."

"Mine's September third."

"I know." She avoided his eyes.

"How do you know that?" He moved a tree branch to the side so she could pass clearly underneath it.

"Your mother would always bring Rice Krispies treats for the class on your birthday."

He sighed, remembering now. "That was until junior high. It became childish. Boy, was I stupid. I could go for a batch of those treats right about now."

Addy giggled. "You just had five pancakes, three eggs, two pieces of toast, and a glass of orange juice."

At his chuckle, she stopped and looked over at him. "What?"

"That was a small breakfast compared to what I'm used to."

She shook her head in disbelief. As they reached a fork in the trail, he let her decide which pathway to take. She took the one that would end up taking them to the top of the hill that overlooked Haven. He followed and when they reached the top, they sat on a large rock in silence.

He loved this view of Haven. From here you could see from one end of town to the other. The main street ran in an arc, cutting the town in half. Houses and businesses spotted both hills surrounding the valley. Mount Powell sat at one end of the town, so that when driving down the main street, you got the best view ever.

His family's land lay in the opposite direction. The location of his house would give it a nice view of the mountain from the back deck. That was if he could clear a few more trees.

"I didn't think I'd like being back here," she said, breaking the silence. He looked over at her and suddenly wondered what it would be like if she decided to leave at the end of the month. His gut hurt at the thought.

"Now?" he asked.

She turned slightly toward him. "It's grown on me. I'd forgotten how wonderful some of the people are."

"Anyone in particular?" He reached for her hand, but she moved away, and he noticed the slight frown on her lips.

"A few." He felt emptiness seeping in.

"I've never been one of those kinds of people who rely on others. I guess it stems from the way I grew up. Learning how to not count on anyone for anything. Even affection," she said as her eyes scanned the view before them.

"That shouldn't be how anyone lives." His eyebrows furrowed as he looked out over the town. His town. Something hit him for the first time in his life. "There was a time when I—no." He shook his head. "When my brothers and I all felt like we couldn't get out of Haven fast enough."

"Has that changed?" she asked, glancing over at him.

"Yeah. It's funny, now I don't even think I could be happy anywhere else," he admitted.

She was silent for a while. "I don't know where I belong yet. I don't even know if I'm willing to stick around here."

The metaphorical boulder that had been sitting on his chest doubled in size.

She chuckled. "I'm out of a job at the end of this month, which means I'll need someplace to park my trailer."

"I have land," he blurted out, causing her to smile.

"I was thinking of asking your mother if I could park at her place since she has that long driveway."

"I'll have electricity and a well by the end of this month," he continued, as if the speed of his words could convince her. "Plus, if you'll allow me to stay with you, it would be easier for me to work faster on getting the rest done so the house can be placed sooner."

"Trent, I . . ." She shook her head as her eyes closed slowly as if in thought. "I don't know what I want, but until I do, I can't continue with this." She motioned between them. "I have some things to think about. Lots of things, actually."

He nodded, feeling as if the boulder had crushed him entirely. "Then park your trailer at my place. I'll have it ready." She started to open her mouth, but he stopped her by raising his hand. "I'll stay at my mother's place until you ask me to stay with you."

CHAPTER NINETEEN

The following evening Addy walked through the middle of downtown Haven, her mind spinning with complete shock.

She had made plans to meet Trent after work at the Dancing Moose, but she couldn't hold in her excitement about the new information she'd learned. She wanted to tell someone, and she'd thought of him first.

To be fair, telling him that she needed a break had loosened the load on her mind. Yet for some reason, her body wasn't feeling that release. She felt wound up tight instead. And the lawyer's news had only increased that tension.

She walked the three blocks across town to the McGowan Enterprises building. The low sun was shining, and the entire town looked like it had been washed clean after the early evening rain.

Even the row of strip clubs she passed didn't bother her—that was until Darla stepped out in front of her. The woman lit a long cigarette and blew the smoke in her direction.

"I thought it's been known for a few decades now that pregnant women shouldn't smoke," Addy said dryly as she started to pass Darla.

Darla's eyes narrowed as she took another drag. "It's my body. My baby. I noticed you going into that lawyer's office."

"Yes," Addy sighed, knowing she couldn't simply sidestep and get away. Darla would probably chase her down to have the conversation she wanted to have with her. Still, she didn't have to give her any more information.

"So? Did your father leave anything for me and his kid?" Darla asked.

Addy's eyebrows shot up. "Why would he?"

"He's the daddy." Darla rubbed her hand over her very flat belly. She was wearing a dark rain jacket that ended just above her knees. What kind of outfit was underneath the jacket, Addy didn't even care.

She continued to rub her hand over her midsection. The fact that she held a cigarette in that hand caused Addy's skin to crawl.

"So you say." She tried to edge aside, but Darla reached out and wrapped her free hand around Addy's upper arm.

"You know it's the truth." Darla's grip tightened. "You could always tell when I was lying."

"That was years ago," Addy supplied calmly. She searched her ex–best friend's eyes to see if there was any way to tell now if she was telling the truth. The funny thing was, she couldn't.

"The baby is your daddy's. He showed up one night at the bar, just as I was closing, then he forced himself on me." Darla's eyes narrowed as she took a step closer.

Addy saw her lie for what it was as she stepped back and her shoulders scraped against the brick wall. The fact that the woman was almost a foot taller than Addy and almost twenty pounds heavier caused a quick moment of fear to spike through her. Then again, most of that height was from the pair of spiky heels she was wearing.

"I'm owed something. He gave me some money." Darla bared her teeth in a mean smile. "Ten grand. Told me he was going to give me the same amount every month."

Addy held in her temper. She'd been prepared for a fight, but Darla had brought her A game.

The lawyer had discussed the ten grand missing from her father's account. Knowing her father had given it to Darla made Addy's skin crawl, but then she got an idea to turn the tables.

"Did you blackmail my father?" she asked loudly and stepped toward Darla. She couldn't hide her smile when the woman took a step away from her. "Even after you blurted it out in the grocery store? Did you think he'd pay again after you spilled the beans to everyone in town?"

She took another step and watched Darla back away even farther.

"You know, if you really are pregnant, I and my lawyer will want proof. Even then, we'll demand a paternity test to prove it was his."

Darla had been looking worried, but now she smiled. "How? Your father is dead."

"DNA." Addy raised a brow. "I share his DNA. They should be able to match it to me, and if not, I'll exhume my father's body before I give you one more dime of his. Don't bother me again until you have proof that kid, if there is one, is my blood."

She turned and walked the rest of the block to Trent's building, reveling in the psychic win.

When she entered, she took a deep breath and leaned back against the glass doors. *Boy, that felt good.*

"Running from the law?" Rea chuckled as she looked at her over her reading glasses.

"I wish it was the law." Addy dropped her bag on a waiting room chair. "Just a former best friend turned stripper, turned . . . possible . . . what? Mother of my supposed half-sibling?" She got a headache just thinking about it.

"I heard about that mess." Rea shook her head and pulled off her reading glasses. "I'm sure we will find out soon enough that Darla is lying."

"I hope so. I can't tell when she's lying anymore." Addy stopped at the end of Rea's desk.

"She's had years to practice since you left town," Rea said. "Are you here to see Trent?"

Suddenly Addy remembered why she had come here in the first place and smiled.

"Yes, is he in?" She glanced down the hallway.

"No, but you can keep me company until he gets back." Rea nodded at the wall clock. "Which should be in about fifteen minutes."

"Sounds wonderful," she said, taking the chair that Rea indicated.

"You look fancy today." Rea motioned to Addy's simple flowered summer dress. She'd found it in the back of her small closet and decided to wear it to the lawyer's office. She'd tossed on her cream button-up sweater over it and had been impressed at how nice it felt to wear a dress again. She didn't own a pair of heels, but her brown dress boots finished the look perfectly. She knew she would be dealing with a dark chapter in her life that morning and wanted a little sunshine to get her through it. So she had taken extra time with her outfit, makeup, and hair.

"I had a meeting with my father's lawyer," she said, taking a deep breath. Since she couldn't tell Trent, Rea was the next best thing. The news was almost bursting from her chest.

Rea's eyebrows shot up. "I heard about what your parents did."

Addy nodded and played with one of the last Band-Aids on her fingers. The stitches had been taken out, leaving only bruises. She knew as much as anyone that Rea didn't care too much for gossip because she'd been the subject of it for years. So her interest was surprising. *Well, here comes a great tidbit.*

"Turns out my dad left me everything he had. Apparently he'd kept his finances a secret from my mother."

"Smart man," Rea said, and at Addy's look, shook her head. "I'm sorry, I didn't mean . . ."

"It's okay. It was smart of him. My mother would have consumed it all like she consumed him." A wave of sadness washed over her.

"Even though she's blood, it doesn't make her family. Take a look at me. I love my son, but . . ." Rea leaned back in her chair. "There isn't a day that goes by that I don't wish he had turned out like my other boys." She smiled over at the picture of the McGowans. It was an oil painting done several years back of the entire family.

Trent must have been around seventeen then. He was just as handsome as she remembered. He'd been her fantasy. Sure, all the boys were handsome, but Trent . . . he made her heart melt just looking at him.

"Does he know how you feel about him?" Rea smiled over at her.

"What?" Addy blinked a few times.

"Honey, I'm not blind. I've been in love a few times in my life."

"Love?" Addy shook her head. "I'm not . . ."

Rea's laughter stopped her just as the door opened.

Addy felt her heart skip as she watched Trent walk in.

He was wearing a pair of gray slacks and a white button-up shirt with a dark-gray jacket. His hair was neatly combed; however, the scruff on his jaw contradicted the businesslike look. He was so damn sexy she felt her mouth water.

"Damn meeting ran over . . ." he said before looking up from his phone. When he did, his eyes locked with hers almost instantly.

She couldn't be in love with Trent. Nothing good could ever come from it.

"Well," Rea said, breaking the silence, causing both of them to glance over at her. "That's it for me tonight. I've got a hot date." She winked at Addy. Then turned to Trent. "I'll see you tomorrow." She flipped off her computer and grabbed her purse. "You'll make sure to lock up when you leave?"

Trent didn't even blink as Rea closed the front door behind her, laughter leaking back through.

"I thought we had dinner plans," he said.

"We do." Addy stood up and tucked her hands together.

His eyes moved over her dress and he smiled, causing his dimple to flash. "You look . . . wow," he said, setting down a circular black case on Rea's desk.

"Thank you." She tried to think of a different subject, anything to change the way he was looking at her now. She knew she had to be strong if she was going to remain on course. She looked down at the case. "Is this for the school?" He'd talked with her about the project, and she'd been very interested in his plans.

"Yeah, they finally approved these." He patted the case, not taking his eyes from her. "It only took them half a dozen versions to finally agree." He shook his head as he wrapped his arms around her waist. "Have I mentioned that you look amazing?"

Addy felt her entire body react to his touch and knew that she couldn't fight her desire to be with him much longer. She was so used to not having happiness, not having someone close to her, that she was losing a hold on her own life. Why couldn't she finally take her pleasures and enjoy life? She wrapped her arms around his shoulders. "No, I believe the word you used was . . . *wow*."

"I can be smoother," he said, pulling her closer.

"Show me," she said just before his lips met hers.

♦ ♦ ♦

Trent pulled them toward the hallway, thinking of nothing other than getting her to the sofa that sat in the corner of his office.

They moved down the long hallway and his back bumped into a door. The sofa forgotten, he pulled on the handle and spun them around, pushing her up against the back of the door as his mouth took hers in a greedy dance.

Her hands were removing his jacket, pulling and tugging at his shirt until he heard buttons pop. When her fingers touched his bare skin, they both moaned.

Her kisses grew more demanding as his hands lifted the sweater off her shoulders. Underneath, he was pleasantly surprised to see her shoulders were bare. The sundress was strapless, which he knew could mean . . . he nudged the dress down slightly and realized that he was the luckiest man alive when he found her bare underneath.

His fingers pinched her nipples slightly, causing her head to fall back to the door, eyes closed. She was more beautiful than he could have imagined.

When he dipped his head and covered one breast, his hands moved down, taking her cotton panties with them until they disappeared from the silkiness of her legs. His hands traveled slowly up her legs as his mouth trailed over her skin.

When he found her, she was hot and ready, which caused his dick to jump. She reached for him at the same time and moaned when she pulled his pants open and wrapped her fingers around him.

"My god," he groaned as she stroked him. "I can't . . ." He thought of how to get this to last longer, but nothing sprang to mind.

Instead, he dipped his fingers into her and a cry escaped her lips as pleasure racked her. Her body responded so fast, she instantly wanted more and doubted she would ever get enough. Damn, she was hot. Too hot.

"Hurry," she moaned after she'd come back to him. "I can't wait." She'd already built back up.

He nudged her skirt up with one hand while rolling a condom on with the other, then stepped between her legs. He entered her in one quick jerk and had them both crying out in pleasure.

Her nails dug into his shoulders and her legs wrapped around his waist. He held her body between his and the hard door.

A bead of sweat rolled down his back as he pumped his hips faster. His mouth took hers, consuming the sexy sounds she was making.

His fingers found her hair and tugged until she leaned back, exposing her neck for him to nibble on.

He'd never had so much passion build up before. When he felt her tense, his own release caused his knees to shake.

"Are we in a closet?" Addy asked as their breathing leveled after a few minutes of silence. He was still holding her up against the door, her legs still wrapped around his hips.

He opened his eyes and glanced around. "Damn it."

She chuckled. "You can be so smooth."

He leaned his forehead against the door with a laugh. "You made me crazy with this outfit."

"Hmm," she purred. "I'll have to get more dresses, then."

His fingers ran over her bare shoulders gently. He felt and heard her breath hitch. Instantly he grew hard again. In one quick move, he hoisted her up in his arms and opened the door to his office.

When he laid her down on the soft sofa in his office, she smiled up at him.

"You get high points for that move," she said.

"Are you keeping score?" he joked, as he came back down to her, losing himself in pleasure once again.

CHAPTER TWENTY

When they walked into the diner, it was half an hour before closing time.

"Just made it." Katy walked over to them with menus as they took a seat.

Addy's face flushed, and she tried to hide her blush behind the laminated paper. Trent had shown her just how smooth he could be. So smooth she would have gladly fallen asleep, naked, on the sofa at his office.

Maybe it was her state of mind, but the low-lit diner became one of the most romantic places ever.

Trent filled her in on his uncle as they waited for their food to arrive. His mother had found a local nursing home that could care for him. Trent had told her that her uncle hadn't spoken since his heart attack, but that so far, most of his motor skills were still functional.

"He was lucky you were there," she said.

"I'm the reason he is the way he is now," Trent added with a frown.

"*He's* the reason he is the way he is," she corrected. "I ran into Trey the other day, and he filled me in on why you feel guilty. You didn't do anything wrong."

"I should have . . ."

"Trent, should I feel guilty about my father?"

"No!" He shook his head and reached for her hand.

"Then you shouldn't feel guilty for what happened to your uncle. You did what was best for your family, and he was very lucky you were there to save him."

Addy had let some of her own guilt go. She was right. If Trent shouldn't carry guilt around, neither should she. But she knew who should feel guilty, and she had every intention of finally getting to the bottom of things with her mother.

"You never did tell me why you came to my office," he said as he reached across and took the half of the burger she offered.

"Oh!" Her expression lightened. "I wanted to tell you about my meeting."

"With your dad's lawyer?" he asked and snagged a fry off her plate.

"Yes, he left everything to me. Everything he had."

His eyes met hers. "Nothing for your mother?"

She shook her head. "No, everything went to me."

"Which is?" he asked.

"I don't know." She pulled out the clump of papers she'd shoved into her purse. "I didn't have a chance to look."

She straightened the papers and moved closer to him so they could both look.

"Addy," he said after scanning the document. "He left you everything."

"Yes," she said, her eyes tracking the words as well.

"No," he said as she looked up at him. "I mean everything. Not just his personal stuff. Your parents' house, the cars, his life insurance, everything."

She blinked a few times. "The house? But . . ." She grabbed the sheet. "What about my mother?"

She'd had a hard time making sense of the document, given the memories of how the assets had come to her. Trent moved his empty plate aside, wiped his hands, then took the packet from her.

He flipped the pages. "Well, according to this, the house was his before they married. It appears it was his inheritance. He paid for the cars and your schooling out of his accounts, along with all the bills."

"But that doesn't make sense. She's always bragged about all the money left to her from my grandparents."

"She may have money too, but she didn't use it on any of those things." He set the paper down and watched her.

"What do I do?" she groaned.

"You're asking me?"

"Yes." She leaned back, looking into his eyes. Things had changed in the past few weeks, but one thing remained. "I trust your judgment. Should I tell my mother? And then what? Kick her out of her home? What if she doesn't have any place else to go? Or, worse, any of her own money?" Her chest tightened the more she elaborated, and she felt her breathing hitch slightly.

Trent reached and took her hand in his.

"Hey, you don't have to do anything tonight. How about you sleep on it for a few days before deciding?"

Since her head was swirling with a million new questions, she simply squeezed his hand in agreement.

They left the diner and headed back to her place. With the excuse that she had too much to think about, she kissed Trent good night and watched as he drove away.

Thoughts of her mother and her finances kept her up most of the night.

By morning, she'd made up her mind to make a visit to her mother's place. She ate breakfast quickly and dressed even faster. Then she spent almost an hour coming up with a plan.

Addy drove through town and headed down the street to the house she'd always known as home. The two-car garage lay to the left as she pulled in the driveway.

She thought back to the last time she was there. Down the stairs via a smaller deck, a pathway led to her father's private workshop. Images flooded her brain, and she had to pump the brakes and grip the steering wheel until the feelings passed.

She pulled in and parked near the garage, knowing there were two cars parked inside. A newer Buick town car that her parents drove to church and anywhere they went together, and an older Toyota sedan that her father drove on his own.

When she got out, she realized that her mother was watching her from the now-open front door.

"Come to kick me out?" she said.

Addy stopped and took a deep breath. "No." She was relieved that her mother knew the stakes. "I've come to get a few things out in the open."

She approached the door. Her mother turned and went into the house, not waiting to see if Addy followed her.

As she walked in, she noticed that nothing had changed. She didn't know what she'd expected, but seeing everything still in place felt wrong somehow.

Her father's reading glasses and the book he'd been reading were still sitting beside his chair in the living room. Sadness threatened Addy's composure, and she had to look away.

"I heard you met with that lawyer. I don't care what he says, I own this place." Her mother crossed her arms.

"Well, no, I do, but that's beside the point." Addy moved over and sat down, then motioned for her mother to take her chair.

She hesitated for a moment, then sat.

"Beside the point?" her mother repeated. "I would think that after everything that's gone on, that would *be* the point."

Addy shook her head. "I'm not here to talk finances."

"Why are you here?" Her mother shifted slightly and for the first time in her life, Addy realized that the woman looked nervous.

"Oh, I don't know, maybe because you're my mother."

Her mother looked as if she'd been slapped. Still, she remained silent.

"Does that mean anything to you?" Addy leaned forward.

"Of course it does," her mother shot back. "I've sacrificed a lot for you."

"Have you?" Addy broke in. "Really? Name one thing."

Her mother's chin rose and her eyes narrowed. "You were always such an insufferable child."

Addy stopped herself from jumping up and walking out. Instead, she held her ground. "And you were such a superior, hypocritical, self-righteous mother and wife. You never once really cared for me. Most mothers involve themselves in their daughters' lives, enjoy their company. You, however, went out of your way not to deal with anything I did or desired. All you ever cared about was what you wanted. Do you want to know why your husband made sure not to leave you a dime? All you have to do is look in the mirror and ask yourself what kind of wife you were to the man."

She stood up slowly, looking down at her mother. Looking deep in her matching blue eyes for a hint of remorse. Seeing none, she continued.

"I came out here in hopes that I'd see a shred of decency. But I can see now there isn't an ounce of it in you." She took a deep breath. "I'm not going to kick you out. I'm not like you. But I will demand several things in order for you to remain in your cozy domain." She pulled out her list. Her hour that morning had been hard, but it had been worth it to come up with a plan of attack. She knew this was her one chance to get her mother's attention—to change the woman and make her something better. She was confident that if her mother followed this list, she would become a woman Addy could like. "If these are not met on a monthly basis, you will be removed from my property. If they are met, you're free to live here." She looked around. "Free to continue your mundane existence."

Her mother gasped as she took the list from Addy. "What do you mean 'volunteer for eight hours a month at the local library'?"

Addy sat back down. "I mean that for one full day, you will drive yourself to downtown Haven, in a car that will now be in my name, and go to the library. You will read to the kids and stack or log in books or whatever other tasks Kim, the head librarian, gives you."

Her mother's eyes narrowed, and she looked back down at the list. "And 'eight hours at the clinic'?"

"Yes, pretty much the same deal there. One day a month you will spend emptying bed pans"—her mother's face grew slightly red—"delivering meals, or doing whatever else they need from you. The same goes for the vet clinic."

"I don't like animals."

Addy tilted her head. "It's high time you learned to enjoy them. I've provided phone numbers and contact information for each place."

It wasn't too much for one person to do, but she knew her mother had never worked a full day in her life. Still, she had been proud to come up with six things her mother could accomplish for the town while trying to broaden herself.

The fact that her mother was even looking at the list told her that she was more desperate for money than Addy had thought.

"I don't know what this last one is." She held up the paper. "'Bonco'?"

"Every Thursday night, there is a group of women who meet at the library and play games. Bonco is an easy-enough game for you to learn, and it's fun. Plus it will get you out of the house and meeting people your own age."

"I know people my age. We've attended church since . . ."

Addy shook her head until her mother stopped talking.

"I know what it means to attend church with you," she said. "You arrive on time, only speak briefly to the preacher and certain prominent families in town, then leave. The people you'll be seeing here are far from the group you're used to showing off for."

"I won't do it." Her mother set the paper back down.

"Then I'll expect you out of the house by the end of the month." Addy stood up again. She knew she had to call her mother's bluff and decided to play hardball. "I'll have my agent put the house and cars up for sale . . ."

Her mother gasped. "You'll do no such thing. This house has been in the family for generations."

"My father's family for two generations. I don't intend to make it three." She made her way toward the front door, leaving the list on the coffee table for her mother. "I'll be checking in on you periodically," she said without looking back. "And each contact has instructions to let me know if you don't show up. Good night, Mother."

She walked out and paused a moment on the front patio to take a deep breath. She smiled when she realized that suddenly she felt free, more empowered than she had her entire life.

This called for a gallon of mint–chocolate chip ice cream.

◆　◆　◆

Being out in nature was one of Trent's greatest passions. A few days after that memorable office meeting with Addy, he spent the morning flying his small plane over the next few sites that were ready to close up. He needed the bird's-eye view to scope out the possibilities for the land.

The first site was due to finish in the next few months. A parking lot housed the work trailer, then there was the actual drilling site. The pumps would remain, but the massive drilling rig and parking areas would need to be replaced with trees and sod. Drilling was messy work, especially in the spring.

Then, before landing, he flew over his own land and couldn't help but smile and dream.

Someday soon he'd have his house and driveway in. He had plans—not just for trees and shrubbery, but a spot for a garden and an orchard. Maybe even a small artificial pond to water cattle or horses. Which meant a place for a barn and corral.

In his mind, Addy walked through the garden and stopped to pat one of the horses. His dreams of his new home intertwined completely with the woman he hoped would share it. The more he thought about it, the more frustrated he got that she was slipping away from him. No wonder he had needed to escape his office—the memory of the evening they had spent in it together consumed his mind while he sat behind his desk. It had been too hard to focus on work, and he'd needed the fresh air to clear Addy from his thoughts.

When he landed, he drove down to the current project and pulled on his gloves to help his crew plant more than a dozen ponderosa pine and Douglas fir trees, each roughly six feet tall.

After quitting time, he pulled into the driveway at his mother's place. His guard went up instantly as he parked behind a patrol car. He slammed his door and rushed into the house without thinking about the mud trail he was leaving behind him.

"What's wrong?" he said, standing in his mother's kitchen. He noticed Tony sitting at the kitchen table with a plate of food in front of him. There were even candles flickering and a table cloth.

His mother jerked her head toward him and frowned. "What's wrong is the mess you're making in my house." She half stood up, then stopped herself and sat back down. "Now kindly go take those filthy boots off and clean up your mess on my newly mopped floor before I come over there and . . ."

He held up his hands and backed up slowly. "Okay, but what's he doing here?"

"Tony is having dinner. He was invited. You were not." His mother nodded. "Now go."

Trent's eyes moved to the man, whose cheeks turned bright pink, his gaze darting everywhere but Trent's direction.

Trent made it back to the doorway and squinted. "Like . . . a date?"

"Go!" his mother said firmly.

He backed up, pulled off his boots, and took out the broom and the mop. He spent a few minutes cleaning up the dirt he'd tracked in.

At least he was pleased to know that he interrupted the rest of their dinner by cleaning up his mess. His eyes stayed glued to Tony as he cleaned. The man knew to avoid his gaze.

"There," he said after putting the mop away. "Now can I get . . ."

"No, what you can do is go take a shower and let us finish our dinner." His mother waved him toward his room.

He crossed his arms and was about to argue when his mother gave him the look. He turned and marched to his room without another word.

He showered in record time and dressed. But by the time he walked back out to the kitchen, Tony was gone and his mother was doing dishes as she hummed to herself.

"What was he doing here?" he asked again, leaning against the countertop and reaching for a slice of chicken that was left in the pan on the stove.

His mother looked over at him. "Tony is a dear friend. We were having dinner and catching up on old times."

He focused on shredding the chicken piece smaller, to avoid meeting his mother's eyes. "Was that it?"

"Of course it was, what else would it be?"

"Where's Trisha?" He glanced around.

"She's having dinner with Kristen and Tyler tonight," his mother said as she finished putting the dishes in the drying rack.

"Was that a date?"

"I'm not sure what that was. I ran into Tony at the grocery store and he asked me to dinner. I offered to cook, so he came over."

"You had candles," he said, glancing over at the long white stems that were now blown out.

"Sometimes candles are nice." His mother sighed. "It's been almost a year," she said, wrapping her arms around him.

"I know." He ran his hand over her hair.

"Don't be upset because I like a little attention."

"I'm not," he said. "I like Tony. Really," he emphasized when she snorted. "It's just . . . it's hard to think about . . ." He shook his head. "Never mind."

He howled with pain as his mother pinched his side. "There, now remember that pain every time you think about . . ." Her eyes narrowed.

He chuckled and rubbed the red spot.

"Now what are *you* doing here?" she asked, getting back to the dishes.

"I was here for clean clothes and a long hot shower, but I settled for clean clothes and a quick hot shower."

"Trailer life not suiting you?" she asked.

"Addy has a lot of things to think about. She says she needs some space." He tried not to let his frustration about being pushed away show on his face, but the fact was he was starting to lose his mind and patience.

His mother moved closer to him. "Well, while you're here, you might as well eat these leftovers and talk about it. Grab a plate."

CHAPTER TWENTY-ONE

Addy enjoyed showing Estelle the ropes. The woman was a natural organizer, and Addy only had another week before her time was up. She knew once she informed everyone of the McGowans' intentions, the group would most likely be moving on to join the rest of the FREE members.

She hadn't had too much time to stop and think about her own future. Other than she knew she wanted to keep a close eye on her mother for the first few months.

She had received word that her mother had called the library and scheduled her first volunteer day.

When she told Trent about her plan, he'd told her how proud he was that she'd done something so wonderful.

She was coming back to her trailer from Estelle's tent late one evening when she bumped solidly into Brian.

His hands went to her shoulders. Instantly her guard went up. She tried to take a step back, but he held on to her. She'd always tried to avoid being with him alone since he usually gave her the creeps.

"I . . . um, heard about your old man," he said, loosening his hands slightly. He wasn't hurting her, it's just that she didn't like being so close to him. "I'm sorry. I know how hard it is. Dealing with suicide."

This behavior was so out of character for him that it took her a moment to remember that his own father had killed himself long ago.

"Thank you," she said, relaxing slightly.

Just then, footsteps sounded close by and Trent walked onto the path. His instant frown when he saw the two of them dimmed her smile. Then she realized Brian was still holding her arms.

She took a step away and toward Trent, instantly blocking him.

"Brian was just talking to me about my father. Saying he was sorry." She reached over and took Trent's hand. His entire body tensed, ready for a fight.

"Don't get all bent out of shape, McGowan," Brian sneered. Gone instantly was the thoughtful man who'd just talked to her, replaced by someone who was ready for a fight. "I'm out of here."

She tugged on Trent's arm as she threw a "Good night, Brian" over her shoulder. He'd already disappeared quickly into the darkness.

"What did he want?" Trent said when they reached the trailer.

"Like I said, I just bumped into him. He was sorry to hear about my dad." She opened the door and climbed inside.

"That man has been trouble since the day he was born." Trent moved over and sat down.

She shook her head at the frown on his face. "I've been handling Brian since long before you gave me a second look," she said as she grabbed a bottle of water to cool her sudden temper down. "Just because you now have eyes for me doesn't mean I can't handle a little unwanted attention." She put her hand on her hip.

"He's an ass," he growled.

"You used to be an ass too." She walked over to the fridge to look for something to eat.

"That was different," he said.

"Oh?" She glared at him, then pulled out her gallon of ice cream and started scooping some into bowls. "How so?" Anger food. Maybe the ice cream would work better than the water.

"I wasn't a psychopath." He crossed his arms.

"I don't think Brian is either. I think he's just . . ." She set Trent's bowl down and tilted her head, thinking about it. "Misguided."

Trent laughed sarcastically. "Right." He nodded toward the gallon container. "Why are you having ice cream?"

"Well, initially it was because my mother showed up last night for Bonco and I was going to celebrate. But now it's because you pissed me off and I need something to cool myself down with."

"What the heck is Bonco?" he asked, breaking her angry streak.

She was thankful the conversation moved to her mother and away from Brian for the remainder of the evening.

By the time Trent left her place, she felt like everything had taken a turn for the best.

Her life really was starting to feel like she knew where she belonged. The fact that it was with Trent McGowan was still cause for concern. Sure, she was starting to trust him more and more, but there was something deep down inside her that struggled with allowing him in all the way.

♦ ♦ ♦

That weekend started out like shit. Bessy was acting up. It took Trey and Trent almost two hours to change out a spark plug, which happened to cause Trent to bang his knuckles more than a half dozen times. Now he had bloody knuckles and a sour attitude.

By lunchtime, the rain had started and his mood went from sucky to worse.

Just as Trent finished up his cold turkey sandwich and stale potato chips, Addy drove up. He slogged his way to her muddy Jeep in the rain. "What are you doing here?" he asked, as she rolled down her window.

"I came to help with the work," she said, glancing around his land.

"I think our workday is a wash," he said to her through the opened window. "Why don't you head back? We're just going to try and finish things up so the electrician can do his job tomorrow."

She surprised him by getting out of the Jeep and smiling. "I'm not going to let a little rain spoil my time." She checked out the sky. "Besides, it looks like it might clear up in a few minutes."

"You don't have to get all wet and muddy . . ." he started, but she was already walking to where his brothers sat huddled under a make-shift tent, finishing their own lunches.

"Well," she said, stopping in front of them. She was wearing an older pair of jeans that hugged her in places he had to stop and admire. She wore a rain slicker, and a black cap covered most of her head. Her hair was tied back in a tight braid that fell to the middle of her back. She looked ready to work and prepared to get muddy.

"Really," he said, catching up to her. "I think we can handle . . ." He dropped off when she turned and gave him a look that said he wasn't getting rid of her anytime soon.

"Where do you need me?" she asked.

"You can drive Bessy," he suggested. At least that way she'd be inside a glass case out of the rain. Besides, he'd finished most of the hard work already. The land where his house was going to sit had been cleared. The foundation smoothed out. They had cleared a small patch where her trailer would sit; all they needed to do now was spread the gravel that had been delivered earlier that morning.

The electrician was due to arrive first thing in the morning and set up a hookup for the trailer before starting on the main house power cable.

The well had been finished, but the plumber was currently installing a fresh-water line and drain for the trailer.

Trent figured that after the house was in, they could keep the trailer parked in the spot full-time. He might even build a small covering later for it to sit under.

"Really?" She turned to the machine and smiled.

"Of course, you'll need some schooling first." He took her hand and walked with her over to Bessy. He helped her up into the machine, then climbed in after her. When he shut the door, he smiled down at her.

"See, this feels nice and cozy. I knew you two would like each other."

She chuckled and pushed his knee playfully.

"Show me how this beast runs."

"Oh, now, you're going to hurt her feelings. She's a sexy little thing." Trent flipped on the ignition and had Bessy purring. "See, she likes you."

Addy rolled her eyes. "What do I do?"

For the next half hour, he taught her how to push the gravel into place. He and his brothers had set up stakes earlier for the gravel area, and by the time he jumped out of Bessy and left Addy alone to finish the job, she was an expert.

"She's pretty good at that." Trey slapped him on the back. It had stopped raining less than fifteen minutes after Addy showed up. Now the sun was shining and burning Trent's neck and arms. He pulled on a hat to keep most of the sunshine out of his eyes as he helped chop and haul the wood to the massive pile they had going.

"You'll have plenty of firewood for years to come." Tyler twisted to stretch his back. "We both will."

"How's it going over there?" Trent asked Tyler. He felt bad that he hadn't been able to help his brother out more, but he'd been so busy trying to get his house ready he had spent less and less time over at his brother's land.

From where they were, he could just make out the double-wide trailer Tyler and Kristen lived in. He knew that he would be able to see their house once it was done.

"Electric and plumbing are in, and we're ready to pour the foundation." Tyler looked up at the sky. "As soon as we can guarantee the weather."

"Yeah, we'll probably pour at the same time. Once my place is set here, I'm all yours on my spare time." Building a home was a hell of a lot harder than having a kit home set in place.

"If you have any left. It seems to me that Addy would get a lot of your spare time," Tyler joked as he walked away.

By the time Addy was done leveling the gravel, Trent put her on the job of clearing the road. The rain had caused several sinkholes, and he sent her off down the pathway to make sure they were smoothed out before the second load of gravel was delivered next week.

He was thankful she had a Jeep so she could get in and out of the area until he could get the entire pathway smoothed out. The fact that it was almost a quarter of a mile had caused him some headache.

At sundown, he rode with Addy back to his mother's house since she had planned on a big dinner for everyone. He let Addy use his shower first and then climbed in after her to rinse off.

When he walked into the kitchen, it was to a room full of laughter, including Addy's. She was hugging her legs against her chest as she sat with her back against the fireplace. Her long hair was still damp from the shower and her face was clear of any makeup. She looked amazing. She looked *right*.

When she noticed him, she patted the spot next to her on the stone hearth and scooted over. He walked across the room and sat next to her.

"Your mother was just telling us about the time the three of you got into it with a skunk."

"It was Trey's fault," Tyler said. "He wouldn't stop trying to get the cat to come to him," he said, laughing.

"What did I know? I was six," Trey chimed in, chuckling.

It felt good, so good, to have his family there, to have Addy by his side. Even now, Kristen and Trisha had become so much a part of the clan that they felt comfortable adding to stories or poking fun at the three brothers.

He could tell Addy had loosened up by the end of the evening to where she truly felt part of his family. He couldn't explain what that did to him. How it made him feel. Other than that he wanted more.

As they drove back to her trailer, she filled him in on Estelle's progress.

"She's as ready as she'll ever be. Actually she is in a much better position than I was. I didn't have someone to walk me through all this," she said, pulling the Jeep to a stop. "It wasn't as if Beau or Joy had enough time to show me the ropes. We were busy in California fighting to save the condors."

"I bet that was amazing. I've only ever seen one on TV."

"They're bigger than they look." She turned to him and smiled. "I never thought I'd be scared of a bird, but . . ." She shivered visibly. "They've got almost a ten-foot wingspan. Just watching them . . ." She sighed. "They're almost prehistoric."

She'd done and seen so much since leaving Haven. He realized he'd squandered his short time away from the town. He hadn't done anything except focus inward. He had never really set out to help anyone other than himself. She had touched and helped so many others that he couldn't even begin to appreciate how wonderful she was. His hand tangled in her hair, gently tugging her toward him over the center console until they touched lips.

"You're amazing," he said softly next to her skin.

"Why? Because I fight for birds?" She gave him a teasing smile.

"No, because you fight for what is right. You make the world a better place for birds . . . and for me." He kissed her again.

CHAPTER TWENTY-TWO

Addy lay in Trent's arms that night, unable to sleep. Her mind kept playing over the wonderful evening she'd had with his family.

She could tell that they were a unit. Completely connected in every way.

She had wondered her entire life what that would feel like. Did he know how lucky he was? How lucky they all were to have one another?

Would she ever feel that way herself? Could she feel that way with Trent? What was still stopping her from accepting that he was good for her?

Thoughts of her mother kept surfacing.

So far, in the past week, her mother had been trying. Addy had contacted a few of the ladies who played Bonco and asked them how it went. Everyone gushed at how wonderful her mother had been. She'd even brought a dessert to share.

Which was one of her mother's classic ingratiating moves. But Addy was still willing to wait and see how she handled her first volunteering job.

It was strange. The more she thought about it, the more she had been forced into a maternal role in that regard. A month ago, Addy would have been solely focused on how her mother made her feel, how she'd done or said something to hurt her. Now she didn't even think about that side of their relationship. Her main goal was to mold her mother into a better person.

There were two more days until the end of the month. She didn't tell Trent, but she was feeling kind of anxious about moving onto his land.

She'd even considered moving her trailer to her mother's driveway. But as soon as the thought surfaced, she'd rejected the idea. The farther away from her mother she was right now, the better.

For the past few years, Addy had lived in parks, next to a group of people she knew. If she needed something, she only had to step out her front door and ask someone.

Trent's land was miles from anywhere. Sure, Kristen and Tyler's place was about a mile across the valley. Gail and Trisha were a little farther away. All of them less than five minutes away by car.

But the thought of being alone out there was different than she was used to. Though if she expected her mother to change, so could she. Since she'd left Haven, she'd kept people at arm's length. Never allowing herself to grow close to anyone. Maybe now she could afford to let someone in. Someone like Trent.

Addy spent her last two days working for FREE filling in the small group on the next assignment in North Dakota. She was asked several times why she was looking ahead when things still hadn't been settled with the McGowans.

"They close on the land in two days," someone said in the small meeting that following evening.

"I understand. Part of my job"—she glanced over to Estelle and nodded—"part of *our* job is to always have the next location prepped and our team prepared. I've been assured that in two days, the McGowans will hold a small press conference to let the public know what their intentions are with the land they have purchased. We've agreed to hold off until we know more."

"Does Beau know?" Brian asked.

"Yes." She looked in Brian's direction and smiled. "After having a meeting with Trent McGowan, it was his idea to go into a holding pattern. Now since tomorrow is my last day, Estelle has baked cookies and provided drinks." She smiled. "So if there is no further business . . ." The small group remained silent so she motioned for everyone to enjoy the food set out.

She walked with Estelle to the back table and knew instantly she wasn't going to be able to avoid Brian.

"Do you have a second?" he asked, holding a small plastic glass and a cookie in his hands.

"Sure." She nodded toward a set of chairs, but he set the cup and cookie down and opened the flap of the tent.

She held in a sigh and followed him outside into the darkness. He continued to walk until they were a few feet from the tent.

"What's up?" she asked when he finally stopped.

"I wanted to say that I was sorry."

"For?" she asked.

His eyes avoided hers. "I was pretty sure I knew what path I wanted to go down in life."

She stood silently, waiting for Brian to continue.

"I had a lot of pent-up anger for this place." He sighed and looked off into the darkness.

"I felt the same way," she supplied.

He nodded. "Yeah, I got that from you. At least when we first came back. I continued on that thought until . . . recently."

"Everyone can change. That's the good thing about life." She touched his arm.

He glanced down at her hand. "There was a time, shortly after I joined FREE, that I thought we were supposed to be together."

Her hand dropped and she frowned slightly at the meaning behind his words.

His eyes moved up to hers. "But now I understand where I belong. What my purpose is." He took a step back, and she wondered where the strange look in his eyes had come from. "I'm sorry for the things . . . for everything," he said again, then turned and walked away.

She watched him disappear down the trail and wondered what that was all about. Then one of the newer volunteers poked his head out and called, "Addy, you're missing your own party."

The next morning, she found out that Brian had left the camp. When she asked the group that he'd been staying with, they didn't know where he had gone.

She spent her final day with FREE preparing for her speech at the press conference, which was to be held at city hall that evening. She'd gone to the last meeting unprepared and didn't want to be caught unready this time.

Just before the meeting, Addy took her time dressing in her nicest slacks and blouse. In the back of her mind she knew Trent would enjoy the outfit. She thought vaguely about shopping for a few more outfits to fit her new life—and for a few things she knew Trent would like that went under her clothes.

Trent had stopped by around noon and had lunch with her, but then had gone back to his mother's place.

"Our plan is to show a unified front." He had taken a deep breath. "Which means showing up together."

"I understand." She had silently been thankful for the extra time alone before the meeting. "Go, I'll see you there."

He had leaned down and kissed her until her toes had curled up.

"We'll be free of all this after tonight and you can start your new life tomorrow." He smiled. "Moving day."

"Moving day." Was leaving FREE the best thing for her? She no longer felt the desire she had when she'd started the job years ago. Sure, she still wanted to fight against injustices, but her desire for something more outweighed that.

Her stomach was in knots when she walked into the meeting hall. Even though Estelle was there next to her, Addy immediately searched the crowd for Trent and his family. When she spotted them, she relaxed a little.

She took a seat near the front as the room filled up with townspeople. When she looked around, she realized that she knew most everyone there.

Then she was shocked to see another familiar face.

"Isn't that your mother?" Estelle asked.

"Yes." Addy stood up and walked over to her. "Mom?"

"Oh, I didn't expect . . ." Her mother shook her head. "Of course. I had forgotten you'd be here."

"What are you doing here?" she asked.

Her mother's eyebrows shot up. "It is on that list you gave me." She pulled the piece of paper from her purse. "Attend every town meeting." She shook the paper in front of Addy.

"Oh, yes, I'd . . . forgotten." She sighed. "I've been preoccupied. Would you like to sit with us?"

Her mother followed her to the front, and Estelle moved down one seat so Addy could sit in between them.

"What's this one about?" her mother asked as they waited for the mayor to call the meeting into session.

"Well, there are several issues that will be addressed." She looked down at the meeting agenda she'd been given at the door.

"Will you speak? It says FREE on the list. Isn't that who you work for?"

"Yes, I've prepared a short talk."

Estelle leaned over so she could see her mother. "Your daughter is a very good speaker. You should have heard her last presentation."

Addy held in a chuckle. She'd botched it the last time she'd stood in front of her hometown. Now, however, she was more prepared.

♦ ♦ ♦

Trent sat up front and tried not to fidget. He hated talking in front of a group. Even if he only had a few things to say and he knew everyone in the hall, he hated it.

He sought out Addy and was surprised to see her mother sitting next to her. The two women's heads inclined toward each other as they spoke and looked down at a paper.

For the first time, he realized how much they looked alike. He'd never thought that before, maybe because of how Victoria had acted, but now, something had changed in the woman.

When Addy looked up in his direction, he wiggled his eyebrows and glanced over at her mother. Addy gave him a thumbs-up just as the mayor called the meeting to order.

He sat and waited his turn to speak. When his brother stood up, the entire meeting hall grew silent.

Tyler read from the family's planned speech. Trent watched a few reactions around the room. Then he noticed Dennis Rodgers standing in the back corner with a few of his men.

The man had a smirk on his lips like there was some inside joke Tyler was missing.

A lot of reactions bubbled up when Tyler told the crowd their plans of building an education center. And when he informed them that they planned on releasing their father's drilling methods to the public, more outcries and questions came from the crowd.

Over a dozen hands rose when Tyler asked the group if they had any questions about their plans.

There were many questions about how the school would affect the population. Where would people live? What kind of money would this bring into the town? What did this mean for the drilling portion of the McGowan business?

Trent helped his brother answer most of them. There would be several buildings with dorm-like apartments for rent. The school would bring in big-oil employees from all over the world and offer certification programs, which would bring more money and business opportunities into Haven.

They tried to answer everything quickly, but the mayor broke in and mentioned that any further questions could be discussed after the meeting or in private.

"Sorry, people, we could be here all night if I don't stick to the schedule." She checked her agenda. "Next up is Addy Collins for FREE, Friends Respecting Everything Environmental. Addy, you have the floor."

Trent watched Addy stand up and move to the microphone and wondered what she was going to tell everyone. He could tell she was nervous, but she took a deep breath and relaxed slightly.

"I want to thank this board for hearing our concerns and thank the town of Haven for hosting our group for the past few months. In light of this wonderful news from McGowan Enterprises, our group will be departing Haven. We'd like to invite anyone concerned about their environment and the world we all live in to join FREE in our future endeavors." She took a breath. "Some of you may have heard that I will be staying on in Haven for a while." He watched her face flush slightly. He realized that he couldn't imagine life without her.

What would he have done if she'd decided not to stay in Haven? If she'd decided not to be with him? Things had changed so much in the past few weeks. How had he become so dependent on having her in his life?

"I want to thank every one of you for the kindness you've shown me in the past few months since I've returned home. I'm so honored to have been welcomed back so easily. If you'd like to find out more about FREE, I've placed packets at the rear table." She motioned toward the back where Dennis and his group stood.

Trent's eyes stayed on the group of men as Addy finished her speech.

When the meeting was adjourned, he and his brothers were bombarded with questions. Most of them from members of their own crew.

"We'll be holding a corporate meeting Tuesday to answer most of your questions," Tyler said loudly over the growing crowd. "But I believe I can put most of your main concerns to rest. This in no way changes your current employment with McGowan. We will be starting a new hiring process once construction is underway. For a list of those positions, come to the meeting on Tuesday evening."

It took Trent almost ten minutes to wiggle free of the crowd. He knew he left his brothers facing a firing squad of issues, but he just had to talk to Addy. He wanted to tell her how proud he was of her. How lucky he was that she'd decided to stay.

He slipped out the side door that opened to the dark parking lot and started making his way toward her Jeep.

A hard blow slammed the side of his head; his left ear rang as pain shot through his entire body. He easily dodged the next fist that plowed in his direction. But the one after that landed solidly across his temple.

Something crashed as he started falling toward the cement, and everything went black.

CHAPTER TWENTY-THREE

Addy said good-bye to her mother in the front hallway and walked outside toward her Jeep. By now, there were only half a dozen cars left in the parking lot. She heard a scuffle and turned just in time to see three silhouettes vanish around the corner of the building.

She gripped her keys with apprehension and quickened her pace when a door to the building opened and the light shone on a figure that remained huddled on the ground.

Fear shot through her as she recognized the dark blazer and sheer size of the man laid out on the cement.

She rushed toward him just as someone shouted from the doorway. "Help!"

They reached Trent at the same time, and Addy realized that it was Gail who knelt beside her. Addy's hands shook as she reached out and touched Trent's neck to feel for a pulse.

"He's alive," she cried out. "Someone call an ambulance." She glanced up quickly and saw Tyler and Trey running toward them.

Tyler sprang into action and applied pressure to Trent's head, stopping the flow of blood from a large gash just above his left ear.

"The ambulance is on its way," someone called out to them.

"Trent?" Gail cried out in a shaky voice. "Honey, open your eyes."

"Mom," Trey said with kindness. "Why don't you take Addy inside?"

"I'm not leaving him," Addy said.

Then Trey looked directly at her. "Take my mother inside."

Addy understood then and looked up at Gail. The woman's eyes rounded. Panic and shock had set in. She reached over and took Gail's blood-soaked hand with her own. "Let's stand back so the paramedics can get to work on him." She took several steps away from Trent as Tyler and Trey held him in place.

When the ambulance arrived, Addy and Trent's family were shuffled into a car and driven across town to the clinic.

They walked, shaken, into the brightly lit building. Tyler spoke to the man behind the desk, then turned around. "Okay, now it's a waiting game." He motioned to the chairs.

Trey, Kristen, and Trisha joined them and they all took seats. In strained tones they assured one another that he'd be okay.

How can they chat? Addy sat in silence as conversation continued. She wasn't even aware she still held Gail's hand until Gail reached over and patted the back of their hands. "Sweetie, he's going to be okay. It's not the first time he's had a bump on the head." Despite the lighthearted voice, Addy could hear her fear.

"There was so much blood," Addy said, exhausted, looking down at her still-covered hands.

"Why don't we go and wash up? I could use a cup of coffee." Gail pulled her up from the chair.

Addy followed the woman blindly into the washroom and scrubbed her hands clean. When she looked in the mirror, she realized that her shirt was covered with dry blood as well.

"Don't mess with that now," Gail said when she started to clean it. "We'll scrub that out later." She sighed and looked down at her own ruined shirt. "How about that drink?"

Addy nodded and followed her out. Then stopped and took the steaming cup Gail handed her.

"I . . . I don't drink coffee," she said.

Gail chuckled. "I know, honey, that's hot chocolate. Trent says it's your favorite."

Tears stung her eyes. Trent cared so much about her that he'd told his mother about her hot chocolate addiction.

"Oh now, don't start that just yet," Gail warned. "Not until we know how he's doing." She grabbed her own coffee from the vending machine and took Addy's arm to walk with her back to the waiting room.

"He's okay," Tyler said as they reached him. "The doctor just came out and said they're taking him back for scans, but he's awake and yelling to see us. I was just heading back there." Tyler turned to Addy and nodded. "I think he'd like to see you first."

Addy handed Gail her cup and followed a young nurse down the hallway. The nurse showed her to a small area where Trent sat up, his bloody shirt ripped wide open. There were several sensors taped to his chest and a pressure cuff on his arm.

When he looked up and saw her, he smiled. At that moment, she knew it was too late to deny the fact that she was in love with him. Had been in love with him for years. Gone was her worry about his past playboy nature. When she looked into his eyes, she knew that he was no longer that man. Instead, she only saw the honest, kindhearted, caring man he was now.

She rushed to his side and fell into his arms. She heard him groan and instantly jumped back.

"Easy," he said, then groaned again. "Damn it," he said. "They did a number on me."

"Are you okay?" she asked, scooting so she could sit beside him on the bed.

"They seem to think so." He grinned at her. "I knew I always had a hard head." He shifted and wrapped his arm around her. "I'm sorry I scared you."

She shook her head. "You'll have to apologize to your mother, who is waiting out there to make sure you're still alive."

He looked at the nurse. "Can she come back?"

"Only two folks at a time," the nurse said before disappearing down the hallway.

"Before she comes, I wanted to tell you . . ." He pulled her closer. Her heart jumped in her chest. "I'm so happy you decided to stay in Haven." She felt her heart kick into beat again.

"Me too." She looked over as Gail walked in.

"You idiot," Gail said, stopping next to him and wiping a tear from her eyes. "What did we teach you?"

Trent smiled. "To duck."

"Or run and grab your brothers. Never try to fight by yourself." She shook her head and laid a gentle finger over the stark-white bandage over his left temple.

"They didn't give me much of a choice this time."

"They?" Gail frowned.

"Three of them," Addy added. "I saw three men running away."

Trent nodded. "I can't be one hundred percent sure, but I'd wager anything that it was Dennis and his goons."

"Did you see them clearly?" Gail looked at Addy.

"No, it was too dark," she replied, squeezing Trent's hand.

Just then the nurse came back. "I need to take him in for a CT scan," she said.

"Don't worry about me," he said to his mother. "You always said I was hardheaded."

Gail chuckled and then sniffled.

When they stepped back out to the waiting room, Mike and another police officer were talking to Tyler and Trey. Gail filled them in on the new piece of information.

"Dennis and his gang?" Tyler asked his mother.

"That was Trent's thought, but we're not sure. Addy saw them a little better than Trent did."

Everyone turned to her, and she had to take a sip of her hot chocolate that Trey handed her. It was lukewarm, but the sugar gave her the spike she needed. She closed her eyes and tried to play back the image in her mind.

"It could have been. One of them was shorter, two were taller."

"How tall?" Tony asked.

"Six foot, six one?" she guessed. "They passed in front of the side door."

"How tall was the shorter one?"

"Maybe five eight?"

"Was there anything else about the trio you could tell us?" Mike asked.

She tried to think, but all she was getting was the fright of seeing Trent motionless on the cement.

"Addy," Trey said, getting her attention. "You'd just said good-bye to . . ."

"My mother," she supplied. "In the front hallway. We stopped off at the bathroom, then she told me . . ." She held in a sob. "That she was impressed with my speech. Estelle had left a few minutes before. I walked out front with my mother, then started for my Jeep in the side lot." She closed her eyes to retrieve the memory. "I heard a noise, someone grunt. I looked over and saw the three men cross in front of the side doors, then disappear around the back of the building. Two tall ones, a shorter one. They all had on dark pants, dark jackets." She shook her head and opened her eyes. "Now it seems like one was carrying something. Maybe a pipe or a baseball bat?"

Gail gasped but regained her composure.

"Go on. Anything else?"

"I was half a parking lot away. The most I can tell you is that two were tall, one shorter."

"What about hair color?"

"Dark," Addy said with certainty. "All three of them. But then again, they could have had hats or beanies on. It was evening already, so it was hard to see."

"It's a start," Mike said. "We'll have to talk to Trent when he's available." Mike turned to go, but then stopped just inside the door. "Do you think this could have been some disgruntled workers? I mean, with everything you had just revealed at the meeting, wouldn't some of your crew be out of work or changing job titles? A lot of people don't like change."

The room was silent as everyone thought about the possibilities. "We'll keep our ears and eyes open. You can see Trent after we do," Tyler said as he wrapped his arm around Gail. "He has to explain why he was dumb enough to allow three men to jump him in a dark parking lot."

◆ ◆ ◆

"I'm not a baby," Trent barked out, then instantly retracted it when his head spun. "Shit."

"I'll let that one slip." His mother smacked his fingers gently. "Now drink your soup."

"Yes ma'am," he said with his eyes still closed.

He was at home, thankfully, released a few hours after being hauled into the clinic.

His scans came back clean, even though he had a few stitches just above his left ear, and, according to the doctor, a knot on his head the size of a golf ball. Not that he was going to reach up and test the size for himself. He didn't want anyone touching his head until it stopped spinning.

"You know, you're lucky," Addy said next to him.

"Hmm?" He opened his eyes. The way he figured it, the less he spoke, the better he was.

"Lucky I came along when I did. I think I spooked them off." She glanced over to Trey and he watched a grin pass between them.

He would have glared at his brother if he didn't think it would cause his eyesight to blur.

"Oh?" he said.

"Yeah, so, um, I heard there was this thing between the McGowan brothers." Addy raised a brow.

Trent groaned and closed his eyes when he remembered the pact that he and his brothers had made when he'd been seven. They'd been snot-nosed boys with skinned knees back then, and none of them had ever believed they'd ever kiss a girl. *Ever.* Since they had cooties.

"First of us who has to be rescued by a chick gets to eat shit." Trey chuckled.

"What are you? Five?" Trent asked, keeping his eyes closed since it helped with the pain.

"Just saying." Trey laughed again.

"Thurston McGowan the Third, did I just hear you curse?" Gail said from across the room.

Trent started to chuckle but stopped when pain lanced his skull. "You did it now," he said.

"Sorry ma'am." Trey frowned.

"Thurston? Why do you go by Trey?" Addy asked.

"Because he's the third." Tyler laughed. "Not only the third son, but Thurston McGowan the Third: Trey."

Addy shook her head. "Really?" She smiled. "Thurston, huh?"

"Now that Dad's gone, will you go by Thurston?" Tyler asked.

"No," Trey said, his brow furrowing at Tyler's new joke.

"What's wrong with Thurston?" Gail said, setting a bowl of chicken soup in front of Trent. "It's a nice strong name." She pursed her lips. "Your father . . ."

"Always went by T. J.," Tyler finished. "At least with all of his close friends."

"Yes, but I never called him that." Gail smiled and sat across from Trent. "Have your second bowl before it gets cold."

When he was finished with the soup, his mother took the empty bowl. "Well, at least your appetite isn't gone," she said as she made her way into the kitchen.

"How come we didn't get any soup?" Trey called after her.

"You didn't get knocked around," she called back.

"The night is still young." Tyler smiled and flinched toward Trey, who sprang up, causing everyone to laugh.

"What?" Trey smirked. "Too scared to take me on tonight?" he said, taunting his oldest brother.

"Don't you dare," their mother said from the kitchen. "I'm not in the mood to sit in that waiting room one more time tonight."

"I think I'm going to go lie down." Trent started to get up, but Addy held him in place.

"What about me?" she whispered. "I am not leaving you alone tonight." She looked toward the kitchen where his mother stood, washing the dishes.

"Mom, Addy's going to stay with me for tonight," Trent called out. His mother turned and sighed, then nodded.

"Addy, I expect you to follow my rules."

She smiled. "Yes ma'am. I'm just worried about him."

"Let me know if something changes." His mother waved them away. "Go on, the lot of you. I need a shower and bed myself." She yawned.

Addy helped Trent down the hallway as the rest of his family left. When she shut the door behind her, she helped him sit on the edge of his bed.

He could have done everything himself, but he let her gently undress him until he sat on the bed in his boxers. When she nudged him to lie down, he pulled her with him.

"I still have my clothes on," she said.

"Not for long," he whispered into her hair.

"Trent, I promised your mother."

"What? That we wouldn't have sex under her roof?" Her hair brushed his face, the smell and feel of it enveloping him. "There are other things we can do besides having sex."

CHAPTER
TWENTY-FOUR

The next morning, Addy found it hard to look Gail in the eyes. She hadn't technically broken his mother's rule, but they had come very close. For his part, Trent acted entirely normally.

She tried to keep the thought out of her mind that he was able to act so nonchalant because there was a chance he'd broken his mother's rule long ago. Which caused her to once again second-guess being with him.

She'd been so scared seeing him hurt last night, she'd allowed herself to get twisted up with emotion. Sure, she knew she wanted to be with him, but she still didn't know for how long.

She watched him eat three helpings of his mother's blueberry pancakes and an entire bowl of scrambled eggs all by himself.

"You're in a good mood today, Trent," Trisha commented, looking in Addy's direction.

Addy quickly glanced away as she blushed.

"Why wouldn't I be?" Trent's smile grew. "It's moving day."

Addy stopped the fork from going to her mouth. "Um, but . . ." She blinked a few times. "Are you sure you're up to it?"

Trent chuckled and winked at her. "Perfectly. Nothing short of a flood is going to stop moving day."

"Be careful what you ask for." Gail sighed and shook her head.

"Trent, we can move anytime, after you've recovered more," Addy said, concerned about his health. He'd just been hurt, and now he was wanting to help her move her trailer to his land. And she could use a little more time to think.

Not to mention that she'd moved her trailer across the country several times all by herself in the past few years. Why did he think he had to help her today?

He shook his head and she noticed just a slight twinge. "Nope." Then he frowned. "Unless you've changed your mind?"

"No." It was her turn to shake her head. "Of course not." Where else was she going to go? She couldn't really afford to stay at the state park without a job.

"Good, then I guess you're moving today." He pushed his plate aside and finished off his coffee.

Addy quickly looked to Gail and Trisha for help, but both of them just shrugged and smiled at her.

"If you need any help . . ." Gail said.

"Mom, it's a trailer. Addy's been dragging it around the country for a few years now on her own. How hard could it be?"

Addy couldn't stop the smile when he repeated her own thoughts.

Two hours later, she held in a chuckle as Trent cursed again.

"You'd think that adding wiring to a Jeep would be easy," he said under his breath. "Almost done."

"You said that ten minutes ago," she teased as she handed him a screwdriver that he was trying to reach.

"Yeah, but now it's really almost . . ." He leaned up and twisted his arm again. "Done."

"I should have made sure the wiring was correct for my trailer when I bought it," she said.

He scooted out from under the Jeep. "I didn't even look at the connections. But it'll work now." He smiled. "Ready?"

She got up and dusted her jeans off. "Yes." But was she? He was excited that she was moving to his land, and he talked about moving into his house when it arrived, but there were still a lot of unspoken things between them.

Something I'll deal with later, Addy thought.

Trent drove the Jeep as they made their way through town and toward his property. On the way, they stopped off at the grocery store to buy more supplies.

She was pleased to see the new large windows in place. They had even removed the old sign that had been twisted and lying in a heap in the parking lot since the explosion.

When they entered, several people waved or said hello. A few stopped and asked how Trent was doing.

"Just a bump and a cut." He rubbed the small bandage covering his stitches. "I've had worse from Tyler and Trey," he joked.

She knew he was making light of it all and could tell that he was still hurting.

The foremost thought on everyone's mind was who had jumped him. Everyone had their own speculation, and it was almost eerie how many suggested the same names.

Walking through the grocery store with him was a new experience. She had to keep reminding him that her fridge was only ten cubic feet and that she only had two small cupboards for food—most of the stuff he was trying to buy wouldn't fit.

"It just means more runs to the store." He put a few things back. "Until the house gets placed, then I'll have a large freezer in the garage that you can store more stuff in."

She held her breath, not wanting to have that discussion yet. How long did he expect her to stick around? How long did she think she'd stick around? Things were still up in the air.

They turned a corner, and Addy stopped as she saw Darla piling a case of beer into her cart.

Addy's eyes went next to a large box of tampons in Darla's cart. Leaving Trent behind, she marched down the aisle and stopped short of her ex–best friend.

"So, congratulations." Addy crossed her arms.

Darla glared at her. "Congratulations for what?"

Addy reached in, picked up the box, and tossed it at Darla. "For pulling the wool over everyone's eyes for a few weeks." She stepped closer and smiled as Darla chucked the box back into her cart. "For pushing my father over the edge. Enough that he'd end his own life. Congratulations for taking the one person in my life that loved me unconditionally." She didn't know what caused her to move closer, but she was revved up. She was inches from Darla when Darla put her hands up and shoved, very hard. Addy fell back a step and almost tipped over a display of fruit.

Addy saw red. She didn't think—her body reacted. Her fist swung out, catching Darla on the chin. She'd kicked Darla's butt once before. This time, it was even more personal.

Darla flung her body at Addy, sending them both falling backward into the fruit. Limes and oranges rolled everywhere as the two of them twisted around, pulling, tugging, biting each other.

Addy had Darla on the ground, the woman's hair wrapped tightly around her fingers, when strong arms lifted her completely up. She had ripped Darla's shirt and a chunk of her hair remained in her fingers. Addy rejoiced when she noticed the blood coming from the liar's mouth.

"You're the reason my father killed himself," she screamed.

"You're crazy! Just like your old man," Darla cried. "She needs to be locked up." Darla looked around. "She hit me."

"You hit first," someone called out. "I saw everything."

"Tell them," Addy said, knowing that the fight was over since Trent had a good hold of her arms and one of the bag boys had helped Darla up but kept ahold of her arm. "Tell them you lied about my father." Something reminded her of the missing money she'd seen in her father's paperwork and how her last encounter with Darla, after she left the lawyer's office, had gone. "Tell them you blackmailed him for ten thousand dollars before he died."

Darla's eyes sparkled. "I didn't lie." She looked around. "I lost the baby." She even had the nerve to try and fake a sniffle.

Addy jerked against Trent, but he held her still. "Let it go. Someone called Mike already," he said into her ear.

She relaxed slightly. "Everyone in town knows what you are." More of her anger ebbed as she thought about that statement. "I don't know why I was ever friends with you."

Addy thought about what her mother was undergoing and how she could tell that she was at least trying. She doubted Darla would ever try to change, even if threatened with losing everything.

"I'm okay," she told Trent, who looked into her eyes and, seeing it for himself, let go of her. She moved forward slowly until she was less than a foot from Darla. The woman's large fake breasts were almost falling out of her ripped shirt, her hair was a rat's nest, and even her makeup was smeared.

"There will come a time"—Addy gritted her teeth—"when you'll need some help. Remember all the people you've burned, because I know we'll remember what you did to us. I feel sorry for you."

Darla laughed. "You? You feel sorry for me?" Her gaze ran up and down Addy as if she wasn't good enough to feel sorry for someone like Darla.

Addy nodded. "It must be very lonely where you're standing. It'll stay that way." She turned back to Trent. "I think we're done here." She took his hand and tugged until he followed her back to their shopping cart. Without looking back, she pushed the cart to the checkout and waited as Trent paid for everything.

"Are you okay?" he asked when they were outside.

"Yeah." She watched as a police cruiser parked beside her Jeep.

"Let me do the talking."

She unloaded the groceries into the trailer and took her time putting everything away as Mike and Trent talked outside. When she heard laughing, she stepped outside.

"It seems that most of your employees left the meeting last night and went out drinking together. Everyone is corroborating that, and so it's looking like our list of suspects has shortened to just a few."

Mike noticed her and a big smile broke out on his face. "Did you really pull her hair out?"

She rolled her eyes. "Men."

"I've already talked to a few people as they were leaving. It seems to me that she started the physical stuff. Do you want to press charges?"

"No." She shook her head and shut the trailer door. "She's not worth it."

"Are you sure you're okay?" Trent asked again.

"Yes. I just want to go." Addy watched as Darla walked out of the store. Her shirt still flapped open, but her hair had been fixed slightly. Of course that would be Darla's first choice. She marched straight over to Mike.

"Are you going to arrest her? I want to press charges."

Addy sighed and went toward the Jeep without acknowledging Darla.

Trent was there, opening the door for her. "Let's go home," he said.

She looked up at him and smiled. "Sounds wonderful."

♦ ♦ ♦

They drove in silence for a while but on the outskirts of town he spoke. "May I just say you're a badass?"

She looked over at him. "Why? Because I can beat up a stripper?"

"No, because you can beat up a woman almost double your size. You had her down on the ground in five seconds flat." He shook his head. "That was hot." He'd hoped to get a smile from her and enjoyed her laugh.

When she turned and looked out the window, he reached over and took her hand.

"You don't really think she was the reason your dad killed himself, do you?" he asked.

"I think she was one of the reasons. I know my mother would have been embarrassed enough about the display that she would have hounded him. Was it the final straw?" She shrugged. "I'm not sure. But as far as she needs to know, she's the reason."

It took him a few minutes to back the trailer into the spot just like he wanted it. Finally he unhooked the trailer and parked her Jeep next to his truck.

They spent a few minutes hooking up the electric, water, and drains, and stood back to admire their work.

He wrapped an arm around her shoulders. "Home sweet home." He leaned down to kiss her.

"Trent." She sighed. "I still may not know where I want to be in life." She gazed up at him. "But I'm happy I have you."

He leaned in for another kiss, wrapping his arms around her waist, just as they both heard the car starting up the driveway.

"Our first visitor." He smiled down at her, then kissed her deeply again until the car rounded the drive and came into view, followed by another two.

They stood there as first his mother parked, then his brothers. Trent wasn't surprised the entire McGowan clan showed up less than half an hour after they had pulled in.

His brothers delivered a large homemade picnic table, which they set up just under the awning of the trailer. His mother and Trisha had cooked plenty of fried chicken and potato salad for everyone. They sat in the warm sunlight and enjoyed the weather, good food, and company.

Trent told everyone about the run-in with Darla in the grocery store. At first everyone was concerned, but then laughter followed when Addy mentioned how she still had some of Darla's hair stuck in her bracelet.

"I've never been proud of my boys wrestling or fighting, but after the other night, I'm glad they can handle themselves." Gail turned to Addy, then to Kristen. "Maybe my boys can show you both enough to protect yourselves. At least show you enough if Darla comes around again."

"Tyler has been training me." Kristen smiled.

"Yeah, but we'll have to postpone the rest of your lessons until after Junior is born," Tyler added.

Trent's eyebrows shot up. "Do you know it's going to be a junior?"

"Not yet," Tyler admitted. "But one can hope."

Kristen patted his hand.

Watching them together, Trent was reminded how imminent their wedding was. He had been so occupied with getting his land ready, he'd put off planning for his brother's big event. He still had a week and a half left, which was plenty of time to make sure his mother's backyard was all set for the big event.

"When does the house arrive?" Trisha asked him.

"Well, about a week after we pour the foundation." Trent sighed. "If the weather holds, I'm hoping by the end of this month, we'll have a lot more room."

"We'll need a bigger place to hold all that food you eat," Addy joked, and everyone laughed.

CHAPTER
TWENTY-FIVE

It was hard to describe the next few days. Addy still didn't quite know what to make of it. Word had gotten out about her scuffle with Darla in the store. Apparently she wasn't the only one who blamed Darla's actions for her father's death.

And then the remaining group of protesters from FREE left Haven. Somehow, the town felt a little emptier after they were gone.

Next, Dennis and two other men were taken in for questioning. All three of them, however, were released when their alibis checked out. Mike had come out and given the McGowans the news about that directly.

Last, two days later, Darla was fired from her job at the Wet Spot. The owner of the establishment, a retired military pilot and local character by the name of Cam Everton, made a point to stop by the trailer to give Addy the news himself.

"I heard what happened." He shook his head and looked down at his hands. "I've lived in this town for the past ten years, and I know there's lots of talk about my establishment, but I try to run a clean place. When one of my girls does something like that . . ." The older man sighed and shook his head again. "It just isn't right. I knew your father." Addy's eyebrows shot up and Cam stuttered through a quick explanation. "Not that he came in my place for . . . he liked the food."

Addy laughed. "Cam, I get it. This town owes a lot to the kind of places you run. It gives the workers something to do and keeps them entertained. Not to mention"—she laid a hand on his arm—"you do have great steaks."

His smile flashed. "The best in the state."

"Thank you for coming all the way out here and telling me the news directly," she added.

"It was no big deal. I'd been meaning to stop by after I heard your father passed. He really was a good man. We don't see too many of them coming in anymore. Not since . . ." He looked over to where Trent was chopping wood across the field. "Well, anyway. I'll let you get back to your work."

"Thank you again for letting me know."

"No problem." He turned to go. "Oh, I forgot to mention this, but I know there was some question as to how your Jeep fire started. I talked to Mike the week after, he asked about the brand of cigarettes that Darla smoked."

"Yes?" Addy's heart skipped.

"Well, she doesn't smoke Gold Crest, but I do. I was questioned and all, but I didn't think to mention that all my girls know that if they run out of smokes, they're free to take one of mine if they leave me some change." Cam looked over toward her new Jeep. "That day, I had three cigarettes that someone paid for."

"Was Darla working that day?" she asked.

"Yeah, Mike asked me that too. She started at eleven and worked until nine that night."

"Did she ever leave during the day?"

"She would leave all the time. Smoke breaks, trips to the grocery store for supplies for the kitchen." He shrugged. "Who's to say if she did any of that on that day? I wasn't tracking her too close."

"Thank you, Cam," Addy said, walking him to his truck. "I appreciate you letting me know."

She watched him get behind the wheel and drive away.

"Everything okay?" Trent asked, wiping a bead of sweat from his brow with a handkerchief, then tucking it into his back pocket.

"Yeah," she sighed as she turned to him. "Cam just wanted to let me know that he fired Darla."

"Oh?" he asked, moving closer.

"Apparently he didn't like the way she'd handled the entire situation with my father."

"He blames her?"

Addy nodded. "Looks like the entire town does." She wrapped her arms around his waist and held on. "You're all sweaty."

"Yeah, I was thinking about a shower, then remembered I have a bunch of stuff being delivered over at my mother's house for the wedding this weekend."

"Oh?" She moved closer. "Can I come watch you put it all together?"

"I was hoping you would. We were going to grill out. Tyler had a few steaks he was going to throw on the fire."

"Sounds perfect."

"You're deep in thought," Trent said as he pulled into his mother's driveway.

On the drive over, Addy's mind had drifted to her own mother. She was showing signs of improvement. She'd already spent a day at the library and a day at the animal clinic.

The vet had called Addy the following day to mention that her mother was a natural around the animals. She had been particularly taken with an older Pekinese dog who had been abandoned by its owners on the side of the road.

She couldn't imagine her mother being a dog person; she had never allowed any pets in her house. But that was why it was on the list—animals brightened lives. Especially since her mother had that big house all to herself now. Maybe Addy would stop by the clinic later that week and see how much the dog was, perhaps as a peace offering to her mother.

Addy glanced over at Trent. "Are you a dog person?" she asked.

His eyebrows shot up. "Yes, why do you ask?"

She shook her head. "No reason. The vet told me that my mom took a liking to a Pekinese."

Trent made a funny face at her.

"What?" she asked, shifting in her seat to get a better look at him.

"That's not a dog. That's a rat in a dog's fur."

Addy laughed. "What, pray tell me, makes a dog a dog in your book?"

He shrugged. "I don't know, something bigger than a football."

She laughed and shook her head at him. "What about cats? Do you like those?"

He nodded. "Yeah, when I build a barn, I'll have a few to keep the mice away."

She cringed. "Okay, yeah, good plan."

"How are you around horses and cows?" he asked, running a hand down her braid.

"Hmm. I've never been around horses or cows."

"Never?"

She shook her head. "Nope."

"Come with me." He tugged her out of the truck and led her down a pathway around the house to a large barn near the back of the property.

As they made their way toward the barn, Trent let out a low whistle. Suddenly two horses stepped out of large doorways on the side of the building and made their way over.

"That is Hank, my father's horse." He pointed to the larger tan horse. "The other one is Grace, my mom's mare." Grace was a silver beauty. Her mane looked like it had been brushed until the hair crackled.

They stopped at a padlocked area. Trent put his booted foot up on the rung and reached out to pet Hank between the eyes.

The horse looked like a big dog, lapping up the attention.

"Go ahead, she won't bite." He nodded to Grace. "Let her sniff you first." He took Addy's hand and held it out for the horse.

Grace sniffed her fingers with her soft nose, then nudged her hand as if to say, *Go ahead, get to work and start petting me.*

Addy laughed when the horse actually leaned into her hand.

"She's beautiful." She wrapped her arms around the horse's head and held on.

"I think she likes you."

"Grace likes everyone," Gail said with a laugh from behind them. "I was just about to go out, would you care to join me?" she asked Addy. "I have some boots that will fit you."

"Go." Trent nudged her. "Mom will ride Hank, you can have Grace."

"I . . . sure," she said, smiling.

"Well, I'm heading up to take a look." Trent gestured to the house. "Looks like they delivered everything already."

"Early this morning." Gail smiled. "It's all ready for you boys to plant. I called Tyler and Trey when I saw you drive up."

Trent kissed Addy quickly. "Have fun."

"You too," she called after him.

◆　◆　◆

Trent and his brothers would have preferred going on a nice, easy horse ride than rearranging their mother's backyard.

There were more than a dozen large bushes to yank out and transplant along the edge of the yard, plus they had to level the ground and lay new sod in the middle of the yard where the wedding would be held. Over a dozen wisteria trees had to be planted near the edge of the yard, where the men moved the homemade archway their father had built years ago. They set the largest trees on either side, so the fresh blooms would hang down through the archway.

When Trent stood back a few hours later, he looked around with pride. The entire area was circled with white and purple blooms.

Tyler had purchased recycled rubber pavers that they laid from the back steps of the house down to where the aisle runner would take over.

"The chairs and tables are going to be delivered Friday night," Tyler said. "We can set the chairs up in rows. There should be about a hundred and fifty."

"What about the tables?" Trey asked, trying to focus. But something had him looking around. Trisha had started the steaks and the wonderful smell was driving them all crazy. The three of them were sweaty and muddy and starving.

"How about putting them in the side yard?" Trent said, walking with them over to the area where they had grown up playing football. "We have a little sod left, we can fill in the spots." He stopped and looked. "Move a bush or two . . . The sun sets on this side, so there should be a beautiful view of the fields in the evening while everyone's eating. Plus it's closer to the steps for the caterers to deliver the meals."

"We can hang up some of those lights," Trey said. "In the trees." He nodded to the row of fir trees. "Those ones that look like Christmas lights."

"Outdoor string lights." Tyler smiled and slapped Trey on the back. "Good thinking. I can pick up a few strings of them tomorrow."

"Any word on how the investigation is going?" Trey looked to Trent. "I mean, *someone* knows something about you being attacked."

"It's funny. More than half the town thinks it was Dennis and his goons, yet we can't get anyone to corroborate where he was at the time. Except, of course, his goons themselves."

"The police have talked to him a few times now and still nothing," Tyler pointed out.

"I know, Mike filled me in. Since they don't have any proof . . ." Trent let out a deep sigh. "They can't get anywhere."

"What about his trial for kidnapping?" Trey questioned.

Tyler ran his hands through his hair. "Stalled since all the paperwork went up. We've given them everything we have, but . . ."

"Dinner's ready," Trisha called out.

Trent turned in time to see his mother and Addy walking up the trail from the barn. The women were smiling, and he knew that Addy had enjoyed herself.

They all gathered on the deck and ate dinner, discussing the wedding plans, as the sun set. As the light dimmed, they glanced over to the side yard and determined the lighting would make for a perfect addition.

"Cam stopped by before we came over," Trent said as he sipped a beer.

"Cam?" Trisha asked.

"He owns the Wet Spot," his mother said. "Nice man, retired air force pilot." She turned back to him. "What did he want?"

"He fired Darla," Addy said.

"Good for him," Trisha added.

"Mom," Kristen moaned.

"Cam told me that"—Addy looked in Trent's direction—"there was a chance that Darla started my Jeep fire."

Trent tensed. "Why didn't you tell me that?"

"Because I wanted to tell you when your mother was present so she could convince you not to go down there and do something stupid."

"Smart woman," Trisha said under her breath.

"Do you think she started the fire?" Kristen asked.

"I wouldn't put it past her. She probably just wanted to mess up the inside of the Jeep. I doubt she even knew I had propane tanks in the back," Addy said.

"Is there any way Cam would know for sure?" Trent asked.

"No. He said he leaves his smokes where the girls can grab them, leaving change for each cigarette. It could have been anyone who knew where he kept them," Addy answered.

"Back to square one," Trey chimed in. "It's just strange, two fires in Haven in under a month. They have to either be connected or the second was inspired by the first."

"What do you mean?" Kristen asked.

"Well, I spoke to the fire inspector, a nice older guy by the name of Kevin," Trey continued. "He said that when there are two or more fires so close together, you either have one arsonist or a copycat. Someone who was inspired to start a fire because of the first one."

"That could be anybody," Tyler said.

"Yeah, anyone with a grudge against Addy," Trent added.

"That list should be very short," Kristen said, cocking an eyebrow at Addy.

"One," Addy sighed. "Just one."

CHAPTER TWENTY-SIX

"How do we prove that Darla set my Jeep on fire?" Addy asked Trent as they lay in bed that night.

"I'm not sure yet, but we'll come up with something," he said. His arm was wrapped around her shoulders, and she snuggled against his bare chest.

"Too bad there aren't any cameras outside of the grocery store." She yawned.

He was silent for a while, thinking—mentally tracking the path Darla would have taken from the Wet Spot to the grocery store more than two blocks away.

"Maybe Granger's Market has cameras?" he said absently. "I have to make a run there tomorrow. I can check with them."

She nodded and wrapped her leg around his. He closed his eyes, enjoying the feeling of her curled up against him.

"Did you enjoy the ride with my mother today?" he asked.

"Yes, I found out that I love horses. I just wish I could have one."

He could tell she was on the verge of sleep. "Why can't you?" he asked.

"Can't," she said, her voice slurred. "Won't fit in my trailer."

He held in a chuckle and decided to let her sleep as his mind ran over every step between the strip club and the grocery store.

First thing the next morning Trent walked the same path. Stopping at every business along the way, he even poked his head into one of the other local strip clubs and asked about cameras. They had cameras inside and at the back door but nothing out front. Since he was there, he asked to see the footage from the back door, just in case Darla had walked down the alley instead of the main street.

Trent made it all the way to the grocery store without any luck. Granger's had a video of the front, but the manager told him that they recorded over each tape the next day when there weren't any issues. Still, he was going to check with the owner to make sure the owner didn't switch tapes out. The guy would let Trent know when he found out.

As he went along, the buzz in town continued to be his brother's wedding. Everyone asked him about it, told him how excited they were to join in the festivities. And some even hinted at how he'd be next.

He laughed that thought off, but deep down, he questioned it. Why not marry? His mind kept nudging him at the thought. It wasn't as if he wanted someone other than Addy. She was it for him. Of that he was 100 percent positive. So what was the holdup?

His mind thought about the new plans for McGowan. About how in less than a month they would be breaking ground for the Thurston McGowan Flathead Drilling Training Center.

Just thinking about it had his excitement building. He hadn't yet talked with Addy further about her role in all that. He was hoping that her agreeing to stick around was her way of telling him she wanted to be a part of it.

He made his run to Granger's, loading up the extra sod and a few more bushes that he planned to plant around his own land. Since Addy mentioned that she liked the wisteria trees, he got a few of them to plant around the trailer.

Just as he was coming out with a full cart, he noticed Dennis walking in. The man had a look on his face like he owned the town.

"Heard you had some bad luck the other night," Dennis said.

Trent decided to keep going, but then Dennis stuck a boot out and stopped his cart from rolling.

"You still haven't learned, boy, to keep that nose where it belongs," Dennis said.

Trent felt his temper rise, though he realized that if he started something, it would be him sitting in the jail cell instead of Dennis. So he pulled the cart free and continued walking instead.

"I knew you McGowans were always pussies," the man called after him.

It took all Trent's willpower to suck up the anger and just load up his truck. Still, as he drove back home, the anger boiled under the surface, ready to burst free.

That was until he saw the small black blob sitting at Addy's feet outside of the trailer. Her grin nearly reached her ears as the tiny puppy wiggled to get free from her hold. Addy's fingers were tight on the end of the leash, but the puppy was tugging against the restraints.

"What's this?" Trent asked, shutting the truck door and going directly to her.

"A gift," she said, letting go of the leash. The black dot rushed to him. He knelt down to rub the tiny dog's head, and the puppy proceeded to pee on his boot.

"For me?" She nodded and he stood. "It's not one of those small portable dogs, is it?"

She shook her head. "No, he's only two months old and, as I quickly found out, not house-trained yet."

He picked the dog up and walked toward her as the dog tried to lick his chin.

"What's his name?" he asked, sitting down next to her.

"I don't know, you haven't named him yet." Addy laughed, reaching over and gently tugging on the puppy's ears.

"Wow," he said, thinking about it. "How about Happy?"

"Sure. He's yours to name."

"Why?" Trent leaned away and looked at her. "Why did you get him for me?"

"He's not the only gift I got today. I stopped by the animal clinic to check in on that little Pekinese dog that my mother liked."

"And?"

"Ralphie was very happy to see my mother when I dropped him off at her place."

"How did your mother take it?"

"She was in love." She smiled. "For the first time in my life, I watched tears come into her eyes." Addy shook her head as her smile fell away slightly. "Funny. I never thought I could crack that shell of hers. Even when Dad died, she didn't shed a tear."

"Some people hide their emotions very well."

"Yeah, I suppose. But today I could tell that she was genuinely happy." Addy reached over and took the puppy from him, gave it a huge hug, then set it down so it could run around at their feet.

"Maybe that was just what she needed," Trent said.

"What about you?" Addy asked. "What do you need?"

He smiled quickly. "You." Her eyebrows shot up.

"And?"

"Is there anything more?" He drew her closer. "What do you need?"

She shook her head and sighed. "I still don't know."

He felt something close to fear close his throat. "Until you do, you don't plan on going anywhere, do you?"

She shook her head again, causing the breath he'd been holding to release. "No, there isn't any place else for me."

"You make that sound like it's a bad thing. Don't you like it here with me?" he added after a very short pause.

"Yes, I do. But I just don't know how long . . . things will last."

"If I had my way, they'd stay like this forever," he said, feeling a sudden need to convince her.

She nodded and leaned against his chest. "Did you find anything out today?"

He allowed her to change the subject given the sudden tightness in his chest.

"No." He stood up. "But you're not the only one who can give gifts. Come with me."

His new dog, Happy, followed him to the truck and sat down with a small plop as Trent pulled out the first tree.

"For you." He watched her expression turn from sad to happy.

"Oh, they're beautiful," she said, moving around to see the rest of what he had in the bed of the truck. "Where are you going to put them?"

"We are going to decide that together," he said, reaching in and handing her a shovel.

◆　◆　◆

Addy stood back and dusted off her hands. *Two can play this game,* she thought as she looked at the pot of flowers she'd just organized. Two massive silver pots stuffed with blooms sat on either end of their picnic table. When Trent came home from work, she had a few other surprises in store for him too.

She'd gone shopping at one of the small boutiques in town. Nothing fancy, but she'd found the prettiest dress for Kristen and Tyler's wedding and had splurged to buy a new pair of heels.

Since the wedding was less than two days away, no one in town had anything to chat about other than who would attend, what they would be wearing, and who would be with who. Even gossip about the recent fires and Kristen's kidnapping fell to the sidelines. Addy had been thankful that everyone had found something more positive to talk about.

She pulled out the water hose that Trent had purchased and wrapped up next to the spout and rinsed off the remaining dirt around the flower pots.

She stood back and smiled, then turned around when the sun peeked out from behind a cloud. Her breath caught in her chest at the beauty. The spot Trent had picked was slightly up on the side of a small hill so that they overlooked the same green fields his mother's place did, just at a different angle. Thick trees covered the hillsides surrounding the opening. There was a small creek that ran directly through the grassy land. The view of the mountains was something everyone who lived in Montana would never get tired of, including her.

She could see the old red barn that held the horses, and if she wanted, it would be a short walk over to say hello to Grace and Hank. Glancing down at her watch she decided, with her few remaining free hours, to take the short walk. Grabbing a light jacket, she locked up and started across the sun-drenched field.

Trent had taken Happy with him to work that day, saying he wanted the dog to get used to going everywhere with him. He'd gone out and bought him a dog bed, forty pounds of puppy food, bowls for food and water, and toys. Tons and tons of toys. Now everywhere she stepped in the trailer, something squeaked under her feet.

Still, she didn't complain. Especially after Happy crawled next to her and cuddled as she slept. She knew the dog was small now, but the vet had told her that he would end up being around sixty pounds. She just hoped the dog could wait until Trent's house got there to do most of the growing.

The smell of fresh grass under her feet mingled with the scent of Douglas fir. She'd forgotten how much she loved spring in Montana.

How large everything looked, how wonderful it felt to know the place you were in, the people around you.

Her mother had told her that since she was living out there all alone now, she had purchased a new cell phone. She had even texted Addy a few pictures of Ralphie with some new toys. The dog looked so happy and so did her mother.

Addy made it to the back gate and easily climbed over the fence. She had taken about a dozen steps when the two horses came running around the barn and headed straight for her.

Her first instinct was to run back the way she'd come, but then she realized that they were rushing to her because they were excited to see her. Just like big dogs.

She laughed as they came closer, both of them making plenty of noise. Hank had a huskier neigh, while Grace's was higher pitched.

They didn't slow down until they were a few feet from her, then both of them halted like someone had pulled on their invisible reins. They walked directly up to her and started rubbing themselves against her, almost causing her to fall over.

"Well, hello to both of you too." She laughed and stood in the field, enjoying them both.

"I wondered what they were up to—they were making so much noise to get out of their stalls," Trisha called out. "They must have heard you coming."

She'd been so busy with the horses, she hadn't seen Trisha approach from the barn.

Addy waved to the woman. "Yeah, I was pretty loud getting over that fence." She nodded back to the gate area.

"No one can get past Hank, he has hearing like a bat," Trisha said as she stopped directly next to the horse.

"I thought I'd come over and see these two. I'm trying to get used to being around horses."

Trisha cocked her head. "Gail told me that she took you riding for the first time. If you ever want to go, just come on over. I can show you how to saddle them up and cool them off if you want."

"That would be great. I don't think I'm ready for solo riding yet, but . . ."

"No problem." Trisha smiled. "Gail or I am always around. We always have time to take these two out."

Addy sighed and leaned against Grace. "She's such a sweetie." She chuckled when Grace nibbled on her shirt.

"I heard you got Trent a puppy?"

Addy laughed. "Yes, Happy. It's the dog's name," she added when Trisha looked at her in question.

"What breed?"

"Full-blood mutt. Dr. Shultz, the vet, says he'll grow to about sixty pounds."

Trisha and Addy started to walk back to the barn. Both horses fell into step and followed them. "He seems like a nice man."

"Yeah, I never really knew him, or a lot of others in town. My mother didn't like animals. At least, she didn't while I was growing up."

"Oh?" Trisha asked.

Addy stopped walking and instantly had Grace snuggling into her shoulder again.

"You may have heard the rumors." She sighed. "My mother was very abusive to my father and me. Now, however, I can tell she's trying."

"I heard." Trisha nodded. "How does that make you feel?"

Addy didn't know why she felt compelled to open up to the woman. Maybe it was the kind look in her blue eyes. Or maybe it was the fact that Grace was letting her lean on her and showing Addy unconditional love, which made her feel so safe that something shifted inside her.

Either way, Addy swelled with a string of feelings that she hadn't even really owned up to before, let alone wanted to say out loud to anyone.

She leaned against the gentle horse as tears streamed down her cheeks and told Trisha everything her mother had done to her in the past. How she felt about it and why she struggled with feeling secure in her relationship with Trent. Trisha stood there, listening to everything Addy said with kindness in her eyes.

When Addy felt her chest tighten and felt like she was out of breath, she stopped.

Trisha looked at her closely. "Don't close your mind to the possibilities around here because of your family. From the sounds of it, you have your mother on the right path to being a better person. You deserve happiness, despite how the woman raised you."

They both glanced over to the house. Sometime during their talk, the sun had sunk below the hills. Several lights had been turned on in the house, lighting the place up, making it look even more glorious. "This is a great place to heal, and a great family who love unconditionally." Trisha placed her hand over Addy's. "Come around anytime you like. Opening up is sometimes the best medicine for healing." She leaned in and placed a soft kiss on Addy's cheek. "I'm happy your mother is learning to love from such a wonderful young woman."

Addy thought about the conversation as she walked back to her trailer.

The floodlight Trent had installed a few nights ago acted as a beacon, directing her to their little home.

CHAPTER
TWENTY-SEVEN

The day before Tyler and Kristen's wedding came and Gail's house was a flurry of activity. For Trent's part, he was running around trying to help set up all the large round tables on the side yard while his brothers hung up the string lights Tyler had purchased. Addy and Kristen were in the house, helping Trisha and his mother get things ready for guests.

The work continued until late in the afternoon. They had taken a longer time than planned setting up a small dance floor since they had to rearrange the tables to make room. But the finished product looked amazing. Tyler flipped on the lights, and Trent could tell with the cream-colored tablecloths and dark rose centerpieces in place tomorrow, the atmosphere was going to be perfect. His mother and the ladies came out to survey the work.

"What about a bachelor party?" Trent asked, toasting with his beer.

"I don't need one." Tyler smiled and hugged Kristen to him. "It's not like I'm going to miss those days at all."

Kristen chuckled. "Right. The days of the oldest McGowan sweeping women off their feet are over."

"The only woman I want to sweep off her feet is you. Of course, it will probably be because you have those stupid fur boots on and there's a foot of snow on the ground," Tyler joked, causing Kristen to smack his shoulder playfully.

"You like my shoes," Kristen said in reply.

"Sure, when that's all you're wearing." Tyler kissed her.

"TMI," Trisha laughed. "TMI."

"I think Happy needs a friend," Gail piped in.

"Oh?" Addy glanced down at the small dog lying at their feet.

Happy had tagged along with Trent all day without any issues. The little dog loved riding in his truck on errands, loved playing in Gail's backyard, and had even had some quality time with Hank.

At one point Trent had lost track of the puppy and had found him over near the barn, sniffing around Hank. He had stood back and watched as the old horse actually played with the puppy for almost ten minutes straight.

"Yes, I've been thinking of getting another dog. It's been years since Sneezy passed away," his mother said.

Addy sat up at that. "Wait a minute. *Sneezy?*"

"What?" Trent said, smiling.

"The seven dwarfs?" she said. "You name your dogs after *Snow White?*"

He looked over at his mother. "It was her idea."

"We've had a Grumpy and a Sneezy. Good dogs, both of them." She nodded down to the black blob currently snoring at his feet. "Each name fit perfectly, as does Happy with this little guy."

"Should have named him Sleepy," Trey said, chuckling. "Or Snorey."

Everyone laughed.

"What?" Trey asked.

"There was no Snorey," Trent supplied.

Trey shrugged. "How would I remember? I was five when I watched *Snow White* last." He leaned back and crossed his arms.

"He still has a few brothers and sisters at the clinic," Addy said to Trent. "Someone dropped them off after finding them in a box in an alley. I can check with Dr. Shultz Monday, if you want."

"Let us know too," Tyler said, glancing over at Kristen. "We were talking about it earlier today. Of course, it will have to keep until we get back from our honeymoon."

"How many brothers and sisters?" Trey asked.

Addy looked over at him. "Six total."

"Hell, might as well sign me up too." He shrugged. "That way we can keep the family together."

His mother chuckled. "We're just a bunch of softies." She reached down and picked Happy up. The small dog stretched, did a circle in her lap, and then fell back asleep.

"Told you. Should have named him Sleepy," Trey said.

"You can name yours Sleepy. This one already has a name, and it fits him just fine," Gail said.

An hour later Addy and Trent left his family and started walking back to their site. Trent carried the still-sleeping Happy home as Addy walked beside him.

"You're quiet." She'd withdrawn as the evening went on, he noticed.

"Just deep in thought," she said.

"About?" He reached over and opened the gate in the middle of the field separating his land from his mother's and let Addy step through, then latched it again.

"How different your family is from mine." She sighed.

He reached over and took her hand after shifting Happy slightly so he could have a free one.

"From the sounds of it, your mother is making an effort."

"She is," she said. "And I hope she will continue to make changes, but some part of me still can't let go of the hurt. Part of me will never really trust her."

He squeezed her hand to stop their momentum. They were standing in the middle of his land, the full moon hovering above them, as his small warm dog snored softly in his arms. He'd never felt more complete than at that moment.

He knew that Addy was still struggling with making a decision about her life, but he hoped that over the next few months, he'd show her that she was where she belonged. Here, with him and Happy. In marriage or not, so long as they were together.

"I hope you trust me now," he said, scanning those blue eyes of hers. Even in the darkness, he could see the change when her eyes softened as she looked at him.

"Yes." She smiled. "There was a time in my life I didn't think I could ever trust you either. I think it never really had anything to do with you but with my mother instead."

He drew her close, Happy tucked between them. "Sometimes time heals wounds, other times, people change. Just like this." He leaned in and covered her lips with his. "I never thought I could be here, like this, with you. Now I can't imagine ever not being like this." He sighed when he felt her stiffen slightly. "Please don't overthink things tonight. Just know that I never thought I could be this happy. Never."

After a moment, she nodded, then intertwined her fingers with his and started walking again. "I invited my mother to the wedding tomorrow," she said when they reached the trailer. "I hope that was okay."

Trent nodded and smiled as he laid the small dog down in his new bed, even though they both knew Happy would end up on their bed by morning. "Yes, I think Kristen and Tyler wouldn't mind." He rose and took her in his arms. "Now," he said as he started kissing her, "tell me again about that sexy dress you bought for tomorrow." He nibbled down the column of her neck.

"I thought you were too tired?" She slowly rubbed her hips against his, sending a wave of heat traveling through his entire body.

"I'm never too tired for you," he said before his lips took hers again.

He could have spent all night enjoying the feel of her lips against his, her body rubbing slowly along his length.

But soon Addy pushed him back onto the bed, and he helped her remove his boots.

After she tossed first one boot toward the front door then the other, she stood at the end of the bed and slowly removed her own clothes. She inched up her shirt, then tossed it down. His eyes tracked her every movement as she tugged down her pants, then stepped out of them while she watched his expression with equal intensity.

"You're so beautiful." His voice sounded scratchy as he felt the air lock in his throat.

Her fingers walked up his legs, then worked on his jean clasp. He let her tug his pants down his hips and off his legs. Her expression turned greedy, seeing him ready for her.

He couldn't stop the gasp when she wrapped her fingers around him, then followed with her lips. A groan escaped as she moved her mouth on him. His fingers dug into her hair as he threw his head back and concentrated on what she was doing to him.

"My god!" he moaned, his hips moving with her motion.

He'd been holding in his feelings for her, afraid of scaring her off. It was too soon to tell her that he wanted her here, with him, for the rest of their lives. Especially when he knew that she hadn't even decided what she wanted to do.

But as she climbed higher and his hands instantly went to her hips, he looked up at her and knew that he didn't want to hold in his feelings anymore. Not now, not when there was a chance it could help her decide to stay with him.

He rolled, sending her sprawling on the bed, gazing up at him. He quickly pulled on a condom before her legs wrapped around his hips, holding on to him. Skin to skin, he slid into her and let those feelings flow out.

◆　◆　◆

Addy lay there, trying to catch her breath. Her ears rang, her head floated a mile up in the clouds, and her body was vibrating from the aftershock that was Trent McGowan.

His heavy body was still pinning her to the mattress, but her arms and legs had long since released his body. His lips still nuzzled against the spot below her left ear, sending goosebumps traveling down her arm every time he let out a breath.

When her mind finally cleared from the fog, she remembered his words. Everything he'd told her with every pump of his hips.

Addy, I've been so in love with you. I can't imagine my life without you. I want you so bad, to be here with me like this forever.

She felt her mind snap into gear as her body settled. When he moved, he took her with him until she was cupped in front of him, his arms wrapped around her.

"Did you mean all that?" she asked, breaking the silence.

"Yes." She felt him kiss her neck. "I'm sorry if it scares you, but . . ." He sighed. "I couldn't hold it in any longer. I've been wanting to tell you for a while."

"What's a while?" she asked.

He howled with laughter, shaking the bed and her along with it. "The day you drove back into town."

She squirmed around to meet his eyes. "You couldn't have known all that when I first got back."

"Sure I could." His fingers tangled in her hair. "Part of me knew all that before you left."

She shook her head. "I don't . . ."

"Believe me?" He kissed her. "Believe me. I've told you the reason I never hit on you. It was all true. You were the one that got away. The one I would have always wished, dreamed, that I'd asked out." He shook his head. "I was stupid back then."

"You couldn't have felt that way about me. You didn't even really know me."

"I knew enough. I knew you were one of the kindest, most sincere people I'd ever met. I remember once in grade school, when a bird had flown into the window, you jumped in to stop Brian and his friends from tossing it around. Then you carried it in your shirt into the school nurse. You spent almost a month nursing it back to health before letting it go."

"You remember that?" She sat up slightly and looked down at him. Even *she'd* forgotten about Mr. Thomas, the name she'd given the hurt bird. "I didn't release him," she admitted. "I only told people I did. Mr. Thomas died a few days later."

"I'm sorry," he said simply. "See, even now there is sadness behind those blue eyes for a bird that died years ago."

She shook her head. "I thought I had you pegged." She took him in—*her* man. His hair had grown out again. Reaching up, she brushed it away from his eyes. "You need another haircut."

He laughed. "So?" he challenged, taking her hand and stilling it.

"So?" She sighed.

"Addy, are you going to leave me hanging here?"

She gazed deep into those hazel-brown eyes that filled her waking and dreaming life now. "Trent McGowan, if you're trying to get me to say that I love you back . . ."

His quick smile and the flash of that sexy dimple was her answer. She caved.

"I've been in love with you since first grade. When I saw you in your gym shorts and no T-shirt playing basketball with your brothers on the playground." She leaned in and kissed him. "But as an adult, I believe I really started loving you the moment you kissed me, the moment you made me yours."

He brought her against him, tight; their limbs tangled as their lips fused.

"Stay with me?" he asked between kisses as he claimed her again. "Move in with me, build a home, have dogs, horses, and kids with me."

"Yes," she said, tears sliding down her cheeks. "Yes to all of it."

He stopped suddenly, looking at her. "Yes? As in . . ."

"Trent McGowan, you are not going to spoil this." She used her legs around his hips to get him back down to her. "I'll expect a proper proposal . . . later." She yanked on his hair and had his lips back where she wanted them, against hers.

CHAPTER
TWENTY-EIGHT

Trent stood, in his monkey suit, in front of a crowd of about a hundred and fifty people. He wanted to reach up and remove the bow tie, but he knew his mother was watching him closely. His eyes scanned the front row and sure enough, her eyes narrowed as she looked at him. As a reply, he gave her a big smile, and in return she nodded her head slightly.

He scanned a few seats over, and suddenly it wasn't the material around his neck that was tight.

Addy looked . . . amazing, damn hot, sexy as hell, and totally his.

He didn't think even Kristen in her wedding dress matched Addy's beauty today.

The blue dress she'd chosen matched her eyes perfectly. A deep slit traveled down her chest, exposing the sexy valley between her breasts. The sleeves were slight, barely passing her shoulders. Her kitten heels added a few inches to her height and caused her hips to sway when she walked.

Some of her long dark-amber hair flowed in tight little ringlets over her shoulders, while some of it was piled up on top of her head. Silver earrings bobbed from her ears as she talked. She even wore a matching necklace that lay directly against the spot he loved to kiss.

He almost missed the main-event kiss with that thought, but Addy pointed and he turned in time to see his brother kiss his new wife.

For the next hour, they talked to almost everyone who had come to the wedding—everyone Tyler and Kristen had invited, as well as Addy's mother. The woman actually had a smile on her face and was laughing at what the person sitting next to her had said.

"Looks like she's having fun." Trent nodded to where Victoria was.

Addy's eyes traveled to the spot. "Yes, that's Dr. Shultz. They seem to be getting along very well."

He turned her toward him. "Does that bother you?" He had heard the sadness in her voice.

"Some." She took a deep breath. "But I know that no matter what my father did, they weren't right for each other."

"Who knows," he said, glancing over her head again at the pair. "Maybe they're just talking about her new dog."

"Ralphie," she supplied.

He shook his head. "Did she name it? Or did it come with that particular attachment?"

"She named him." Addy smiled. "Why? Don't you think it's as unique as Happy?" Her eyebrows shot up, then she turned on her heels and walked toward their table.

"Hey, you let me name him," he said after he'd pulled out her chair and they sat. "I wonder how he's doing in his crate?" Concern flooded him.

"I'm sure he's fine. We need to kennel train him sooner or later. He can't always go with you everywhere."

"Why not?" He checked out the crowd. "I doubt anyone here would mind . . ."

Just then Kristen and Tyler took their seats nearby.

"She looks amazing," Addy whispered to him. "She's actually glowing. I never thought it was a real thing."

He agreed. He couldn't help but smile as his brother leaned over and said something, causing Kristen to laugh. "Yeah, both of them are so happy, it's almost sickening." He reached under the table and took her hand in his.

"I hope we don't look that pathetic," she joked.

"Worse, I'm afraid. They're an old married couple now. They are allowed to act like that."

"Oh?" Her eyebrows shot up.

"Yeah, we still have some time." He leaned closer. "I was hoping for a fall wedding."

"Fall?" She blinked a few times. "This fall?"

"Why not?" he asked.

"Because you still haven't officially said the words."

"I haven't?" He frowned, then scooted his chair back with force and knelt before her. He didn't realize that the crowd had grown quiet or that every eye at the wedding was on him. All he cared about was her.

"Addy, I've never thought I'd have someone like you in my life. Someone so kind, smart, caring and someone who takes my breath away when you look at me and smile." She smiled now and he gasped dramatically in response, getting a larger smile and a joyful laugh from her. "You light up my nights, fill my days with joy, and I can't imagine spending another day on earth without your promise that you'll stay with me for the rest of our lives. Make me the happiest man at my brother's wedding." He winked at Tyler. "Well, maybe the happiest single man here," he said to broad laughter. "Marry me, please," he said when the laughter died down. He pulled out the small box he'd hid from her for the past few weeks. One look at the ring and he'd known it was perfect for her.

A large oval dark-blue topaz sat between two smaller mystic-blue topazes in twisted shapes. The ring was so delicate, so unique, that he knew it had been made for Addy.

She allowed him to slide it on her finger, and he suppressed a sigh of relief when it pushed perfectly into place. Tears were slowly streaming down Addy's cheeks, and he stood up and kissed them away.

"Yes, Trent McGowan, I'll put you out of your misery and marry you," she teased, then laughed when he swung her up into a deep kiss.

"My top," she gasped into his ear. "I don't want to flash everyone here."

He turned her so that he was blocking her from everyone's view as she fixed her dress quickly. Then he turned them back around as everyone cheered.

"Congratulations, Addy and Trent. I hope you two will be as happy as Kristen and I are," Tyler broke in and everyone turned to him. "Now that my brother has stolen a little of our spotlight," Tyler continued as everyone laughed, "I'm supposed to tell everyone that dinner is ready." He motioned to the long tables that sat along the side of the house.

Addy and Trent were bombarded with congratulations before everyone joined the lines for food. Trent took Addy away with him to the front of the house under the shade of a tree and kissed her until they were both too full of love to continue.

"We'd better go join the group," she said, leaning against him.

"Soon." He kissed her one more time. "I have another surprise for you. It's taken some doing, but . . ." He glanced down at her feet. "You may want to slip those on." He nodded to the pair of boots his mother left for him by the back door.

"Trent?" She narrowed her eyes at him.

"Trust me." He smiled. "You'll like this. But we have to be a family before . . . so while you put those on, I'm grabbing Happy. Back in a second."

◆　◆　◆

Addy sat down on the folding chair and slipped off her heels and replaced them with the boots.

When Trent came back, he'd removed his tux jacket and held Happy in his arms. The puppy was so excited to see her that he almost wiggled out of Trent's arms.

"What's this all about?" she asked as they walked to the barn. "Slow down, I'm in a dress."

"I know, but . . . it's kind of part of the whole thing."

"What? The proposal?" she said, trying to keep up with him.

"Yeah," he said over his shoulder.

"Trent." She came to a complete stop when her gaze fell on his next surprise.

"Do you like her?" Trent asked, setting Happy down to run and play with the most beautiful, stark-white horse Addy had ever seen.

Drawn by the horse's grace, Addy took a step forward, then another until she came up against the fence. The horse spotted her and threw her head up in a greeting. Addy laughed and held out her hand like Trent had taught her.

The horse, ignoring Happy now, approached her. She sniffed Addy's hand for a moment, then nudged it and forced Addy to pet her. Addy laughed again and rubbed her mane.

"She's gorgeous." Addy looked back at Trent. "She's mine?" When he nodded, she leaned in and threw her arms around the horse.

"What are you going to name her?" Trent asked, standing beside her. Addy looked at Happy, running around the horse's hooves, and remembered his family's tradition. Then, without even a hint of a smile on her lips, said, "Blackie, clearly."

Trent laughed and shook his head. "Really?"

"I think Snow is better suited." She broke into a grin. "What about you? Don't you need a horse to ride along?"

"Watch out there. If all goes right . . ." He held up his fingers in his mouth and whistled. Nothing happened. "Okay, let's try it again." He did it again, this time louder.

Then she saw a speck of black through the trees, and suddenly a handsome black stallion was rushing toward the fence line.

"I've been working with him for a few days at Bob's place," Trent said. "He delivered him and Snow early this morning."

"Let me guess—Prince?" she asked, nodding at the stallion.

"Actually I was thinking of Charming." He grinned.

"He's perfect for Snow," she said.

"You're perfect for me." He kissed her.

As they returned Happy to his kennel in Gail's bathroom, Addy pulled off her boots and slipped on her heels once more.

"I'm starving," she said when they finally got in line for the food.

"Did you like your present?" Trisha asked as she joined them in the food line.

"She's perfect," Addy said. "Have you seen her?"

"I walked down this morning and helped unload her." She winked. "We'll keep them both here until Trent can get his barn built."

"I can't wait to ride her."

"I helped Trent pick her out," Gail said, joining them. "I test-rode her myself. She's gentle, just like Grace."

"I named her Snow," Addy supplied.

"Of course you did," Gail said. "Trent already named Charming before he'd even agreed to purchase him."

Addy looked over at Trent, who just shrugged. "You just know when it's right."

By the time they sat down to eat, her heart was almost bursting with love. His family was so gracious. They had all admitted in one way or another that they knew he was going to propose to her, making her wonder if they had taken a family vote on it or if he'd just told them ahead of time.

Either way, they had proven to her that they were a group that she wanted and would be proud to call her own family.

"I need to go talk to my mother," she told Trent. She didn't want her to ruin her perfect evening, but she knew there were some things she had to say.

"Want me to come with you?" he asked.

"No, I think this is something I have to do on my own." She stood up and squeezed his shoulder, then made her way through the crowd toward her mother.

"Do you have a moment?" she asked, nodding toward the back deck.

Her mother stood up and followed her to a more private place.

Instead of stopping at the base of the stairs, she climbed them and stood to overlook the large, open field. She could just make out their small trailer across the way.

Her mother stopped next to her. She'd worn one of her flowered skirts with a cream blouse. An outfit Addy had seen her wear a dozen or more times to church. It was one of her favorite colors on her mother.

"You look wonderful today," Addy started.

"Thank you." Her mother glanced down. "Your father always liked . . ." Her voice dropped off. "It doesn't matter."

"No, go on."

"I don't know if you'll believe me or not, but I loved your father very much."

Addy knew that if she didn't put everything on the table now, it would eat at her and build into something she wouldn't be able to control later. Trisha's praise in a tough moment lingered in her ear.

"It's hard to believe that from what I witnessed," Addy said truthfully.

"I understand." Her mother watched the field. "They're a nice family." She looked over to where the party was still going on. Kristen and Tyler were currently cutting the cake.

"Yes, they are. I'm very lucky."

"I know I didn't always show you . . . I'm working on changing things. When your father . . . I . . ." Addy saw tears slide down her mother's face. She'd never seen her mother cry before, except when she got Ralphie.

"Mom?" Addy stepped closer.

"No." Her mother shook her head. "I didn't mean . . ." She took a handkerchief out of her purse and wiped her eyes. "I never cry."

"Maybe that is part of the problem?" Addy suggested. "Showing emotions doesn't make you weak. It makes you human like the rest of us."

"I'm stronger than that."

She watched her mother's shoulders straighten. She knew that move so well; she'd seen it every time her mother would get upset. Addy moved closer and laid her hands on her shoulders. "Mom? You don't always have to be strong."

"Yes, I do." She laughed bitterly. "I was taught that tears were a weakness. My father never . . ." Her mother trailed off, and suddenly more tears flooded from her eyes. "It's all his fault." She sniffled.

"Who? Dad's?" Addy asked. Her mother nodded, then shook her head quickly.

"Yes—no, my father's. He . . . he used to . . ." Her mother closed her eyes and took a deep breath. "Did you know that my father was one-quarter Cheyenne?"

Addy felt a little shocked at her mother's reveal. "No, I never knew. You never talked about your parents."

"I never talked about them because your father rescued me from them." She sagged against the post. "I grew up on the reservation in a shack. I met your father when we came into town one day for groceries. He was so strong and handsome." She sighed. "He helped me load all my firewood, then took me into the shop and bought me a sandwich. No one had shown any interest in me before him."

Addy shook her head. "Why did you always tell everyone that you came from oil money?"

"I was embarrassed." She turned to her daughter. "Your father loved me so much that, at least back then, he didn't care."

"Why?" Addy asked after a moment of silence. "Why were you so mean to him, then?"

"At first it was because he was unhappy. I could tell before you were born that he'd lost all interest in me. I guess over the years I just became bitter, almost as mean as my own father. The day I got home from having lunch with your father, my father found out about it and beat me. I couldn't stand up for almost a whole week."

Addy reached out and laid her hand on her mother's. "I didn't know."

"No, nor would anyone in this town. I knew how people talked. So your father and I came up with a story. One that everyone in town would believe. We eloped in Helena, then went shopping, and I got a new hairstyle and a new last name to go along with my story. No one in town suspected I grew up less than twenty miles from here."

"What about your family?" Addy asked.

"Your grandfather passed away a few years back. I'm not sure about my brothers."

"I have uncles?" Addy asked, surprised.

"Two of them. I haven't seen them since the day I left. I received a letter telling me about my father's death."

"What about your mother?"

"She died giving birth to me. Maybe that's part of it. It's not like I had great examples." Addy's mother shook her head. "Either way, Richard's death has opened my eyes. I'm so tired of being filled with hate and rage."

"Then don't be," Addy said. "You still have a lot of time left. You can turn your life around."

"I only wish I would have opened my mind before your father did . . . what he did." More tears streamed down her face.

"We can't change the past, but we can grow from our mistakes." Addy embraced her. "If you need any help, I'm not going anywhere."

After a long, silent hug, her mother leaned back. "I really like working with the animals and kids. I never thought that volunteering would be so . . . rewarding." She tilted her head. "I didn't do a lot of things right in my life. I'm not sure what I did to deserve you giving me another chance. But I promise you, I'll prove to you that I'm worth it."

"That's all I ask." Addy smiled.

"Now let me see that ring." Her mother's hand enveloped hers with gentleness for what felt like the first time.

CHAPTER
TWENTY-NINE

Trent reached for Addy when she sat down next to him. "Everything okay?"

"Yes, everything is . . . right." She squeezed his hand. He could tell something had changed. She was teary, and he could see the emotions building behind her gaze. He was about to lean in for a kiss when his mother caught his eye. She was waving at him with a look on her face that said trouble.

"Something's up," he said. "I'll go see what's going on." He got up.

"Should I . . ."

"Stay, I'll be right back." He moved quickly to the back of the crowd. "What's up?" he asked his mother, who looked even more panicked now.

"Trey was helping Mr. and Mrs. Etheridge to their car when Carl showed up."

"He's here? I thought . . ." He furrowed his brow. "Wasn't he living in a home?"

"No," his mother sighed. "I didn't want to tell you boys yet that he had improved and is pretty much back to his old self. I heard that he got kicked out of the home last week. He moved back into his trailer. Apparently he was . . . well, it doesn't matter now. The point is he's out front, drunk, and demanding to talk to Tyler."

Trent glanced back at his brother and knew that he wasn't going to let his uncle spoil this day for him or Kristen. "I'll go help Trey." He jogged to the front of the house.

Trey was no match for the old man, not even now after his heart attack. Even though Carl used a cane and weakness on one side of his face slurred his words, the man was still bigger than both Trey and Trent together. If he went down, they'd need all three brothers to get him back up.

Trey had his uncle's arm, holding him back as he talked.

"Now's not the time," Trey was saying over and over. When he saw his brother, he relaxed slightly.

"What seems to be the problem?" Trent said, gaining his uncle's attention.

"The problem is . . . I've heard what you brats are doing with my company. I won't stand for it." The old man's voice rose.

"I'd be happy to discuss this further with you if you'd care to come into my office on Monday morning."

"What? So just like last time you can yell at me until you kill me off so you can have all my stuff?"

"Uncle Carl, we haven't taken anything from you. In fact we've given you plenty over the years." Trent took his uncle's other arm and started leading him to his old clunker of a truck.

"I'm not going anywhere. I've got a right to be here. I'm family. Everyone here has a right to know what you've done to your own kin. Your father owed me." Trent could see a stream of slobber falling from his uncle's chin and wondered if the man should really be on his own.

"Uncle Carl, why don't you come see me Monday and we can come to an agreement," Trent suggested again.

That seemed to get his uncle's attention. "You're the second boy, right?"

Trent was a little taken aback that the man who'd known him his whole life was now looking at him like he couldn't remember who he was. He wondered if perhaps his uncle hadn't recovered fully.

"I'm Trent, yes sir." He nodded.

His uncle's eyes narrowed. "That one takes after Thurston." He glared at Trey. "You and your brother looked like that slut of a woman my brother married."

Trent's hand tightened on his uncle's arm. "I'd be careful what you say about our mother," he warned. He didn't care if the man wasn't back to his old self, no one talked about their mother like that.

"Why? You going to hit me like your old man did every time I called that bitch out?"

Trent and Trey dropped the man's arms at the same time, almost causing the man to fall forward.

"From where I'm standing, you're trespassing," Trent said with a calm he did not feel. "I have every right to call the police and have them haul you in."

"Go right ahead." The old man actually moved closer and Trent wondered if most of the slurred speech had been because of the booze instead of the heart attack. "I've been pushed around by you and your family for long enough. Your father stole something from me, and I won't rest until I get what I deserve."

"Our father didn't steal anything from you, old man," Trey countered. "I'm getting Mike from the party." He started to head toward the back, but Trent stopped him by putting his hand on his brother's arm.

"Go on," Carl urged. "I'm done here anyway." He turned and marched with his cane toward his truck. "I'll get mine. You wait and see."

"Make sure he's gone before we let any guests up here," Trent said to Trey. "Make sure Mom didn't hear any of that either," he whispered just before Trey jogged back down the pathway.

He jumped into his brother's truck and followed his uncle back into town. His uncle parked at one of the local strip clubs and went in.

Something clicked in his mind. If his uncle was working with Darla, the recent attacks would make more sense. But he knew he was probably being missed at the party—he and his brothers would have to follow up later.

Trent turned the truck around and drove back to the party. When he joined Addy again, he was still in a sour mood. Most of the wedding party had died down, but Kristen and Tyler were still dancing slowly as the lights twinkled overhead.

"Trey told me that your uncle was here," Addy asked, looking worried. "Is everything okay?"

"Yeah, he was. Everything will be better if you dance with me." Trent took her hand and pulled her to the dance floor. Thoughts of what he'd seen kept trying to creep into his mind, but he pushed them away and held on to the current moment.

Embracing her, he felt all the tension leave his body. "I followed him into town to make sure he got where he was going okay."

Addy sighed and looked up at him. "He's still family."

"Yeah, but the kicker is he thinks he's due everything my father worked hard for. The man has always been a drunk. I never remember him working a full day in his life, yet he thinks he should get everything."

"You're a good brother, keeping that from Tyler and Kristen today."

He smiled as Tyler looked around and, with his arm linked with Kristen's, started toward the door.

"They're trying to sneak out," he whispered.

"Oh?" She glanced over. "We have to throw the rice."

"Hang on, Trey and I were up here early setting up something . . ." Trent motioned to his brother, who was already in position.

When Tyler and Kristen reached the front path, Trent nodded to Trey, who pulled a string.

Tyler and Kristen were bombarded with more than six full bags of rice from above.

Everyone turned, laughing, as Kristen let out a squeal and Tyler yelled.

"How did you do that?" Addy asked.

"It was a lot harder than you think. First, we had to set up the boards, then use pulleys . . . needless to say, I'm very thankful it worked," Trent said.

"Okay, since we can't sneak away, we'll say good night and thank you to everyone left," Tyler said, spitting rice out of his mouth and brushing it from his hair. He turned to Trent. "You're in charge until I get back. Don't screw it up, little brother."

Trent saluted him. Then the guests followed the couple and waved at them as they drove away.

♦　♦　♦

Later that night, Addy sat with Gail and Trisha on the back patio. Gail had turned on a small propane fire pit that warmed them as they watched the night stars above.

Trent and Trey had changed into their normal clothes and had taken Happy on a walk down to see Snow and Charming.

"What a wonderful day," Trisha said, leaning back in the patio chair while sipping wine. Gone were her high heels, replaced with warm, fuzzy socks.

"It was perfect," Gail said, matching Trisha's relaxation. "I guess that makes us officially a family now." Trisha held up her wine glass and Gail tapped it with her own.

"I had a nice chat with your mother today," Gail said to Addy.

"So did I." Addy smiled.

"Things seemed different," Gail added.

"Yes, they are."

"How does she feel about you getting married?" Trisha asked.

"We actually had a fairly productive chat—she loved my ring." Addy angled her hand back and forth in the firelight. She'd been looking at it all night herself.

"It is beautiful." Gail smiled. "My boys can sure pick good women."

Addy laughed. "Well, you raised some good men."

"That we did." Her smile fell away slightly.

"Did I see you dancing with Tony?" Addy asked. "I think he has his eyes on you."

Trisha snorted. "He wants more than just his eyes on her."

Gail giggled. "He can want until his heart bursts. I'm not that easy. Did I ever tell you what Thurston had to do to convince me to marry him?"

"No." Trisha sat forward slightly. "What?"

Gail giggled as she took another sip of wine. "Let's just say he had to convince me that he was going to be the man for me. Flowers, chocolates, and dancing." She sighed. "Oh, that man could dance." She closed her eyes, and Addy saw a tear slide down her cheek.

"You miss him." Trisha reached over and took Gail's hand.

"It's like I skip every other heartbeat." Gail snuggled back into her chair. "I know I can never truly be happy like that again, but . . ."

Addy started thinking about her mother as the three of them lapsed into silence. What if her mother found someone else to spend her time with? How would Addy feel about that? She figured she would deal with that if the time ever came.

Trey and Trent returned a few minutes later.

"Ready to head home?" Trent said. "This little guy is exhausted."

"You or the dog?" Trey joked.

"Oh, which reminds me, I talked to Dr. Shultz, and he is going to hold Happy's two brothers and a sister for you guys. Now all you need to figure out is who gets the girl."

"Tyler and Kristen already said they wanted Bashful."

"Which is?" Addy laughed.

"The girl," Gail said. "I'm going to see which one looks like a Doc. Then Trey can have . . ."

"Dopey." Trey smiled. "If his brothers are anything like him, there's bound to be a Dopey in the pack."

"We'll see you guys tomorrow," Trent said, helping Addy up. She bent down and picked up the small dog, who had trotted over and laid down at her feet.

"I think he's gotten bigger already," she said. Trent reached over and took the dog from her after Happy had covered her chin in kisses.

"Night," everyone said as Addy and Trent made their way through the house toward her Jeep.

Happy curled up in the back seat as Trent drove toward their place.

"When does the house get here?" she asked.

"Fifteen days." He groaned. "Not soon enough." He smiled over at her. "Not that living in a one-hundred-square-foot place with you is a burden, it's just . . . it will be nice to be able to stand up in a shower again."

She laughed. "Yes, I've missed taking long, hot bubble baths."

"Did I mention there will be three bathtubs?"

She shook her head.

"I have the house plans if you want to look them over?" He paused as he waited for her answer.

"I'd love that," she said. "Maybe . . ." She bit her bottom lip. "I want a garden."

"Good, so do I." He smiled as he parked. "I was thinking just along there." He pointed to the darkness, but in her mind she knew exactly where he meant. "We can have a small orchard of fruit trees back behind it." He leaned over the steering wheel. "The barn for the horses, over there." He pointed in the opposite direction. "A corral." His finger moved over the dash, and she could imagine everything as if it were full daylight. "There's even enough room for a chicken coop."

"You've thought of everything. Where will the playground go?" she asked. She'd always wanted kids but worried that it might be better if she didn't have them, given her family history. Now, however, seeing the changes in her own mother, she believed that there was no way she would end up like her and felt like she could dream again.

"There." He gestured to where the backyard would be after the house was placed. "There are five bedrooms, think we can fill them all up?"

"We can try." She felt her heart flutter and knew that it was because she was finally where she belonged.

ABOUT THE AUTHOR

Jill Sanders is the *New York Times* and *USA Today* bestselling author of many romance novels, including the Pride Series, Secret Series, West Series, Grayton Series, Lucky Series, Silver Cove, Entangled Paranormal Romance Series, and Haven, Montana Series. Her sweet and sexy stories—available in print and audio in every English-speaking country—continue to lure new readers and are currently being translated into different languages.

Jill is an identical twin, born to a large family in the Pacific Northwest. She relocated to Colorado for college and a successful IT career before discovering her talent as a writer. Now she makes her home along the Emerald Coast in Florida, where she enjoys the beach, hiking, swimming, wine tasting, and, of course, writing. Visit her at http://jillsanders.com.

28535617R00167

Printed in Great Britain
by Amazon